TERRIBLE LIZARDS

A DINOSAUR HORROR ANTHOLOGY SUPPORTING THE RSPB

EDITED BY
KYLE J. DURRANT

CONTENTS

For everyone who hasn't let their
love of dinosaurs die
And for birds all over the world

A Note on Content Warnings

This is a horror anthology, which means some stories may contain themes or events that could cause distress to some readers.

Reader discretion is advised.

For a list of content warnings, please turn to the back of the book.

INTRODUCTION
KYLE J. DURRANT

Dinosaurs have fascinated us for over two centuries, and it's easy to see why. These diverse and often gargantuan animals dominated the planet for many millions of years, leaving their legacy in the rock for us to uncover and study. Since the first fossils were extracted from the earth and dubbed "terrible lizards", society's imagination has been afire with possibilities.

Furthermore, our knowledge of dinosaurs is constantly evolving. In fact, there are those who say that we're going through a dinosaur renaissance. Every week, it seems, there's a new species uncovered; every month a new study comes out that alters how we think about these animals. Perhaps the most famous case is Spinosaurus. Is it a formidable sail-backed Tyrannosaurus-killer, or a paddle-tailed aquatic fish-eater?

In the time between me writing this introduction and the release of this book, the consensus may have changed half a dozen times. The study of dinosaurs is a reminder that science is always advancing and that the facts are always being updated. We're not being lied to – we're improving our understanding.

Another of the prime examples of this is that today we know that "terrible lizards" is a misnomer. They weren't lizards: they were bird-like reptiles. They weren't terrible: they were remarkably evolved and efficient creatures. In fact, many were likely gentle giants. Famously, Maiasaura is known as the "good mother lizard" because there is evidence that they devotedly raised their young. Indeed, dinosaurs were remarkable creatures with habits and lifestyles as complex as any animal alive today.

Which brings us to the dinosaurs that flourish among us. By now, it's become common knowledge – especially among dinosaur fans – that birds are the living descendants of these remarkable animals. And just as humans are apes by virtue of our lineage, so all birds are living dinosaurs.

If you're in any doubt of that fact, I implore you to look at the cassowary. Those clawed feet are remarkably similar to a very famous dinosaur, wouldn't you say? And the fact that these fleet-footed carnivores persist, in some form, into the modern world...that is *terrifying*.

The book you are holding is a testament to our enduring fascination with the Dinosauria. Thirteen authors who share an interest in these prehistoric beasts have come together to tell some horrifying tales featuring our favourite extinct animals. What's more, these stories will contribute to the protection of the dinosaurs that remain.

All proceeds from this anthology are being donated to the Royal Society for the Protection of Birds (RSPB), helping to maintain their habitats and fund medical interventions when needed. Just by holding this book, you have helped the remarkable species of bird that call this planet home.

That's something to be proud of. And it means the hard work is done, so you can sit back and enjoy this selection of dinosaur-themed horrors.

Now, admittedly, some of these stories don't feature dinosaurs. You will also come face-to-face with plesiosaurs and pterosaurs – swimmers and flyers, respectively – that whilst not dinosaurs, are still close relatives. And I hope you'll agree that they are every bit as terrifying as their more famous counterparts.

On the subject of famous faces, you will certainly recognise certain species, such as Tyrannosaurus Rex and Velociraptor...but there are some more obscure varieties here, too.

I must say that I was overjoyed with the variety of stories I received. I feel that every story accomplishes something original, with unique twists on how dinosaurs can interact with humanity to become horror monsters.

As you read these stories, allow yourself to return to the first time you watched Jurassic Park. Feel awe and terror combined as you imagine these hungry predators from prehistory stalking through your hallways or stomping through your garden. Embrace that fear.

Dinosaurs are fascinating. And for the purposes of this book, they are terrifying.

Kyle J. Durrant
Editor

TERROR ON CENTRAL PARK WEST
A. W. MASON

They were there for less than ten minutes before the bones began to move. And at first, nobody noticed.

Richard Lipschitz was not only born with an unfortunate name, he was also born with the uncanny ability to draw unwanted attention to himself. In his brief twelve years so far on planet Earth, he had transferred elementary schools twice, suspended each time for fighting (although the only fighting he would admit to was fighting back tears of shame) and now attended a middle school miles away from where he lived. This was instead of the junior high two blocks down from his parents' apartment – a special request approved by the school board in an attempt to distance Richard from his old schoolyard tormentors.

He was easy prey for bullies of any persuasion to feast on. First, there was his weight. Richard wasn't obese by any means, but rather what his mom referred to as "husky", confirmed by the fit of blue jeans he received each new school year. There was another issue of outward appearance that made him a quick target: Richard's parents weren't wealthy and probably weren't considered middle class either. He was gifted one new pair of off-brand sneakers each school year—along with the one new pair of "husky" pants—and if he was lucky, a new tee-shirt or two, not to exceed the value of ten dollars. The rest of his wardrobe consisted of items from thrift stores and second-hand shops. No name-brand Nike kicks or Lacoste polos anywhere to be found.

It bothered Richard, and he wanted to be mad at his parents that he didn't fit in with most crowds at school no matter how many times he transferred. But he was also smart enough to know it wasn't their fault. His anger would be misplaced if he cast it upon them, but it didn't mask the insecurities that seemed to fuel the asshole teenagers who got a kick out of nasty name-calling and the random beatings administered when the school halls were ghost towns between classes.

"Hey, Dick Schitz! You think dinosaurs were all fat asses like you or did they just say they had big bones too?" a spiky red-haired kid snarled at Richard.

As soon as the kid posed the question, a group of teens surrounding him erupted into laughter, guffaws echoing from the fossil displays.

"Shut up, Scott. You know what you have in common with all these dinosaur fossils? You both have the same number of brains in your skulls," another kid retorted. He stood between Scott, the red-haired harasser, and Richard, acting as a human buffer between the two.

The group of teens behind Scott *oooooed* in unison, challenging the redhead to fire back. He peered around the buffer-kid, looking at Richard who seemed to be studying the floor.

"Aww, Richard need his boyfriend Eddie to protect him? Why don't you two faggots go take a stroll somewhere private so you can show each other your own bones instead?" Scott said.

The mob behind Scott pushed past Eddie and Richard, purposely shouldering into them as they moved on. Scott came last, lowering his voice so the chaperone meandering toward the group wouldn't be able to hear him.

"Smell ya later, Dick Schitz."

Richard found that no matter how many schools he transferred to, there always seemed to be someone lined up to make his existence a living hell. However, the great thing about his newest school was that he found an Eddie, a kid held back for his poor academic performances. Nonetheless, he had offered Richard his friendship after helping him pass his American history class the year prior.

In some ways, their friendship was one built out of necessity, but when diving deeper through the layers, it was a friendship that meant more to both of them than either was willing to outright admit.

"Come on, man. Let's go over here and you can tell me about this gnarly looking dude," Eddie said to Richard, pointing at a fossil of a titanosaur.

Regardless of the little scuffle with Scott, Richard had been excited all week, and especially for today. He was excited because, at last, field trip day had arrived. One of the fortunate things about living in The City, and attending school there, was the rich history and the plethora of places to go exploring, much as they were now, at New York City's American Museum of Natural History.

Richard and Eddie's group—as well as Scott's—started their tour on the fourth floor and would eventually make their way down to the ground level, meeting up for lunch with the rest of their class. Or, at least, that was the plan before the screaming began.

"Did you hear that?" Richard asked. He stood, tip-toed, to peer over the exhibit in front of him and toward the source of the yelling. "It sounded like Mrs. Whitford."

Another shrill scream echoed through the museum's top floor. A blood-curdling shriek that reminded Richard of an old movie where a woman finds the mangled corpse of her husband in a piece of farm equipment.

"Look over there," Eddie said, pointing at a cluster of people gathering around a Tyrannosaurus rex fossil. More screams and shouts began to fill the room. A museum employee ran past Richard, nearly knocking him to the floor. The employee shouted into a walkie talkie as he attempted to make his way through the throng of people amassing around the T-rex. It sounded to Richard like the man was trying to get someone to contact emergency services.

Richard and Eddie turned to each other, their startled eyes meeting as their heads aligned. They nodded to each other, agreeing without speaking, that they should go investigate the commotion.

Chaperones and other adults stood fast around the T-rex display, trying to create a human barrier between the crowd and the fossil. Several students held their cell phones up over the onlookers, capturing photos and videos of the scene. Another portion of museumgoers crouched back away from the assembly, crying, unable to be comforted from their hysterics.

Richard used his size to nudge through the gathering and to the perimeter of adults trying to mediate the scene. They directed him away, waving their hands once he made it to the front, shouting at him to get back and leave room for medical personnel.

When Richard was at last able to peek around the chaperone who tried to block his view, what he saw drained his face of its colour. His cheeks felt like they were on fire, a tingling of burning pinpricks dotting the flesh on his forehead. But at the same time, his entire body went cold, gooseflesh filling each tiny crevice on his skin. Beads of sweat began to stand out on his temple, wetting his thick brown hair.

The kid's name was Lawrence. He was Scott's right-hand man when it came to troublemaking and tormenting. But Richard could only recognize that it was indeed Lawrence because his head, stuck in the T-rex's maw, faced the onlookers. The ancient teeth, once used to tear through flesh and bone millions of years ago, now pressed down, crushing Lawrence's skull so that the boy's eyes bulged in their sockets, his swollen tongue protruding between his wrecked jaw. Where the dinosaur's teeth sank in and disappeared into Lawrence's face, streams of sticky red blood spilled out and over the T-rex's jaw as if it had just fed.

At the base of the fossil exhibit lay Lawrence's headless, lifeless body. The ribbons of flesh that used to comprise his neck gushed a slow pulse of gore onto the T-rex's feet. A striped piece of white bone shot through the torn muscle and skin.

"It was only supposed to be a joke!" Richard heard Scott yelling from beyond the chaperone barricade. The lean, mean, red-headed bully looked more like a frightened child, yelling through a hitch of sobs, his eyes and cheeks wet from a deluge of tears.

"It was a joke! I swear!" he continued to confess to no one in particular. "I only dared Lawrence to climb up and stick his head in the thing's mouth so we could take his picture. It was supposed to be funny."

Scott was on the ground now, his arms wrapped around his knees and his head buried into his body. He rocked back and forth, oblivious to the chaos going on around him.

Eddie placed a hand on Richard's shoulder as he made his way to his friend's side. The barricade started to falter. Instead, more of the parents tried to corral the kids to the opposite side of the museum next to the woolly mammoths. Behind the T-rex, a museum employee shouted into her walkie talkie until her voice went hoarse.

"Jesus. What happened?" Eddie asked, surveying the carnage.

"I guess it was supposed to be a prank or something. Lawrence was trying to get a picture with his head inside the T-rex's mouth. The top part of the skull must have come loose and fallen on him while he was up there. But how would that even rip his head off?"

Eddie didn't get a chance to respond to Richard's inquiry before another barrage of screams broke out on

13

the far end of the fourth floor. An even larger commotion began to form away from the site of the T-rex accident, but Richard didn't need to linebacker his way over to the hectic stampede of people running back toward him in order to see one of the chaperones, a man he didn't know by name, impaled on the tusk of a woolly mammoth.

"What in the…" Eddie trailed off, seeing what his friend was now looking at.

The crescent shaped bone of the mammoth protruded through the chest of the adult as he gripped the tusk with both hands, looking down at it with dumb fascination. A steady river of blood flowed from the wound in his chest and trailed down past his khaki slacks. He attempted to scream, but only a wet gurgling noise, like percolating coffee, came from his mouth.

Several museum patrons, including Richard and Eddie, stared, frozen in place, watching in horror as the chaperone tried in vain to back himself off the tusk. And then something happened that snapped Richard from his trance. With a swift jerk to its left, the mammoth whipped its head, flinging the impaled chaperone off its tusk and into a display board explaining the eating habits of the Triceratops.

The mammoth raised its right front leg into the air, breaking its fixture to the display, and brought it down with a force that installed a network of cracks in the floor. Breaking free of its remaining restraints, the fossil continued to manoeuvre out of the display and onto the main observation floor.

From behind them, Richard felt the ground shake, the unsteady rumbling sending shockwaves from the soles of his feet through the tibias in his legs. The screaming from the mammoth side of the room was temporarily forgotten as Richard craned his neck back toward the T-rex exhibit.

Lawrence's head dropped from the T-rex's mouth as the extinct beast let out a silent roar. The skeleton lunged forward, shattering its restraints, much as the mammoth had. The T-rex's tail swiped across Lawrence's decapitated body, sending it streaking down an open path of tile. A red trail of sticky muck smeared into the floor as the body came to a halt.

Scott, who now sat in a state of catatonic shock next to the T-rex display, didn't bother looking up when the carnivorous giant's foot crashed down upon him. A sickening crunch of bones snapped inside the red head's delicate, human body as the dinosaur flattened him to the ground.

Overhead, Richard felt a powerful whoosh as a pterodactyl flew within inches of his scalp. He turned to Eddie, his eyes two large golf balls set into their sockets.

"Run!" Eddie shouted.

The only problem, though, was there wasn't anywhere to run. An Apatosaurus tumbled out of its enclosure, mowing down a group of classmates scurrying to vacate its destructive path. To the right, a Deinonychus, all seven feet of it, struggled to break through the glass holding it captive. Farther down the way, the titanosaur emerged from a pile of debris caused by two other fossil beasts colliding with one another whilst vying for escape.

The titanosaur snapped its massive jaw at the onlookers, snatching a museum employee by the arm, ripping it off from the employee's shoulder. Eddie and Richard ran toward it while the dinosaur was busy chewing, trying to swallow the mashed-up appendage, and slid behind an empty display case.

The two friends watched as more and more unidentifiable sets of bones sprang to life, some tearing themselves apart in the process while others began to roam the building, attacking humans and other fossils without discrimination.

"This can't be happening," Richard said to Eddie, watching the chaos unfold. "It can't really be happening at all. They're just bones! They're not alive."

As if challenging that statement, a Triceratops crashed into the display they hid behind, sending shattered glass raining down all around them. The beast meandered off, eventually locking bones with another skeleton several yards away.

"We can't stay here. We have to find a way to make it over to that exit and get down to the third floor," Richard said, pointing at a hallway a running distance away from them.

The uproar of ear-piercing cries persisted, taking over the fourth floor. Sounds of breaking glass and crunching metal accompanied the screams as the silent dinosaurs snapped at each other; the poor souls, running blind, tried to seek shelter. Richard glanced back at the exit, a wide set of stairs leading down to the third-floor level. He was surprised to see it empty, neither man nor creature aware of its presence.

"All right. So, here's what we do: once there's a semi-clear path, or at least the fossils are distracted for a bit, we run like hell to that alcove," Eddie panted, motioning to the stairs.

Above them, an overhead light burst, cascading pieces of delicate bulb glass to the floor as another set of flying bones tried to make an exit through the ceiling.

"And we don't stop for anybody," Eddie continued, "no matter what. It's just you and me, man. Once we get down to level three, we'll make sure we get help, but right now we have to focus on getting out of this mess."

"Yeah. Okay," Richard said, nodding his head in agreement. The museum had turned into a bloody battlefield. Severed limbs, headless torsos, and the whimpering agony of bodies with mortal wounds littered the entire hall. The only thing missing was the rapid succession of gunfire emitting from high powered assault rifles.

"Okay then. Let's do it," Eddie said, but before he could get to his feet, Richard leaned in and wrapped his arms around him, embracing his friend in a vice-like grip.

"Thank you, Eddie. Thank you for being my friend and for sticking up for me and for not being an asshole. I just wanted to tell you that."

Eddie, caught a bit off guard at first, hugged him back, patting him firmly on the shoulder. "Yeah man, don't sweat it. I'm glad you're my friend too. But hey, let's get the fuck out of here, huh?"

Richard nodded again and waited for Eddie's lead. The T-rex rampaged past them, chasing four people toward another set of bones. Once the creature passed, Eddie turned back to Richard with eyes like cold steel. The two boys sprang up from their crouched positions and ran toward the stairs, minding the rubble in their way.

The exit was perhaps only fifty yards away, but the path to it seemed to stretch on for miles. Richard stayed close behind Eddie, keeping watch where his best friend was manoeuvring among the debris while also trying to keep an eye over his shoulder for incoming monsters. Somewhere in the distance, an alarm was sounding, a barrage of bleating most likely from a fire exit being pushed open.

Halfway to the stairs, Richard had already witnessed another classmate trampled under the gallop of a Stegosaurus. Looking up at the beast, he also noticed a body mangled up in the knife-shaped plates running along its spine. His stomach rolled and cramped; a warm feeling in his gut wanted out.

Next, he observed the smoke three-quarters of the way to the stairs. He did not see its source, and couldn't imagine how a fire could have started during the melee, all things considered. The overhead fire sprinklers would turn on soon, only making the floors slick with stale water, another obstacle they could do without.

In front of them, ten feet from the exit, a pile of bones and what looked like rock, or concrete maybe, blocked their way. At their heels, an incomplete set of bones hobbled toward them, the ancient creature missing a front and back leg. Eddie jumped up onto the pile of debris in front of them, climbing it like a deadfall. Richard followed behind him, stepping and gripping the spots Eddie had just traversed, making sure not to grab something loose and go tumbling back to the floor.

The pursuing set of bones limped near the bottom of the blockage, crouching down on its one back leg ready to strike at Richard, who hadn't made it over the top of the deadfall yet. He looked back, face screwed up in a terror-filled grimace. He couldn't erase a vision of the old thing's sharp teeth penetrating the soft flesh of his hamstring.

But before Richard could close his eyes and wait for the inevitable, Mrs. Whitford, a large, thick leg bone in hand, wound up like Jose Canseco in a homerun derby and swung at the predator. The bone connected with an audible crunch, destroying the dinosaur's jaw and shattering the orbital socket. The rest of the fossil fell from its leap and careened into the pile Richard clung to, adding to the mess of bones.

Richard, frozen in a moment that could have been fear or gratitude, watched as Mrs. Whitford ran off in the opposite direction, winding up again with a tomahawk chop, ready to wreak havoc on another set of old bones.

A tug on Richard's shirt collar brought him back into this bizarre reality as Eddie signalled for him to crest the pile and make haste toward the stairs. The two boys continued their climb, descending the backside of the pile in a rush of crumbling fossils.

"This way!" Eddie shouted as they approached the stairwell.

The boys ran into the hall beyond the entrance to the stairs and out of sight of the mess they escaped from. They both sat down hard, backs against the wall, and waited to catch their breath.

"Christ, this is bad. They are all going to die in there," Richard said, brushing dust off his shirt.

"Not if we can help it," Eddie said. Something sharp had nicked his temple during their rush out and a small rivulet of blood ran down his face. "We'll get downstairs and have someone call the police, or the military, or something."

"I mean, someone downstairs has had to have heard all this racket, right?" Richard asked.

"I hope so, man," Eddie said. He let out an unsteady breath. "All right. Let's get the hell out of here."

The pair trotted down the steps to the third floor. An eerie silence surrounded them as they walked toward the primate exhibit at the end of the stairs. They paused in the hall.

"Where is everyone?" Richard asked.

Eddie crept forward, half anticipating another fossil to jump out, a set of bones somehow already making it down to this level. But a few feet into the primate

21

exhibit, Eddie stopped cold, his eyes narrowing at something on the floor in front of him.

Whispering, Eddie asked, "What is that?"

Richard moved past his friend and toward what he was pointing at. The shape, perhaps the size of two footballs, became clearer as he approached it. A long spear impaled the shape's chest.

"It's...it's a monkey. I think it's a capuchin monkey."

Richard nudged the primate with his foot and the body turned to its side as the spear fell over.

"I don't like this, Richard. Maybe we should just keep going down the stairs to the ground floor level, go to the information desk, and tell them what is happening."

Richard dropped to his knees so he could examine the monkey more closely. The fur was matted with fresh blood where the spear had pierced its abdomen.

"Hey Eddie, do you think maybe some of these monkeys, you know, reanimated too? Like the dinosaur bones did?"

A faint guttural howl floated in from down the hallway followed by a litany of grunts. Richard stepped back from the monkey, afraid to turn the corner into the hallway leading to the rest of the displays.

"What's down the hall from the primates? What's the next set of exhibits?" Richard asked, words coming in quick bursts.

Eddie looked up at the sign above them, an arrow on each side, one pointing left with the words "Plains Indians and Eastern Woodlands Indians". Now, along with the grunts and growling, came a human sound, like a howling rage, echoing down the hall.

"Maybe we should head down to level…" Eddie started.

An air slicing sound buzzed past in front of them as a decorated spear, easily six feet long, flew by and stuck into the wall with a monstrous *thwock*. The vengeful yelling grew louder and now the sound of several stampeding feet filled the hall. Another spear flew by, crashing into the one already stuck in the wall.

Eddie looked at Richard who then looked behind them and back at the stairs.

"Run!"

BURNING DAWN
WESLEY WINTERS

"I hate dinosaurs."

Stephen Faris took several deep breaths in an attempt to steel himself, but it was no use. How could one prepare for infiltrating a Tyrannosaurus nest? Even armed, it seemed like suicide. Perhaps if he'd been greenlit to use explosives, he'd feel better. But his rifle—as large and powerful as it was—held tranquilizers instead of bullets. He knew they reacted instantly upon implantation in the Rex's scaly skin, but there was something bothersome about putting his life on the line for the function of a loaded dart. Maybe it was because he'd never trusted one before. Or maybe it wouldn't matter what his rifle fired because, either way, he was facing down a damn dinosaur.

"Faris. Update."

Stephen pressed down on his earpiece and said, "I'm here."

"And?"

Stephen swallowed and popped his head out of hiding for another look below. In the crater, the nest was seemingly unguarded. Quiet. There were three eggs, none of which had hatched. Yet. Behind Stephen was a hover-cart for transportation. It was pre-programmed for auto-delivery of the eggs to the compound; all Stephen had to do was load its cargo and press SEND on the device panel or his wristwatch. Either way, he was unnecessary to the delivery once the eggs were boarded and the command entered. There was no risk of him dropping the eggs or being derailed by the mother T-Rex during his escape. He could die, but the transport would go on without him. And that was clearly all that mattered to these people.

"Why was I sent alone to do this shit?" he growled into his earpiece.

"*Matthews got sick. You originally had a partner.*"

"How comforting. And how convenient for Matthews."

"*Relax, Faris. You have the tranquilizer. Those specialized darts will bring down any dinosaur within a second of impact.*"

"Have they been tested?"

"*Of course they have. You're not the first soldier to be sent outside the compound.*"

Stephen closed his eyes and tried breathing deeply once more. The nest was still quiet and unguarded. If he was going to steal those eggs, he needed to get moving before the parents returned. "Why are these eggs so damn important?" he asked the handler.

"Cancer research has taken enormous leaps forward with embryotic materials found in these eggs. The T-Rex is not our only specimen—just the hardest to collect."

"The damn government already has a cure for cancer," Stephen growled into his earpiece, sweat building over his brow. "Just get them to release the shit."

"You know they'll never do that."

"And what makes you think they won't stop you from doing the same?"

There was silence from his handler for a long moment. Then: *"Get moving, Faris. You're burning dawn. The mother will be back soon."*

Since the public discovery of the Rising Island thirteen months earlier, governments from around the globe had set up stakes along the beaches, erecting a variety of compounds for scientific research and development. Stephen was employed by Heinrich & Bastille, the leading team in behavioural studies of the dinosaurs roaming the island. According to them, it had been learned that the Tyrannosaurus would often hunt alone in the early morning as the sun was first rising. Later in the day, they would pack hunt. Unlike in movies, their eyesight was not based on movement.

They could see just as well as eagles and were even equipped with stereoscopic vision for hunting in the dark. Though none of this made Stephen feel any better, he understood why it was better for him to infiltrate the nest now as opposed to later.

"Proximity sensors show you're clear…"

As if he trusted those security walls. Trees were constantly knocked over or damaged by the movement of these enormous beasts; the company sensors malfunctioned on an hourly basis and were of little comfort. But Stephen had a secret companion in his left jacket pocket to calm his nerves and give him strength—a bottle of whiskey. As he stood from hiding, he removed the bottle and quickly took a heavy swallow from its amber body.

The nest awaited him.

Stephen began down the crater as carefully as he could manage, but there was no clear path. He kept the rifle slung over his shoulder and neck to keep it in place as he slipped and slid his way down to the clearing below. Once he'd reached the bottom, he paused to listen to the surrounding forest. He heard nothing but distant birds and insects.

The eggs were roughly a foot and a half long, he surmised on approach. The cart had a soft basket prepared that could safely hold two specimens of this size. Stephen had been tasked with the recovery of one, but more if possible. He scanned the crater and reminded himself there was no easy way out; he'd have to climb to some degree, one way or another. Had Matthews not been "sick", he could have had a rope system in place to make it easier and faster. But on his own and ill-equipped, Stephen would have to use the sling during his escape. Only one egg could nestle against his chest at a time, so there'd be two trips to make, assuming the mother didn't return too soon.

"I'm getting set to carry the first egg out," he whispered into his earpiece as he positioned the sling with his free hand.

"*Keep it steady.*"

Stephen rolled his eyes and grunted with annoyance.

It wasn't easy positioning an egg of that size and weight into a sling strapped to his chest, especially with a large rifle against his back. He bent his knees in the nest to avoid drops of any height. Twice, he fumbled the egg and nearly damaged the shell against the floor of the nest. He took a moment to relax—with another swig of whiskey—before trying a third time. Finally, he secured the egg in the wrap and stood slowly from the nest. By the time he was beginning his climb out of the crater, his back was already aching from the weight strapped across his body. A day of massage therapy would have to follow this mission.

Assuming he survived it.

"You've got company."

Of course, I fucking do, he thought, searching his immediate surroundings for cover.

"Move quicker."

"Shut up, shut up, shut up," he growled in panic, carefully removing the egg from its sling and placing it gingerly in the angled brush. He then removed his rifle and lowered his backside against the incline, sinking himself into the foliage beside the egg. As quietly as he could manage, he readied the tranquilizer to be fired. He had an additional five shots in his utility belt in case they were needed. Though he'd been assured one was enough for a Tyrannosaurus, there was always the possibility more than one dinosaur would rear its ugly head during his recovery of the eggs.

The ground trembled with the approach of something large. Something moving with…a limp?

Stephen clicked on his earpiece. "What's coming?"

"It's not the mother."

"So, what is it?"

From the opposite lip of the crater, a wounded Triceratops appeared. Its horns were red with blood, as was its sheared face. Before Stephen could question its intent, he realized its eyes were mostly shut. The lizard stumbled at the lip, clearly unaware of the drop, and tumbled loudly into the crater a second later. It landed just shy of the two remaining eggs of the nest, where it remained, shuffling listlessly on its side and mewling.

"Shit."

"Is there a problem, Faris? We can see you have a new friend in your vicinity."

"It's dying," he said without clarification.

"What is? Wait...Faris, you need to hide."

Stephen's heart leapt into his throat. "What is it?"

He could hear quickened movement from the direction the Triceratops had come.

"All the sensors are red."

"Meaning?"

"Hide."

The approach sounded like thunder from beyond the crater's lip. Stephen shuffled himself as much into the foliage as he could manage and scooped leaves over his body without restricting his ability to use the rifle if necessary.

Two enormous dinosaurs appeared atop the lip a second later and eyed the dying Triceratops below. They were at least fifteen feet tall and long, similarly built like a Tyrannosaurus. However, their faces were pulled farther out, their were jaws thinner, and their eyes were smaller. They had the face of pissed-off reptilian geese, as far as Stephen was concerned.

"If you can safely do so, send us a picture."

Stephen swallowed hard and damned his earpiece. He doubted any dinosaur could hear his handler's voice but didn't know for sure. Slowly, he removed his left hand from the rifle and turned the face of his wristwatch toward the dinosaurs as they began their descent into the crater.

"Record," he whispered into the watch, bringing it momentarily closer to his lips.

A red light appeared from its side. Stephen nearly cursed aloud, having forgotten the indicator. Luckily, the dinosaurs took no notice of him or the light; they were dialled in on the Triceratops below. As they reached the bottom of the decline and began toward their prey, Stephen filmed a twenty second video before transmitting the file to the compound with a quiet voice command. He then returned his hand to the rifle and steadied his breathing.

"*Keep out of sight, Faris. Those appear to be Carcharodontosaurus.*"

Stephen squeezed his eyes shut in frustration. *As if I know what the hell that is*, he thought angrily.

"*They're bad news. Wait for them to leave.*"

And how long could that take? They were feeding on a fresh kill fifty feet away from him. Luckily, his scent wasn't likely to be carried easily in the breeze from within the crater, but they could still take notice of him before long. All it would take would be a simple slip of his boot or—

The egg tilted against the brush beside him.

Stephen turned his head to glare at the specimen in warning.

Don't you fucking do it, he thought.

The vine nestled at its base bent a centimeter lower, rotating ever so slightly against the weight of the egg.

No. NO.

Stephen removed his left hand slowly from the rifle once more, this time to reach out and steady the egg. But he was too late. The egg began to roll down the decline before he could reel it in towards his body. Though it did not break, it bounced back into the clearing and came to a stop a foot from the crater's curving walls.

One of the Carcharodontosaurus looked in its direction as the other continued its feast of the Triceratops. Curious, it cocked its head and waited for a beat. Stephen clenched his eyes shut and tried not to breathe. Finally, the dinosaur took notice of the previously ignored nest and approached the two eggs that were closest to it. Stephen slowly opened his eyes to see if he'd been spotted. Instead of an approaching Carcharodontosaurus, he saw the enormous creature using its snout to puncture a Tyrannosaurus egg and eat from it.

Now what was he to do? None of the eggs were with him and he was a sitting duck. The eggs were going to be destroyed soon enough or the mother would return to the nest and protect it from further harm. Either way, it didn't look like he'd be going home with a specimen anymore.

Mission failure.

Stephen was about to press his earpiece and request permission to return to base when the ground began to tremble once more from outside the crater.

I can't believe I'm going to be trapped in a Dino ring of death while Matthews watches TV from his fucking cabin.

Both theropods raised their heads and looked beyond Stephen.

Of course she's returning from behind me, he thought unhappily.

A moment later, the Tyrannosaurus roared from atop the ridge above him, her call ear-piercing. Stephen didn't bother craning his neck to observe her quick descent, but instead prayed he wasn't hiding within her pathway. The crater shook as the mother came crashing down the slope, knocking aside trees with the flick of her thick neck. By a mere foot, she missed crushing

Stephen's legs as she passed overhead to charge the nearest Carcharodontosaurus feeding on the egg. Its partner looked up from the gore of the Triceratops and screeched in reply. The Carcharodontosaurus standing over the eggs reared back in preparation for the fight to come.

Stephen took this distraction to roll over and get to his feet. As he quickly climbed up the crater's walls with his body as low as he could manage, the dinosaurs launched into one another below. The ground shook with their collisions, so much so that Stephen lost his footing and slipped more than once. By the time he'd reached the lip and climbed over to where his hover-cart remained in wait, one of the Carcharodontosaurus was bleeding from its neck atop the nest. Beneath it, two of the eggs had been crushed. Only one remained, the egg Stephen had lost along the crater's side wall. It was currently forgotten as its mother and the remaining Carcharodontosaurus continued their bloody collisions, snapping their jaws against shoulders and sides.

"Shit."

He could still get it, couldn't he? These beasts weren't paying him any mind.

Don't be ridiculous, he told himself. To return to the nest during the fight was still suicidal and stupid.

His handler suddenly sounded from within his ear: *"Do you have the specimens, Faris? I see you've left the nest."*

Stephen peered into the crater and watched as the two apex predators did their best to kill one another. "Two were crushed," he explained to his handler. "And the other is, uh…pretty close to a battle."

"What's happening?"

"The mother returned."

"Where's the third egg?"

"Along the side of the clearing."

"Hold your position, Faris. I'm getting a clearance."

A clearance? For what?

As he waited for an answer, Stephen rested his rifle against the tree beside him and took a knee beside the hover-cart to make sure it had remained undamaged by the mother.

"Faris."

"Yeah?"

"I have received clearance to reward you double for retrieving that remaining egg."

Stephen paused. "Did you say double?"

"That's right. And you'll keep Matthews' original take, as well."

Stephen did the math. Bringing home the egg would grant him a payday of sixteen thousand dollars.

He did his best to suppress a smile. "Uh, I'll sure as hell try."

"Let us know when the egg has been secured in your transport."

Stephen returned to the lip of the crater and looked below. Then he collected his rifle and took aim at the Tyrannosaurus. She had to be the priority. And he had an additional five darts. From above the nest, he could safely subdue both predators and return for the egg. He tried lining up his shot along the neck of the mother, but she was moving too frequently. He wondered if the dart would act any less if shot elsewhere. The beast's backside was an easier target, so he shifted his aim and squeezed the trigger. At the same moment, the Tyrannosaurus spun forty degrees with the neck of the Carcharodontosaurus secured in her jaws. The dart pierced the losing dinosaur's eye, blinding it. The Carcharodontosaurus grunted loudly as its legs gave out beneath it and the Tyrannosaurus released her grip. The Carcharodontosaurus collapsed onto its side and began to breathe heavily at its opponent's feet.

Stephen cursed and worked his utility belt for another dart.

The Tyrannosaurus turned its gaze on him.

"Shit!"

He fumbled with a dart and dropped it in the warm soil beneath his boots.

The mother left the side of the dying Carcharodontosaurus and began toward the curving walls.

Stephen collected the fallen dart and quickly tried rubbing it against his jacket to clean it of dirt. By the time it was loaded and he was raising his rifle once more to take aim, the mother was closing in on his location at the lip. He took a step back and stumbled on a root. His shot went awry, and the dart disappeared just above the mother's shoulder. Stephen fell onto his backside and scooted away from the edge of the crater as the Tyrannosaurus emerged.

"Fuckin' hell!"

Rather than load his rifle again with the mother towering over him, Stephen rolled over, scrambled to his feet, and began to run. The mother's jaws missed him by inches.

"What's happening, Faris?"

The Tyrannosaurus emitted a frightening bellow and gave chase. Stephen weaved in and out of trees in hopes it would slow the mother down, but she simply crashed through them with ease. He wondered if he could lose her or if she'd just sniff him out. Maybe if he circled back to the nest, he could still recover the egg. But first, he needed to load his rifle and actually land a dart in the mother. He looked over his shoulder to judge their distance and saw they were about two hundred yards apart. If he went into the open, she'd surely close that distance in seconds. He knew the Tyrannosaurus could run upwards of seventeen miles per hour, whereas he could only go about seven under the weight of his gear.

Before he could reach the clearing, he turned and began to arc back in the direction of the nest. The mother seemed to pause and reconsider her chase. Taking this as a chance to slow enough to reload his rifle, Stephen stopped long enough to recover another dart from his belt before running once more. He was already exhausted and gasping for breath, but he couldn't allow himself to be caught.

By the time he was returning to the crater, his vision was doubling, and his head was spinning. He no longer knew where the mother was because his hearing accounted for little more than a heavy pulsing in his ears. As he approached the edge of the crater and looked below, his equilibrium padded forward, and he lost his balance. Stephen tumbled down the crater wall and rolled to the nest below. He landed six feet from the remaining egg with a thud. When he tried to collect himself from the dirt, he screamed in agony—his left arm was broken. Rolling onto his side painfully, he scanned his surroundings for his fallen rifle. It took him a moment, but he finally spotted it part of the way up the incline, tangled in the bushes.

"You've...got to be...kidding me..."

Head still spinning, Stephen sat up in the dirt and began scooting himself toward the egg with his good arm acting as a hook. His legs were bruised and weak. His whole body seemed to be trembling with exhaustion or adrenaline, a mixture that left him feeling more than a little high and unfocused.

"Faris…are…there…you…Faris…respond…"

The pounding in his ears was lessening, but he could not yet make out his handler's requests, nor was he interested in hearing them. He had the egg back in hand, but how was he to load it in the sling with a bum arm? Maybe if he rolled up against the incline, he could get it to move backwards into the swaddle on its own. As he made this attempt, the ground shook with the approach of the mother above.

"Of course," he grumbled, doing his best to focus on the egg instead. If he could get it on his person before she neared, maybe the Tyrannosaurus would leave him alone in fear of hurting its unborn young.

"Leverage," he thought aloud. "I need the leverage."

The mother began down the slope toward him with a roar from her enormous jaws, one foot crushing Stephen's rifle into the brush along the way. As she moved toward him, Stephen collected her final egg in his swath and quickly stood to show himself to the Tyrannosaurus, stumbling backwards in the process. As his equilibrium tilted and he fell onto his backside, he pulled back the dark cover enough to expose the side of the egg to its mother as she closed the remaining distance between them.

"Look!" he shouted. "LOOK!"

The beast paused over him, her teeth hovering only several feet above Stephen's own. Her breath was hot and putrid. Stephen held his breath, terrified. The Tyrannosaurus tilted her nose to the egg and sniffed twice. Then she backed away from Stephen several feet and raised her head to view him from a vantage point.

Stephen slowly picked himself up, careful not to turn his back on the beast at any point. He kept the egg facing its mother and revealed its shell again once he was steady on his feet. "You hurt me, you hurt this," he said quietly.

The mother stared at him as she shifted her feet every few seconds in impatience.

Now what?

Stephen tapped his earpiece and said, "What are the chances the mother will follow me back to the compound?"

"You haven't shot her yet?"

"My gun has been broken."

"Jesus, Faris."

Stephen continued to stare right back at the Tyrannosaurus as she watched him intently. He was too scared to break their connection in fear it would give him away as weaker than he wanted to appear.

"Will you answer my question or not?" he asked.

"*Studies have shown the parents will sometimes starve themselves to protect the nest from scavengers. So, yes, it is possible she will follow you here to reclaim the egg.*"

"And if she does?"

There was a long moment of silence in which Stephen considered signal interference. Then, "*We will disable the mother and harvest her. An even larger payday for you, assuming things go smoothly.*"

Stephen took in a shuddering breath and said, "Be ready then."

He began to move backward with the Tyrannosaurus's glare upon him. Every five feet or so, she would take a step forward, keeping him within snatching distance.

Damn, he thought. *Can I risk turning or not?*

Just as he was about to look over his shoulder, the back of his boot fell upon the nose of the tranquilized Carcharodontosaurus. He nearly fell in surprise and was horrified to see the Tyrannosaurus had angled herself differently in preparation.

She was clearly waiting for him to make one wrong move.

"Damn you," he mumbled breathlessly. How was he to climb out of the crater moving backward like this with a broken arm?

The mother's eyes suddenly left his. She was now looking beyond him.

What?

He looked backwards and up the ridge. Three camouflaged men were positioned with weapons, one of which was a net gun. They were not from Stephen's company, that much, he was sure.

They were competition.

"Fuck."

The net gun fired, immediately ensnaring the mother's head and miniature arms. She reared back and tried to scream, but her jaw was clamped shut. Stephen remained in place, unsure of where to go. These men would probably capture him, maybe even kill him depending on their company. As he considered his options, however few, the Tyrannosaurus ducked her head low and dragged it across the crater's floor to tear the netting.

"You need to leave, Faris."

Stephen snapped out of his daze and ran at a twenty-degree angle around the thrashing dinosaur, toward the slope leading back to his hover-cart. Behind him, the men began shouting in a foreign language he could not follow. A rifle fired just as Stephen was reaching the incline and slipped; the bullet pierced the ground beside his hand where it fell. Stephen cursed and instinctively looked back. The Tyrannosaurus scraped her head against the horns of the deceased Triceratops and freed herself. The attention of the armed men on the ridge returned to her instead of Stephen. He thanked God and returned to his painful one-handed climb out of the crater as gunfire erupted around the nest. The Tyrannosaurus roared and charged up the ridge toward the men as they scattered, shouting back and forth.

As Stephen crested the slope and leaned against a tree to catch his breath, he looked back at the fight on the opposite end of the crater. The mother was out of the pit now, swinging her open jaws angrily and giving chase. One of the soldiers fell and she hurried upon him. Her head snapped forward like a striking snake and removed the man's arm as he screamed horribly.

Stephen turned away and prepared himself to load the hover-cart with the egg in his sling. As he fumbled to get the egg out of its swath, another gunshot sounded, this time closer. The cart suddenly dipped to the forest floor with a screech and spitting sparks.

"Damn it," Stephen growled, taking refuge behind a tree, securing the egg against his chest once more. One of the soldiers was making his way around the crater toward him. Stephen considered his options. There was still another soldier unaccounted for, being hunted by the mother. Or maybe he was long gone by now. It was impossible to say. The Tyrannosaurus had left the one injured man dying in the dirt to pursue the man now coming after Stephen. Had he realized this yet? Stephen hoped not.

"Get out of there, Faris. We are standing by."

"I'm being followed by another company," he said, pressing the earpiece. "They're shooting at me."

"What about the mother?"

"She's in the mix, too," he said with an uncomfortable chuckle.

"Has your cart been damaged?"

"Yeah. I doubt it's going to work."

"Then run and keep as low as possible. Use the trees to your advantage. Avoid clearings. Once you're upon the beach, you'll have our eyes on you."

"That makes it all better," he said without pressing the earpiece.

The soldier paused to take another shot at him, this time striking Stephen's broken arm, which he hadn't realized was visible. The bullet tore off the cap of his elbow, spinning him to the floor. He screamed in agony and quickly collected himself from the leaves. Another shot zipped by but missed. As he began to move out of

45

hiding, he heard the man scream in surprise—he'd been caught unaware by the Tyrannosaurus.

So, somewhere, that left one soldier remaining.

Stephen ran like hell.

After five minutes, he took refuge behind a large boulder to catch his breath. He didn't want to bottom out again like he had before breaking his arm. He listened for the thunderous approach of the mother, but her movements sounded distant. Maybe he could lose her after all. Unless she knew of the compounds along the beach, which seemed likely enough to Stephen. They'd been there for months, after all.

"Taizai!"

Stephen felt his stomach sink. He turned his head to the right and saw the missing soldier standing ten feet away with his rifle raised. Stephen lifted his good hand in surrender but was unable to lift the other.

"What do you want with me?" he asked.

"Ugoka nai de kudasai."

Stephen shook his head. "I don't know what you're saying."

The soldier moved closer without lowering his rifle.

His handler sounded from within his ear: "*Why have you stopped?*"

Cautiously, Stephen slowly brought his finger toward his earpiece and pressed down on it to speak.

The soldier repeated himself, this time louder and with the poke of his rifle in Stephen's face.

"One of the soldiers has me cornered," he said slowly to his handler.

"*You are close to the beach. Very close. Hang tight.*"

Stephen wondered if that meant help was coming. He removed his hand slowly from his ear and kept it up in surrender. The soldier said something else in Japanese and stared intently at Stephen. Unsure of how to respond, Stephen tried his luck by simply nodding. The soldier relaxed slightly and lowered his gun. He then reached into Stephen's sling to retrieve the egg, all the while keeping his eyes on Stephen's.

"*Faris?*"

He didn't dare press his earpiece. He and the soldier were face to face, both holding their breaths.

"*Make sure that egg doesn't fall.*"

Stephen couldn't help but cock his eyebrow in confusion. A second later, the soldier had the egg freed from his sling and was taking a step backward. Then his head suddenly exploded in a mist of red. Stephen dove forward in the same instant and snatched the egg out of the man's hands as his corpse crumpled sideways. Both men hit the ground as the gunshot echoed through the forest.

"*Hurry, Faris.*"

Stephen stood and repositioned the egg against his chest, all the while trembling with shock. It was then he realized the ground was also shaking.

"*The mother is coming.*"

Stephen ran for the beach beyond the trees. He wasn't far. After a minute, he passed a company soldier ushering him along. In his hand was a sniper rifle, which he raised once more to take aim beyond Stephen.

"GO!" the man yelled.

The thunderous approach of the Tyrannosaurus was just behind him now. The company soldier fired twice in quick succession before turning to run as well. Stephen practically leapt onto the sand of the beach and directed himself toward the stone-laid walkway leading to the compound doors. As he reached them, he heard the soldier turn to fire his rifle again. The sound of the man cursing was cut short by the immediate crunching of jaws closing around his body. Stephen risked a look back and saw the soldier lifted by the Tyrannosaurus and tossed through the air. The doors ahead opened as he neared, several more soldiers ushering him inside. From atop the roof of the compound, several darts were fired at the mother as she turned her attention back on Stephen. She took several in the neck and chest before collapsing shy of twenty feet from the compound doors.

Inside, Stephen stopped running and placed his good hand against the wall as he gasped for breath. Someone moved up alongside him and collected the egg slipping from his grip without a word. As the doors closed, he looked out at the mother Tyrannosaurus and her dilating pupils. Her tongue lolled out of her open jaws, which were painted crimson. Then she was gone, beyond locked doors. A medical officer appeared beside Stephen a second later and gestured for him to take a seat in a wheelchair he'd brought with him. Stephen obliged and laid his head back in exhaustion. The wheelchair turned toward the hall and began in the direction of the compound's medical wing.

Stephen shut his eyes and began crying in relief.

Thank God, he was going to get paid.

THE HIDDEN GROTTO
DEREK HUTCHINS

Just after 3am, Willard Law received the phone call that woke him from his sunken slumber. He rolled, his mind torn mercilessly from its interlude, and grumbled as he answered his phone, speaking softly so he didn't wake his wife.

The phone call in question was from Gary McBride, the Director of the National Speleological Society in Alaska, where Willard lived. What Gary was offering was the chance of a lifetime, an opportunity for which Willard had waited his entire career — the life-altering opportunity to explore a virgin cave.

Willard's body coursed with energy by the time the swift phone call ended, a stark shift from his torpid comportment a few moments earlier.

Gary had been brief in details, but made sure that Willard understood the potential implications of this exploration. "You're gonna wanna take this one," Gary had assured him, in his usual, genial country tone.

Willard stumbled out of bed and threw on a pair of pants and a t-shirt, his hands jittery with excitement.

He'd been caving since his teenage years, and he'd served as the head of his local speleological grotto for the past eight.

Gary had informed Willard that a group drilling for oil had accidentally drilled into a sinkhole, resulting in the potential death of one of their employees. Willard's proposed mission was two-fold: retrieve the body of the employee who had fallen into the cave and provide a preliminary assessment of the conditions inside. However, the final detail Gary had provided had been the most intriguing: *there were trees inside this sinkhole.*

A rarity that meant this expedition would be newsworthy.

"Assemble your team," Gary had instructed him, "and get here ASAP."

After several early morning phone calls, plenty of coffee, and a turbulent drive out into the middle of nowhere, Willard arrived on site. He was the foremost cave expert in this part of Alaska, and that made him in charge.

He greeted the landowner and drillers, who refused to shake his hand.

"About time you showed up," one of them spat. "Pat's been down there for almost three hours!"

Willard squinted in the pre-dawn gloom and thought he could distinguish the outline of the cave opening. He reassured them he would do everything he could to get their friend out of there, but made sure to emphasize that sinkholes were no joke, and that they had to declare the area safe before they could go down after him.

Willard found Duke, his geological engineer, already on site doing just that. Willard watched him from a distance as Duke patrolled the area, testing the ground to make sure it, too, wouldn't collapse under their feet.

As they waited for Duke to give the all-clear, the rest of the team filed in. Willard's 'team' consisted of Jeremy and Ben, two spelunkers who also belonged to the NSS. They could be a little rough around the edges, but Willard had known them for years and gone caving with them dozens of times. He trusted them with his life, and he knew they knew how to cave.

Then there was Micky, a guy who had gotten into caving later in life, but as Willard often said, 'better late than never'. He had a cartography background, and brought the equipment to digitally map the cave once they dropped inside.

Jeneva pulled up next; she was part of Willard's search and rescue team, and would provide any medical treatment that might be necessary to the injured driller — *if* the guy was still alive.

53

And finally, Magdalena Riviera, Willard's go-to biologist. Normally, he wouldn't call a biologist for a caving expedition, but the fact that Gary mentioned trees meant they might run into some unusual fauna down there. He wanted to have someone who understood that better than him. Magdalena had gone on a few spelunking trips with them, and she had sounded eager to join.

The drillers returned to Willard's side only a few minutes later to pester him again.

"Are you in charge? We need to get down there after Pat."

"You're not going down," Willard said, with all the authority he could muster at five in the morning. Typically, he considered himself a pretty chill guy, but he had the useful ability to put all that aside in stressful situations. "We need to make sure this area is safe so we don't make the same mistake you did."

"Hey, boss, you don't have to be a dick."

"I got woken up at 3AM because you idiots were drilling into karst formations…at night. That gives me the right to be a dick. Now, we're going to do everything we can for your friend, but you need to let me do my job."

The men grumbled at Willard's speech, but they backed down.

"You're kinda hot when you go into boss mode."

Willard turned to see Magdalena standing behind him, the pale hair and skin of her albinism contrasting staunchly with the rocky surroundings. Willard smiled. "You implying that I'm not hot always?"

"Don't flatter yourself, you're a solid four."

"I've accepted that, which is why I have to compensate with the physique of a Viking warrior." Magdalena smiled and Willard clapped her on the shoulder. "Glad you could make it out on such short notice, scout."

"Hey boss, we're all clear." Duke flashed him a thumbs up, and in the dawning light, Willard called his team into action.

They advanced carefully toward safety cones that Duke had placed to mark the hole. Edging past the cones, Willard was the first to look down into the pit. The opening was narrow, no more than six feet across. *Just big enough for a man to fall through.* What a morbid thought. The thin ray of light penetrating the darkness revealed a drop that had to be over a hundred feet, and a canopy of treetops, as green as grass after rain. The actual cave floor was hidden from sight.

Ben whistled. "Wow. Of all the spots to drill, they pick the worst possible one."

Jeremy chortled. "Seriously! Now we gotta clean up their mess."

"But you like it messy."

"I always like it messy."

"Okay, guys," Willard said, clapping his hands, "I need you two to get our rappel anchors installed. Make sure you're not drilling into sinkholes."

Jeremy saluted him and the boys set to work. Everyone else prepared their gear, checking their ropes, putting on their gloves, and filling their packs.

Once the boys had the rappel anchors installed, Willard tested them. Nearly four hours since he had received Gary's call. He could tell his team was itching to get down there, but it was his job to make sure they were safe.

He was about to launch into his safety spiel when Gary showed up with a few other members of the NSS. "Can we be your base?" He tossed Willard a walkie talkie.

"Of course. I was wondering if you were gonna show up."

"I always show up," Gary countered, zipping up his jacket.

Willard went over the safety protocols with his team, as well as proper cave etiquette. "Which means no outside contaminants. I'm looking at you, Jeremy."

Jeremy nodded and ditched his cigarette. "Had to get one last one in."

Willard was keenly aware of the dangers of caving. There existed a million ways to die in a cave, and he'd survived many of them. The most likely cause was falling due to faulty equipment or incompetence. You could drown in an underground aqueduct. You could drink bad water and get poisoned. You could breathe in bad air. You could get lost. You could get trapped in a cave-in. You could get hit by a rock fall. The list went on.

Willard descended first. He rappelled down backward, into the pit, his legs leaving the safety of the rocky ledge and allowing himself to fall into the unknown. No human had set foot in this cave in thousands of years, if ever. Except for Pat, Willard was the first. That thought thrilled him, and he secretly hoped this adventure might bring him some kind of recognition. That this would be his contribution to humanity. *Law Cave*, named after the famous explorer, Willard Law. There weren't many places on earth left to explore; underground seemed the only place left to go. But Willard counted himself among the greats like Ponce de Leon and Magellan. *To go where no man has gone before* — that was his mandate, his mission.

Willard felt the leaves of the treetops brushing his thighs, and he continued to lower himself down, breaking through the canopy, until his feet hit the ground. Once he had untethered himself from the rope, he used his walkie to radio up to Gary. "Home Daddy, this is Mole Rat, touching down."

"Copy that, Mole Rat. Sending the next package."

The team rappelled down one by one, until they all landed safely inside the cave.

Magdalena's reaction was the most exciting. "Do you see this tree? I've never seen anything like it! It has to be a new species. Something unique to this biosphere."

While she rambled on about the plants, Willard explored the area, most of which was covered by a plethora of knee-high ferns. "Okay, the body will probably be somewhere close by. Let's spread out and see if we can find it."

They had only been searching for a minute when Jeneva called out, "Over here!"

Willard rushed to her voice, but when he arrived at her side, saw no fallen driller. "Where's the body?"

"I didn't find the body," Jeneva stated. "I found this." She motioned to a leaf stained with a splash of red.

"That blood?" Ben asked, stooping to admire the stain.

"I'll bet you a hundred bucks that's blood." Jeremy walked with his hands on his hips, searching the ground for signs of a crimson trail.

"A hundred bucks? You're that sure?"

"What the hell else could it be?"

"How are we even going to prove that? We don't have the equipment down here."

Jeneva touched the blood stain and rubbed the substance between her fingers. "It's blood."

"So where'd he go?" asked Magdalena, as Jeremy elbowed Ben and motioned for him to cough up the dough.

"That," Willard said, "is the million-dollar question." The reality of the situation rose like a tidal wave in his mind. Someone had died down here, which brought with it the implication that any of them might be next.

"What, do you think he just got up and walked away?" Micky asked.

"PAT!" Jeneva cupped her hands to her lips. "IS ANYONE DOWN HERE?"

The sound echoed off the walls of the cave, and Willard scanned the full chamber for the first time. The enormous space stretched over a hundred feet from floor to ceiling and at least as long as two football fields.

As the others walked around, shouting for Pat, and scouring the ground for a body, Willard pulled Micky aside.

"Hey, Mick. I want you to head to the close end of the cave and start making us a map."

"Can do, boss."

Micky pulled his handheld scanner and began to survey the cave. Sure, they had a body to find, but to Willard, mapping this cave was the more important task. If he wanted the fame, he had to deliver the data.

Shouts arose from the group and Willard became aware of a flapping sound above his head. Something passed through the beam of light from above, momentarily hiding them in shadow. He looked up to see a large, white bird circling above their heads inside the cavern.

"Holy shit! What is that thing?" Ben asked.

Holy shit is right. The thing easily had a wingspan of ten feet, far larger than any bat or cave mammal he'd ever encountered. Plus it was white, its wings feathered, and from what he could tell at this distance, instead of two legs, it had four, and a head that had no beak, but rather a set of external mandibles, almost like a gargoyle.

Willard edged toward Magdalena. "Hey. You ever seen anything like that?"

She kept her eyes on the bird as she gave her response. "No. It's fascinating. This cave has been isolated for so long, it's quite possible we'll find new species down here."

"Of bugs, maybe, but of birds?"

Magdalena shrugged. "Anything's possible."

The bird swooped toward the far end of the cave and Willard heard a scream. He and Magdalena looked at each other, then raced down the rocky slope, ignorant of crushed ferns beneath their feet, hopped over a trickling stream, and arrived on the other side of the 'forest'. From their unobstructed vantage point, they saw Ben standing at what should have been the end of the cave, but instead of a corner of rock, there gaped an enormous pit where the ceiling sloped downward. The stream ran off the edge, creating a waterfall over the lip of the pit.

Willard carefully made his way across the slick rocks to Ben. "What happened?"

"That thing came out of nowhere. It took Jeremy."

"*Took* him? Where?"

Ben motioned to the pit. Willard crept closer to the edge and peered down, not seeing any bottom.

Shit.

"What do we do now?" Jeneva asked.

"We go down after him." As much as Willard hated to admit it, he refused to leave a man behind. He'd wanted this to go as smooth as butter, to retrieve the body and spend the rest of his day exploring this miraculous cave…but he would have to put aside those desires and daydreams of a statue erected in his honour. This was now a rescue mission.

Willard pulled a light stick from his bag, twisted the knob so it lit up, then dropped it over the edge of the cliff. They all watched it fall…

Fall…

Fall…

Until finally it landed with a faint splash in a body of water about a hundred yards or so below.

"Be straight with me, Will. What are the chances he survived?" Ben had paled considerably, and Willard placed a hand on his friend's shoulder.

"I don't know…but we're not leaving here without him."

Willard's head spun as he tried to work through the mechanics of how to descend safely into the void. He and Ben installed a couple of pins in the rock wall closest to them, which would allow them to extend the rope from their anchor line so they could get to the bottom of the waterfall on the same anchor.

With that done, Will hooked himself up, nodded to his team, and pushed himself back over the edge.

He didn't know what he would find when he got down there. An enormous underwater lake? There had to be somewhere for the bird to land. He brought his flotation device ready just in case.

Magdalena shook her head when she saw him pull it out. "You brought that with you? You are such a boy scout."

"Eagle scout, actually," he corrected.

The descent felt like an eternity, each second one leap away from getting Jeremy the help he needed. Finally he felt icy tendrils creeping up his leg and knew he'd reached the water. His headlamp revealed the space to be another enormous cavern. The body of water was a wide, underground river, and off to the left was a rocky surface upon which grew another forest. The rocks that made up the walls — some form of gypsum, Willard guessed — reflected the light from his helmet, lighting the nearest section of the chamber.

He'd never seen anything quite like it.

Willard, now fully submerged in the icy water, disconnected from his rappel line and gave it two tugs, signalling to those above that they were good to come down.

He swam for the shore, reaching for his radio which hung from his shoulder. "Hey Home Daddy, do you copy?"

Only static rang in answer.

Willard cursed. He couldn't get a good signal down here. He hadn't planned to come this far down.

Willard shivered as something slithered past his leg under the water. He didn't want to know what it was, and he didn't want to think about it, but he picked up the pace, splashing his way to shore and climbing up on the moss-covered rocks.

Once he felt safe, he looked back in the water and saw several curving lines moving beneath the surface.

Eels.

"JEREMY!" He called, listening to his voice echo throughout the hollow space. More birds flapped overhead. He traced their movement to a roost on a ledge high off the ground. But he saw no sign of Jeremy up there.

Two people missing. What a mess.

Willard wandered further inland, climbing a jagged rock formation, and gazed out over the land below. This truly was another world. A lost continent below the surface of the earth. The forest stretched on for as far as his eyes could see, and he could see darker spots in distant walls, most likely tunnel entrances, suggesting the cave system was even larger.

The find of a lifetime.

It took a few minutes for the rest of the team to join him, as they had to descend one by one. "How are we going to get back up?" Magdalena asked, the least experienced caver present.

"I've got an ascender in my bag," Ben replied. "We'll have to crank ourselves up. It'll be slow going, but we've got no other choice."

Besides the splashing from the waterfall, this place chittered with life. There were squawks from the birds, strange animalistic communications which Willard had never heard before. But it was the roar that got his attention. A sanity shredding outcry which sent goosebumps down his spine.

Magdalena carefully removed her hands from her ears once it ended. "What was that?"

"It sounded like a…dinosaur," Micky said, looking mighty uncomfortable.

Willard almost told him, '*That's what they sound like in the movies, we don't know what they really sounded like,*' but stopped himself. What if the movies had it right?

"Okay," Willard said, as a way of breaking his shock. "I don't know what that was, and I don't want to find out, but we've got a man to find. Let's find him and get the hell out of here." He had to put on a brave face. Bravery was rewarded later on; bravery was the hallmark of history's heroic explorers.

"You don't have to tell me twice," Jeneva muttered, as she filed past him toward the forest.

They entered the trees, which were spaced far enough apart that there would be no bushwhacking, thank goodness. Every few seconds someone would hiss Jeremy's name, too afraid to shout it, not wanting to draw the attention of whatever had made that cry.

Willard's ears picked up the familiar chittering and he followed it until he saw a white-haired creature hopping across the forest floor. The thing had the appearance of a mole rat, with no eyes to speak of, and had a bulbous body about the height of Willard's knees. He couldn't think of anything in real life to compare it to, but his mind conjured the image of the ROUS's from the film *The Princess Bride*.

Whatever it was, it appeared harmless, and hopped its way over to a strange looking nest of large eggs at the base of a tree.

"Is it just me, or does that thing not have eyes?" Ben asked.

"It's a cave dwelling mammal," Magdalena answered, as she snapped pictures with her camera.

"They must have been living down here so long, they evolved. Don't need eyes to see in the dark."

"It's creepy as hell," Jeneva muttered.

Magdalena approached the nest, snapping more pictures as she went. "I wonder what kind of creature made these."

"Don't get too close to it!" Ben warned.

In a sudden burst of movement, the mole creature snatched up one of the eggs and scrambled off into the forest.

The birds called to each other overhead, their voices a combination of screeching and singing. *Echolocation*, Willard realized. *Their voices are rebounding off the walls so they know where they are.*

A familiar grunting made Willard pause. "Did you hear that? Jeremy?"

Another grunt. Definitely human. Willard searched around until he saw the source of the noise: Jeremy, splayed out on top of a gnarled stretch of tree roots.

"Jeneva."

"I'm on it." Jeneva rushed to his side, already removing her backpack. Her eyes assessed the damage. Jeremy's shoulder actively bled. The bird had torn deep into his muscle. His legs rested at unnatural angles, and it didn't take a genius to see that he must have been dropped and broke his legs in the fall.

The damage looked bad, but Jeremy was still moving. His eyes found Ben and his lips tried to smile. He attempted to speak, but all he could manage was a sickening gurgle.

"Don't talk, buddy. We're gonna get you out of here."

Jeneva did the best she could to bandage his shoulder and set his legs. "Somehow we're gonna have to get him up to the surface. He's not cranking himself up on his own."

Willard's mind already whirled with thoughts on how to feasibly achieve this. They would probably have to send a few people up first, secure him either on a stretcher or with ropes around his torso and with his harness.

Ben and Micky lifted Jeremy in a fireman's carry, and Willard, Jeneva, and Magdalena led the way back toward the waterfall.

Hang in there, Jer. We're gonna get you outta here.

When they reached the edge of the water, Willard told Jeneva to climb up first, then Micky would follow so they could hoist Jeremy up. As she slipped into the water and swam over to secure her harness, Magdalena collected samples of leaves and small bugs in jars. When she went to scoop a white spatter of guano with a small metal tool, Willard couldn't resist cracking a joke.

"Hey Mag, cut the shit, would ya?"

She flashed him a glare as she scraped the sample into a small tube. "This place is a biologist's dream. And I don't know if I'm coming back here, so —"

A scream of pure terror and pain, amplified by the cave's echo, split the air. Willard and Magdalena turned just in time to see Jeneva's body being pulled through the water, then disappear beneath the surface.

Willard raced to the water's edge, eyes scanning the murky face for any sign of movement. "What happened?"

Micky threw up his hands. "I don't know! One second she was fine, then she screamed."

"There's something down there. Something big."

"Well, we gotta go after her!" Ben yelled, but he shrank when everyone turned to look at him.

"Good idea. You do that."

Magdalena pulled a flare from her bag and struck it to life. The burst of light illuminated the water, revealing a massive shadow lurking out of reach below the surface.

"That thing's huge," Micky said. "It's gotta be the size of a whale!"

"Yeah, except whales don't eat people."

Willard realized with a spark of horror that the shape was getting bigger. "It's coming up. Get away from the water!"

Everyone backed up a good ten feet from the shore, and watched as a grey dorsal fin, at least four feet high, emerged from the water. The creature darted toward the waterfall, then once again vanished beneath the lake.

Willard instinctively fumbled for the radio. "Home Daddy, this is Will. We need a rescue team. Do you copy? There's something alive down here and it's got us pinned."

The radio responded with indifferent silence. "Do you copy?"

"What are we gonna do?" Ben paced back and forth, panic rising in his voice. "We gotta get back to our line! We gotta get Jer out of here! *We just lost our only medic!*"

Micky delivered a powerful slap across Ben's bearded cheek. Ben recovered from the shock, then nodded in appreciation to a stern-faced Micky.

"We stay put until we figure that out. No one leaves my sight. Understand? There could be more things out there." Willard paced, his eyes on a pale looking Jeremy, as he tried to think through this problem.

"Hey, boss, have a look at this."

Magdalena waved him over. She squatted above a patch of dirt where a large footprint was clearly imprinted. "Does this look familiar to you?"

Micky stood behind Willard. "Looks like a dinosaur footprint."

Willard couldn't deny the truth to the man's words. That's exactly what it looked like. The three-toed foot, over two meters in length — what else could it be?

"That's impossible," Willard remarked, running a hand through his thinning hair. "It's got to be someone playing a prank. Like Bigfoot."

"Yeah, someone rappelled down a three-hundred-foot sinkhole to leave a dinosaur footprint, and then didn't tell anyone about it," Ben scoffed. "Nice prank."

"Dinosaurs have only been extinct for sixty-five million years. If the event that caused their extinction somehow didn't affect what was living here, and this biosphere is self-sustaining, it's not out of the range of possibility. Somehow, they got trapped in here." Magdalena snapped pictures of the footprint while speculating. "It's a wild theory, but what else do we have to go on?"

"So you're telling me we discovered a cave filled with dinosaurs?"

"Maybe not dinosaurs exactly as we understand them. A lot of evolution can happen in sixty-five million years, not to mention the unique biological needs that arise from living underground. But close enough."

Willard scoffed. "Damn. When we get out of here, this place is going to change all of our lives."

"I wish I shared your optimism."

"I thought this place was a biologist's dream?"

"I'm starting to think it's more of a nightmare."

Willard scanned the scenery around him, uneasy. He couldn't help but feel he was wasting time. "Mag, let me see your camera. I want to take some more pictures of those flowers."

"Are you sure a flashing camera is the best idea right now?"

"I got you, boss," croaked Micky, sliding a camera from his bag. "Anything to keep my mind busy."

Micky limped his way over to the cave wall. The ground where Micky stood was covered with glossy, intertwined vines, leading to a patch of purple and white flowers that hung from a rock wall.

Micky had his camera, ready to take pictures of them. "If I bring one of these babies back for my wife, I'll never sleep on the couch again. I'll say 'Babe, no one else on earth has a flower like this.' Man, I wish I had found this place years ag—"

Willard had a hard time believing what his eyes told him. It looked like the flower had just moved, reacting to Micky's proximity, and spat something his direction. Micky screamed, clutching his face where the excretion had landed. He flailed, falling backward, roaring in agony. Willard stepped forward to help him but Magdalena gripped his arm, holding him back. "Don't."

"Over here, Mick. Follow the sound of my voice."

Blindly, the sobbing Micky made his way over to Willard where they helped him sit and finally got a good look at him. "Take your hands away from your face."

Micky wouldn't, so Willard and Magdalena had to pry his hands away.

Magdalena gasped.

Micky's face was gone.

Just gone. Erased from existence. Whatever the flower had spat at him was obviously some kind of acidic compound which was eating away at Micky's flesh, dissolving his tissue right before Willard's very eyes.

Micky's screams had shifted to autonomous and repetitious moaning. Willard wished there was something he could do, but Jeneva's medical bag had been swallowed by whatever lived in the lake, and he seriously doubted it contained a face replacement kit.

Willard gripped his friend's arm, hoping to give him some semblance of comfort in his final moments. "Hang in there, bud. It's gonna be okay." *I'm sorry —*

Thump.

The earth quivered beneath Willard's feet. He heard skittering in the brush and a flock of birds took flight from the nearby trees.

Thump.

Thump. Thump.

The rhythmic pattern of something walking. Something *big*.

And it was coming toward them, no doubt drawn by Micky's cries of anguish.

"Will…" Ben looked to him for answers.

"Yeah, I feel it. This place just won't give us a break, will it?"

He looked around for some kind of hiding place, but besides the forest, or the water, there was nothing. He snatched the small knife off his belt. He doubted it would be worth much.

No nature program or history book could have prepared Willard for what emerged from the trees. A twenty-five-foot high, bone white dinosaur walking toward them on two legs, its powerful body also

74

possessing two clawed arms. Its face was a massacre of teeth pointing in various directions, nostrils flaring, no eyes to be seen. It resembled no dinosaur with which Willard was familiar. This was a thing born from nightmares.

The beast's mouth opened, emitting a clicking croak that sent shivers down Willard's spine. *It's trying to figure out where we are using sound.*

Don't move don't move don't move. He tried to will his thoughts to the others. *It has no eyes; it can only see you if you move.*

"Forget this!" Ben cried, then took off for the trees along the river's edge.

The thing locked onto Ben at the first flicker of movement. It took less than two steps for it to chase him down. The monster seized Ben in its right claw, his body clenched in its dominant grip, while it tore the top half of his body off in one mighty bite.

Beside Willard, Magdalena quivered. "Don't move. Don't make a sound," he whispered. "It must sense our vibrations."

The dinosaur turned back toward them, almost as if it heard his whisper. Stalking on feet that could crush Willard, it made its way toward them, nostrils flaring as it sniffed the air. The beast reeked of rotting meat and feces. A piece of Ben's intestine hung from between its teeth. Willard closed his eyes and tried not to move. Sweat trickled off his brow, and his legs grew faint.

The face of the monster leaned right in front of him. Inches from his face. If he wanted to, he could reach out and touch a living dinosaur, but that was the last thing he wanted to do.

Willard sensed movement beside him, then heard a thump. Magdalena had fainted.

The beast poked its head forward, snapping its jaw and coming up empty, but bumping her foot in the process. Willard reasserted his grip on the knife, ready to do whatever damage he could to protect his friend.

But then Micky groaned and the dinosaur turned, snapping Micky's dying body in its massive jaws. It lifted Micky up in the air, tossed him up and caught his remains again in its mouth, then moved off into the woods.

Willard waited. He waited for a long time.

At last, Magdalena stirred, and Willard got her some water, filling her in on what she had missed. They sat there in silence for a while, beside Jeremy's body. At some point it had become a corpse.

The lack of light from the other cavers had caused the atmosphere to darken, so Willard pulled his last remaining lightstick from his bag. He set it on the ground beside them.

"I don't think we were supposed to come down here," Willard whispered. He only spoke to keep from going crazy. "What a day, huh? At the beginning we were intrepid explorers, making the world's greatest discovery."

"We didn't discover this place," Magdalena scolded him. "It's always been here. Evolving. Continuing on. Nature is not ours to conquer."

Willard turned and saw that the flowers growing on the wall glowed in the dark. If their team hadn't been demolished by flesh eating dinosaurs, Willard reckoned he would have thought they were quite beautiful.

My fault. It's all my damn fault…if I hadn't been so set on gathering evidence, Micky and Ben might still be alive…

Willard became aware of movement at the edge of the glow from his lightstick. Small creatures, scuttling and crawling their way toward the beacon in the dark. There were more too, gathering around, forming a natural circle. Some bigger, some smaller. Even the birds circled above, eager to check out the gathering below. Several hairy bipedal beings, perhaps descended from ancient humanoid creatures, huddled together, black silhouettes against the darkness.

Willard wondered if they were intelligent. They certainly weren't apex predators. As if in answer to his thought, the ground trembled and the bipeds scattered, along with several of the critters. Not all were so wise, and the large dinosaur snatched up several in its jaws, enjoying an evening feast.

We can't stay here, Willard realized. *It's being drawn to us like mosquitos to a porch light.* And there was no way in hell he was going to turn it off.

Formulating a plan as he went, Willard dragged Jeremy's body over to the water and tossed it in, making as big of a splash as he could. "Sorry, Jer."

"What are you doing?" Magdalena hissed.

"Improvising. Come on!"

Willard slipped into the water and Magdalena followed, while the dinosaur was distracted with its prey.

Willard held the lightstick aloft as he swam toward the waterfall. "We have to find the carabiner."

Magdalena found the line descending from above and began to pull its length through her hands, searching for the end. Willard silently urged her to move faster. He caught a glimpse of Jeremy's body in the distance and saw it disappear, pulled under by whatever lay beneath. His distraction had worked, but how much time had he bought them?

"Ow!" He felt something nip at his ribcage. Looking down he saw a gathering of eels, surrounding him, pecking at his flesh. He did his best to bat them away with his free hand, while holding his other hand above the water, swiping at them with his knife.

"Found it!" Magdalena held up the gleaming carabiner in triumph.

"Great! You go first!"

"What about you?"

"Only one of us can ascend at a time, Magdalena. And you're the hot one."

Magdalena clipped herself in, looking guilty.

"Go. GO!"

She found the crank and began to whip it up and down, pulling herself out of the water. "I'll go fast."

Another eel sank its teeth into his calf, drawing blood. Willard gritted his teeth and growled, kicking it away.

Fully out of the water now, Magdalena looked down, her face transforming into a mask of horror as she saw the swarm of eels around Willard. "Get to shore!"

The water bloomed with blood now. Eels tore at his flesh. The funny thing was that he couldn't feel it anymore. They must have had some kind of natural numbing effect. He smiled up at her.

"Will, what are you doing?"

"No one's going to miss a solid four." He inhaled sharply as a cold chill swam up his limbs. "Get yourself out. Tell them the cave collapsed. Make sure no one else follows our path."

The last thing Willard saw before he was pulled beneath the surface was the image of Magdalena cranking herself upward, back toward the world of men, where reason prevailed and monsters no longer roamed the earth.

There would be no Law Cave.

He smiled. Some things were more important than having his name in history books...like protecting those he cared about.

Then he was lost to crushing blackness.

THE BEAST FROM BEFORE
ANDREW JACKSON

The man walked out of the hills at dawn, reeking of blood and brimstone. A chill wind, soon to warm, blew low across the hardpan, rattling the spines of nearby cacti, rousing crickets, and biting through every scrap of the man's shredded clothing, nipping at the exposed flesh with a million razor teeth. He noticed it little more than the fact his left shoe was missing, or that his right arm was hanging from a strand of sinew no thicker than piano wire; neither this nor the cloud of flies that followed the bloody, jerky swathe of his passage across the rocks, nesting in a vile cloud in his putrefying flesh, and already using him as a breeding ground. He was preoccupied with higher matters.

Jonah L. Sullivan's bloodshot, sand-gritted eyeballs were filled with a deep red glow. Three days ago, when he'd last touched water, he might have recognised the Nevada sunrise for what it was. As he discarded his last worldly possession - a wad of chewing tobacco in his cheek, with a single yellow tooth embedded inside – he began to wonder.

He knew what he was doing was wrong. That was the difference between him and most of them. The dollar-thirty-seven per day didn't justify the things that came out of his lungs, or the way the Earth screamed as they wounded her. He'd hoped that the silent disquiet he'd felt regarding Manifest Destiny and that recent article in the Herald about a little place called Wounded Knee would convince God to overlook his hypocrisy, but perhaps self-awareness only made his sins graver. So, he was *here*, after all. He was disappointed, but secretly not surprised.

Jonah walked towards the red light, leaking vital fluids like a busted lantern.

What *was* it? What the heck was it, that had burst from the ruptured ground like an apocalyptic afterbirth and showed the interlopers what greed *really* was? What was it now, calling at his back; that horrible, bone-chilling wail that made the buzzards in the devil-red sky bank away, flapping like frightened sparrows? If he'd had much blood left, it would have pumped faster at the first distant *thud* from up the trail.

Jonah smiled humourlessly and kept walking.

The path was lined with bones, glinting crimson in the rising sun. Rats, rabbits, birds, some decomposing, some alive and feeding off the dead. The stench of rotting meat stuck in the back of his throat as he passed something that may once have been a horse or cow. Something too big to be prey.

Far ahead, over a short rise, a series of shapeless black lumps rose to meet the red sky. It was probably a town, judging by the rising smoke, the distant clashing of steel on steel, and the cries of sickly roosters. If it was, he had a responsibility to warn them. To tell them about the demon.

But it wasn't. Jonah L. Sullivan was in hell. He'd known it from the moment he'd heard those first screams in the blackness, smelt the awful animal scent of the *thing* beneath the rock. Compared to it, those shapeless black lumps that might just be gravestones or sarcophagi were almost a comfort.

He walked towards the graveyard as the ground trembled behind him, and those strange, almost inquisitive cooing sounds battered against his back. A thick, warm, meaty stench washed over him.

He paused for a moment, confused, as some vestigial, tiny voice inside his head tried to pick one of those dark shapes out of all that red, tried to tell him there was someone there waiting for him. Someone he'd come out here to feed. But then it was gone. And he was in hell.

There was a colossal sniff, as of a titan blowing its nose, and his hat lifted off his head and fell into the dust at the side of the trail. Soon, it was the only sign that Jonah L. Sullivan had ever existed at all.

Six days later

A cold wind sang through Parchthroat Pass, painting the three hunters' faces by flickering firelight. Between them, a jackrabbit sizzled and popped on a long spit.

"Warren Hurst says it's wolves," said Cesar, the youngest. The fire hissed and spat an ember onto his wrist as he turned the meat. His heart skipped a beat and the rabbit trembled under his hand, more from the noise than the pain.

Condor chuckled, his broad back to the others. Slivers of moonlight glinted off his slick, braided hair, and the wolf-tooth amulet around his neck. "Warren Hurst would say the moon was made of gold dust if it bought him a whiskey."

"Patty Greensill saw them too," Cesar continued, eager to impress the deputy. "Hundreds, she said, coming from the mine at night."

"Ditto Patty Greensill, if it meant she could hold court," grunted Sheriff Weatherby.

Weatherby loved fancy words like ditto, being able to recite The Gettysburg Address verbatim. His biggest case since taking office was busting Pickled Pete's moonshine still. Cesar should remember; he'd suffered the little grey-haired man's lecture through a cataclysmic hangover. Condor should have been top dog – he'd won the town election - but the world wasn't fair.

The deputy cocked his head and listened. Cesar tried emulating him, but all he got was the tin-whistle of the wind, distant coyotes, and the *hoo-hoo* of an owl. This far up the mine trail, red rock cliffs loomed over them, suggesting strange, disturbing images at night. It was like being in an earlier land. One filled with giants.

"He is close," said Condor, laying his rifle on the rock and stretching. "Hours at most."

Weatherby worried at some grit between the neat folds of his pants, then produced a little golden dinner-knife on a pearl chain and began slicing up the rabbit. "We must keep our strength up."

Cesar's stomach felt like a dried prune, but he made himself eat. If he wasn't so gosh-darn clumsy, if he didn't always ruin Pa's *systems*, he'd be asleep on the ranch now, rather than out here impotently backing up the lawmen, and a bunch of miners who were probably just late. In a warm bed, listening to animals dying.

"Ever hunted anything before, son?" Weatherby asked between mouthfuls.

Cesar shook his head. "Just varmints, sir. Nothing like this."

The sheriff leant back and laced his fingers across his belly, smearing rabbit grease over his shirt. "Well, what's sauce for the goose is sauce for the gander, and all that."

The other two looked at him blankly.

Weatherby coughed. "By which I mean to say, it doesn't matter how big or nasty our quarry is. He'll turn up his toes just the same." He tapped his hip holster and let out a faint belch. "We're the apex predators here."

Cesar would have felt better if the sheriff's eyes weren't darting like frightened birds behind his glasses.

Even the widely travelled deputy had never seen the likes of the beast that had seen every farmer in town take his shotgun to bed for months – consequently being responsible for old Jebediah Hallam's spontaneous decapitation. The beast drunks and schoolchildren threatened each other with in arguments. The beast that could bite through a cow's spine, snatch sheep whole, and devour chickens, coops and all. But he was the only one who didn't seem terrified.

"Wolves," whispered Cesar. He almost believed it.

Since Ma, Cesar never slept well. He was prone to what Doctor McReady - Lackworth's non-licensed dentist – called *nocturnal perambulations*. So when he became aware of himself, standing on a boulder with his flies undone, warm liquid trickling down his thigh and pooling in his boot, he wasn't scared or even surprised.

The moon was a round silver egg in the sky, but there wasn't enough light for him to read his pocket watch. The pass was quiet, but for the constant creaks and cracks of the stressed rock, and the rattle of small stones moving down the shallow incline. And Weatherby's snoring.

Cesar cast aching, drooping eyes over the sheriff and deputy, just feet away, one wrapped up in a goose feather quilt, the other lying stiff on a thin sheet, cocked like a pistol hammer, seemingly ready to fire at a moment's notice.

He didn't belong here, but at least he might not disappoint Pa. His shot might save the farm, maybe even the town. And then maybe they'd share more than shouts and scrawled notes. But still, he wasn't like Condor, whose eyes and ears made sure Weatherby rarely had to be in his office. There was an old schoolroom legend that the deputy read your report sheet before Miss Kane had written it. It was almost spooky that he hadn't spotted the two glittering orbs in the dark, around the next bend in the rocks.

Cesar felt his heart stop, as a rush of cold prickles raced across his body. His perception of distance was clouded by sleep and the darkness, but those... not eyes. They *weren't* eyes – had to be ten feet off the ground. At least. And maybe four times that distance from him.

A lone droplet of sweat trickled down his ribcage, racing his trembling hand to his belt, and a pistol that wasn't there.

"No..." he whispered. And it was okay, because this wasn't happening. McReady was wrong. He slept just fine, and this was just another dream. In reality, the gun would have been on his hip, and he'd have pumped a bullet through each of those shining black triangles, bobbing almost imperceptibly like undulating chips of pure jet. If he started running now -like his lower body was desperate to – he'd feel like he was moving through molasses, his breath and movements and thoughts sluggish and inadequate, as terror tore his heart through his back. And he'd wake up in bed, screaming, with Pa banging on the wall. Like most nights. A small, awful voice was telling him you couldn't smell in dreams. Couldn't process that faint whiff of spoiled meat that ruffled the hairs on Condor's sleeping head as it came down the valley in little huffs.

Just when he thought the paralysis would erupt in a scream, and bring those terrible orbs down on him, they abruptly vanished. He tensed, listening for the tread of a heavy animal, the rustle of fur gathering in hiding to spring when he moved. But nothing came, and after several minutes of standing like a telegraph pole, shivering in the night chill and straining all his senses into the blackness, he slunk back to bed, defeated and ashamed of himself for his imagination. A dream. Just another dream.

In the morning, he wondered why his boot was wet.

Following a meagre breakfast, Condor led them up the pass, accompanied by Weatherby's tuneless whistling. Buzzards wheeled in a sky half robin's-egg-blue and half the bruise of an oncoming squall. Periodically, gaps in the rock exposed the plains below: rolling dunes, stubby cacti, little clots of bison, stretching to the horizon. Lackworth was only visible by the twisty black smoke of its smelters. The town might as well be the world, its dusty boardwalks and oily smells the only civilisation Cesar had ever known, and the only sign of man for a hundred miles. From up here, that world looked miniscule.

Easy to swallow.

Just before noon, Condor stopped so abruptly that Cesar rode into him.

A wagon had overturned in the crook of a narrow bend, torn fabric flapping in the wind. One mule was gone, the other little but bone. What meagre flesh remained was ragged and black, and the ribcage was just cracked, jagged spurs, as if unbelievably powerful jaws had torn out its still-beating heart. For an awful moment, the sun seemed to ring in his ears, spinning in the sky, and he had to clutch his horse's mane to keep it still. It was the most terrible thing he'd ever seen. But there was worse to come.

Several ore-filled kegs had spilled from the wagon and split, filling the turn with clumps of rock. Between them lay shapes that were horribly familiar, to a young man who'd brought his sick mother her morning milk until the morning she didn't need it anymore.

Condor whistled harshly, rifle instantly in hand. Cesar tugged Pa's old six-gun from his belt, hands trembling, and Weatherby dropped an ornate Volcanic pistol in the dirt with a squawk of frustration.

"How... how many?" gasped the sheriff. Many of the shapes still wore stained shirts and wide-brimmed hats. A startled buzzard took off from a severed leg picked almost clean. Flies covered the corpses in dark, undulating death shrouds.

"Six, by my count." Condor gestured at a rusty repeater, sticking out of the ground like a tombstone. "And armed, much good it did them."

Cesar tried to look everywhere but at the dead mule, the decomposing miners, the endless, sun-dried blood. One appeared to have been crushed, his chest flush with the trail. The strewn ore was covered in yellow crystals and crimson specks. Cesar leaned in closer, fascinated and appalled by human hair sprouting from a hunk of ore the size of his fist.

"Don't... don't even think about it, boy," said Weatherby. "That's our lifeblood."

He wasn't sure what was scarier – Weatherby seeming to care more about the sulphur than the dead, or that he sounded about two breaths from sobbing.

Cesar's horse whickered and stomped, and he allowed her to lead him away, further up the mine trail. One of them was trembling, but he wasn't sure which. A rotten signpost between two rocks proclaimed *Cerberus, .5 miles*. Someone had put a bullet hole through it.

"Do... do you think maybe the mine..." Cesar said, looking up the dusty incline towards the next bend in the rocks, for some reason thinking about floating black orbs.

Weatherby read his mind, seemingly glad to focus on something other than what he could see.

"Cerberus has an excellent safety record," he said. "Considering what we're working with, our accident rates are really quite low, and—"

A sudden scream cut him off, erupting from further ahead. It sounded like a hawk, maybe a red-tail – bone-piercingly harsh, but louder, so much louder. As Cesar watched, a stream of dislodged pebbles ran down the nearest cliff face, and a dozen tiny lizards extricated themselves from hidden holes and ran past the riders, through the muck and gore, without slowing.

Weatherby tugged his collar, face white as marble. "Uh… windy day, isn't it?"

Condor hadn't moved. Admirably, neither had his horse.

"That came from the mine, sheriff," he said.

"Well—" said the little man, and let the word die with the echoing scream.

Cesar gulped. "What if… what if they found something down there? Miss Kane was telling us about these giant monster bones they found in-"

Weatherby swelled up, ready to orate, but Condor cut him off.

"Our Earth is older than us," he said. "Things we shouldn't know swim in her blood. Take from her too long, sometimes she takes back."

Weatherby harrumphed. "The mine feeds our children, deputy. No sulphur, no town. No hope."

Condor halted again shortly, raising his hand until Weatherby ceased chattering. The afternoon sounds blanketed them: buzzing cicadas, ravens' caws, rocks shifting in the canyon walls. The echoing, ¬booming footsteps of something big, something close. A cougar that had been following them, glimpsed only by the deputy, tucked tail and ran, mewling like a kitten.

Weatherby seemed to rise out of his saddle with each distant *thump*, giving the disquieting impression that the very ground was moving. Cesar thought again of school; of gods and demons and... minotaur. He leant in closer to his horse and rubbed sweaty fingers over his gun.

"Maybe it's a bear," he whispered, eyeing a monstrous mound of stringy dung. "Stocking up for winter."

"We don't get bears this far south." Weatherby looked at Condor, fingers white around his fancy pistol. "Do we?"

"This isn't bear trail." Condor indicated the dusty footprints, three-toed and impossibly large. "But the principle is sound. Our friend always returns home. Let's hope he's already eaten."

As they entered the last stretch of the pass, the sun vanished behind a cover of gunmetal grey, almost as if where the three men were going, it had no business.

Cerberus Mine sat at the canyon's end, in a tall, broad basin. The entrances – three of them, to be precise – were set into the rear wall, but two seemed to have fallen in, and perhaps recently, judging by Weatherby grumbling something about productivity quotas before Condor again signalled him quiet.

Discarded pickaxes and shovels carpeted the gentle incline to the mine's entrance, about a hundred feet from the riders. Three more wagons leaned against a large tin barracks, the star-spangled banner dangling from its roof like a hanged man. There was a very large dent in the shack's front side. Nothing moved but for tumbleweed and the crescent-shapes of circling buzzards. It was easier to look up there because looking at the ground was worse. Far worse.

"Make yourself useful," said Condor, to distract Cesar from the sickly reek of spoiling man-meat. "Gather up some of that weed. Drier the better."

Cesar dismounted and set about the task, holding his breath as he stepped around more ruptured miners – mostly just little piles of purple-black viscera and dirty, snapped-off shards of bone.

"It's just meat. It's just meat," he whispered to himself, fighting down his gorge and pretending not to notice the discarded watch-chains and tobacco pouches amongst the carpet of the dead. From the mine came distant *boom-boom* sounds, and a chilling, unearthly noise that resembled an unnaturally deep pigeon's coo.

"Let's draw a line under this," spluttered Weatherby, eyes determinedly focused on a narrow point halfway up the basin wall. "How do we… um."

Cesar returned, his arms full of dry brush.

"How deep does Cerberus run?" Condor asked.

"About nine hundred feet." Weatherby's chest puffed out. "All hand-dug, of course. No shortcuts with sulphur."

Cesar knew – being threatened with the mine weekly - that sulphur was difficult, dangerous stuff. The matchbox in Condor's hand worried him

Weatherby seemed to notice it too, hand halfway to his gun, but before he could fully process what Condor was planning, two things happened almost simultaneously. First, the heavens reopened, and rain cascaded into the basin, and then a monster stepped out of the mine.

Cesar's only comparison was to the geckos that he frequently had to shake out of his sheets. A twelve-foot-high gecko, with tiny, ineffectual arms, covered in scruffy, patchy feathers, and a yawning jaw filled with forearm-length teeth. Two beady black eyes – seemingly far undersized – sat far back in a massive, elongated skull that had the colour and consistency of dried lava. With a sharp twist in his bowels, Cesar realised they looked horribly familiar.

The ground trembled as it slithered from the mine on two huge, stubby legs. Endless, leathery dark skin sparkled in the sudden squall. A fist of noxious air preceded it, filling the men's nostrils with the stench of rotting meat. It didn't react to the party in any obvious way, but as it drew to a halt, standing impossibly *there* in the rain, it didn't need to. As far as it was concerned, they were probably already halfway down its gullet.

In the following silence, only the creature breathed.

"Some things man was never meant to see," muttered Condor. "Stay absolutely-"

Weatherby shrieked, high and cat-like, wheeled his horse around and spurred it towards the trail. The giant head swivelled, nostrils flaring, then it made that low, trilling coo, and took off like lightning.

Weatherby's horse was at full gallop, but the beast closed the distance in five long strides, clamping wide jaws over the screaming sheriff.

Cesar yelled and fumbled for his gun, but his terrified horse chose that moment to kick and bolt, clocking him in the temple and sending him into the dirt. The revolver clattered away. Condor's rifle cracked, but the great lizard merely tossed the sheriff like a toy and tore him in half.

Cesar's body felt fuzzy and strangely comfortable, nose dripping warm liquid. He was aware of someone distantly yelling – probably Pa with a sore head – but that wasn't important. He'd just snatch another half-hour before cleaning the sheep pen. Just-

"Boy!" roared Condor as the monster turned its tiny, dead black eyes on them. Dead black eyes from a dream that wasn't. A string of Weatherby's bloody intestines hung from its mouth. "Get to the shack!" A sudden clap of thunder stole his words. "Find… need… there…"

The words didn't wake him so much as Condor's matchbox striking his chest. On rubbery legs, he pushed himself upright, cradling the matches, and staggered towards the barracks. The thing took a step toward him, and then its right eye exploded.

Condor got off another shot before the monster lunged, and Cesar saw no more.

He fell into the shack, tripped and sprawled into warm, pungent darkness, landed on something more maggot than man and vomited into it. From outside came the sharp crack of Condor's rifle, and those awful pigeon-cries.

Cesar crawled past bunks with built-in footlockers, over hats and hatchets, chamber pots and fly-specked jars of jerky. What could possibly stop a creature this size? Could anything, short of a world falling on it? A long silver gleam caught his eye on a shelf above a crude brick firepit, and he shuffled closer in a low crouch, almost relieved by the smell of the spoiled stew – just pork, thank the Lord - in the pot hanging over the embers. A shotgun! Better, a blunderbuss. Its mouth was almost as wide as that terrible maw. And almost as ancient. Cesar's heart sank as he saw the rust on the muzzle, the absence of trigger.

Cesar cried out, as much in frustration as to blot out the unearthly wails outside and kicked the nearest footlocker to pieces. He knelt to scrabble through the splinters, praying for a pistol, a knife, anything at all. Weatherby's squirming innards kept coming back to him, hanging from the monster's mouth like a tongue. So red, like… his probing, sweaty hand closed on something, the one thing the miners up here weren't supposed to have: a shortcut.

He burst into the storm, heart pounding harder than the creature's footsteps as it cornered the deputy.

Condor danced his horse like liquid, dodging and weaving, twisting and hopping, shooting one-handed, but retreating, always retreating, as the monster pushed him towards the cliff wall. One of its little arms was hanging bloody and useless, but it was too big, too fast.

He brandished the sticks, shouting wordlessly, distracting Condor, who finally stumbled and fell.

Cesar cried out and started forward as the great jaws closed on the screaming horse, but the deputy somehow crawled out from under, vaulted the huge, thrashing tail, and limped the short distance to the shack.

A flash of blue lightning illuminated Condor's tired, old features as he looked from the gorging lizard to Cesar, to the mine. The sounds of the creature's feasting eclipsed the thunder.

"Know what you have to do..." he rasped. "Don't hesitate. Not for a second."

Cesar gulped under the one-eyed stare as the monster threw the husk aside and turned to face them. That razor-grin was almost mocking.

"No." He shook his head. "There must be another way."

"Don't let them come back here, kid." Condor pumped another round into his rifle. "Promise me." He closed his eyes, said a quick prayer in another language, and dropped something into Cesar's hand, which gripped it painfully. Then he was gone.

That terrible eye seemed to snare Cesar, filling him with ice. In it, he saw himself for what he was, without his sapient toys and tricks. Just another helpless, terrified mammal. Prey, for something that had hunted his kind for eons. Over the next thundercrack came a deep, triumphant cry, full of terrible certainty. Then that eye exploded too.

The lizard screamed, blood and yellow ichor painting its teeth, then lumbered after the sound of Condor's shot, footsteps rattling Cesar's teeth. The blind creature missed him by inches, blasting down the mine's throat like a cannonball.

The fuse lit easily, but the rain instantly doused it. He cursed and almost dropped the bundle, thinking of Weatherby, the miners, the man who'd bought him precious seconds. Already, those booming footfalls seemed to be coming back. Only one place was close enough, dry enough.

Cesar stumbled into Cerberus, guts churning with terror. Here, the bones were so numerous they crunched underfoot, glittering pale in the lightning. Someone had tried to collapse the tunnel with a sledgehammer, succeeding only in splintering one of the supporting timbers. Many of the roof beams were in a similar state, and bits of the leathery hide hung bloody from sharp rocks overhead, where the creature had forced its way through a hole not made for it. Egg-like sulphur dust stung his throat, not quite masking the ancient animal reek of the approaching creature.

He could hear that tail beating the walls, see Condor's discarded rifle leaning against the rock wall, just ahead of a wide T-junction leading further into the mine. A hiss of foetid breath blasted through the tunnels and stirred his hair as the match finally caught. He touched it to the fuse, the sudden hissing the greatest sound on Earth.

Cesar stumbled backwards as the blunt, gore-soaked snout edged into view, Weatherby's little dinner-knife lodged in its gum like a gold tooth. The monster roared, exposing a dark abyss behind ice-white shards, and then he was outside again, the lizard mere feet away.

"Some things man was never meant to see," he whispered, and lobbed the dynamite into the blind, screaming face.

The first explosion threw him flat. The second deafened him. Everyone in Lackworth heard the third.

The storm was gone, along with the basin's rear wall – the former Cerberus Mine now merely jagged, broken boulders and spurs of red rock. The ground settled slowly, aftershocks forming depression after sinkhole, before finally solidifying into a loose scree slope to the plains below. The sun was small in the sky and returned only shyly, as if afraid it might yet be consumed. In the dissipating smoke, something groaned and sat up.

Cesar's head felt like the morning after the moonshine, with Sheriff Weatherby knocking politely on his father's door. He staggered upright and brushed dust off his clothes, shivering at the way the surrounding hellscape resembled a devouring mouth. Blinding terror washed over him for a moment, before he finally saw what he'd done. The *thing* had to be dead. If that hadn't killed it, nothing could. Still, as he tripped and staggered down the new slope towards civilisation, he half-expected those colossal jaws to come bursting through the earth and drag him down after them. Into those unknown depths from whence it had come. Maybe to meet its family, hungry and waiting.

He'd abandoned the idea that he might wake up the second time he'd looked into those awful eyes. It was easier to pretend it hadn't happened, that he was crazy. He could laugh at himself, like the townspeople ahead – like Pa – certainly would, before they stopped finding him funny. Something like that didn't... *couldn't* exist. Not now. And yet... attached to Cesar's pants leg was a rain-sodden feather that ran the length of his thigh. They'd call it a new species of bird maybe. But it was an old one. Old, and not quite extinct. He shook it away, kicking frantically until it fell upon the new grave.

Miraculously, his only injury seemed to be to his right hand, still clenched tight and refusing to unlock, ever since Condor had left him. With his left, he prised open the stiff fingers to reveal the wolf-tooth amulet. True, ancient power, to humble any tin star. The sharp end was pointing towards Lackworth; home, and the distant puffs of dust that heralded approaching riders. He had a promise to keep.

A PRIMITIVE PARTY
NICOLE NEILL

"The remains of cattle were discovered this morning by passer-by Mark Willis. They were located when Mr Willis was jogging at the edges of Gold Orchard Avenue, leading from the private Oakridge Ranch. Described as appearing like the victims of an animal attack by the witness, this is yet to be confirmed by the authorities. Oakridge Ranch, known publicly as the supplier of all American beef for our serving armed forces, has been reached for a comment. Privately, the ranch has often been accused by the native population of being built to spy on the local population and keep an eye on their loyalty during war efforts."

"Rubbish," Danny Bryer scorned the radio report.

Danny's sister Alice looked up from the kitchen table at his comment. She had only been half-listening to the radio while picking at a slightly burnt waffle.

The kitchen had all the illusions of a cliché home, right down to the red-and-white chequered cloth on the round table. It matched the look of an All-American homemaker's domain but held none of the soul. Two months of trying to make it a home and Alice still

105

viewed it as an inferior copy. The attempts to bring the holiday season into it had not proved successful, with the bunting of paper bats and ghosts hanging limp and lifeless instead of terrifying.

"Are you going to eat that or study it?" Danny pointed at the waffle. "Come on Alice, we need to head out."

Danny took a deep swig of his cup of lukewarm coffee before cocking his head to the side door as he heard steps on the tiles leading up to it. His bright blue eyes twinkled with amusement as the door opened inwards to admit their neighbour and Alice's friend, Elisa March.

Elisa entered the home full of music and sunshine, smiling and humming as her light feet made a dance out of her steps. The teenager had a glow of energy and vibrancy within her that lit up her eyes, heating the brown to copper, and adding a healthy smudge of dusky pink to her cheeks.

"Good morning, Bryer children," she greeted chirpily. "Look what I have here."

Elisa held up a piece of black card with generic white ghosts patterning it. With a bright smile she held it out and waved it up and down excitedly.

Danny took it from her with a small smile, though his blue stare showed disinterest. He turned the card over quickly in his hand.

106

"A Halloween party invitation. Interesting," he said sardonically.

"With no clue to the host, which is interesting," Elisa commented as she wagged her finger at Danny.

Danny glanced up at her and shook his head, before looking to Alice who had stood up from the table. "Well, it's starting at seven so I guess it can't be that wild. You know dad will want you back for ten."

Alice cocked her head and forked out her tongue before shaking her head. "Back before there's time to have fun," she grumbled.

"Yeah. Anyway, let's get in the car kids," Danny ordered. He held up his hand and gestured to the door Elisa had entered through.

The trio headed out to a cool, sunny morning. The grass of a neatly clipped lawn shone damp with the remnants of the pre-dawn's frost, and a chill in the air hinted at fog to come.

Alice and Elisa hopped into the back of the waiting Jeep, one of the obvious tells that they were part of the army base. Big, green, and entirely environmentally unfriendly, its engine grumbled through a neighbourhood of almost identical houses with mimicked lawns. The base did its best to resemble suburbia, an image that lasted until you reached the barbed wire-topped fences to escape.

Alice cast her eyes up to the metal fences and suppressed a sigh. Every morning for the past six months she had glimpsed them, but she still couldn't suppress the feeling of imprisonment they caused.

"So what are you dressing up as tonight, Alice?" Elisa pried.

Alice glanced over to her friend curiously. "You assume I have a costume for a party I just heard about?" She spoke with enough sarcasm to match her brother's earlier tone.

Elisa elbowed Alice playfully. "I assume you have a costume for Halloween, something which I hope you have heard about before now."

"Right, that thing."

Danny snorted from the driver's seat and shook his head as he suppressed a laugh.

"What about you Danny?" Elisa glanced up to the rear-view mirror and smiled at him.

"I'm on patrol tonight. No costumes for me," Danny explained as he glanced back to her.

Danny wound down his window and offered up his I.D to the patrolling soldier by the gates. They nodded to each other before Danny eased the jeep out.

"I'm going to be a cat," Elisa announced happily.

Alice watched as they passed by paper pumpkin lanterns hanging off lampposts and some bad looking bedsheets ghosts fluttering in the wind from tree branches. She appreciated seeing a familiarity in the decorations even if the buildings still appeared foreign to her. She realised the irony of her thoughts given she was the foreigner here.

The small stretch of suburbia switched to tall trees undressing for fall as they headed up a bumpy stretch of road to the high school. Although it was a twenty-minute drive away from their homes, the school belonged to the army base as well, serving to educate all the army brats. It was believed that they might have some comfort and companionship with kids in similar circumstances. Alice felt it kept them isolated, stuck in a bubble from the locals, ensuring they would never really familiarise themselves with the people whose land they occupied. Alice wondered what Halloween parties were like here; dressing up, carving pumpkins, and eating caramel apples seemed universal, but she wondered at the truth of that.

The Jeep dipped down and shook as its wheels bumped along uneven road.

Danny cursed, reaching for the brakes as the vehicle slipped down into the earth.

"This is one hell of a pothole," he grumbled as he tugged up the handbrake.

Alice stared out the window, mystified, peering down to the odd grooves in the road they had sunk into.

"Weird shape for a pothole," she murmured.

Elisa's gold hoop earrings jingled as she turned her head to the window.

Danny unbuckled his seatbelt and jumped out of the Jeep. He cursed again as he stumbled in the uneven dirt. His blue eyes widened as he stared down, and then he turned round to take in what had upset their journey.

"Is...is that an animal print?" Alice asked the question as she joined him.

She moved ahead and let out a soft "Woah."

Danny followed his sister, halting almost instantly as he took in what she did. The prints were large and deep, three- toed with sharp points, formed in pairs as they veered off to the right. Danny turned his head to follow them, and his mouth parted slightly as he took in the trees there. They looked like something had charged into them, bending them back with its force. What alarmed the young soldier most was that the surviving trees standing nearby were about sixteen feet tall, meaning whatever had pushed the others back to the point of almost snapping stood around a similar size.

"Alice!" Danny yelled out his sister's name as he glimpsed her racing forward to the trees.

Alice's long, copper-brown hair danced like a flame as it fluttered up and back behind her as she hurried over to the damaged trees. She stepped off the edge of the road, heading into the boundary of wilderness, intrigued by the tracks leading in there.

Danny hurried after his sister as a moment of absurd terror bubbled up in him for creatures non-existent. He caught up to her with ease and grabbed her left arm to secure her.

"Hey!" Alice glared up at her brother.

"Maybe don't run off into unknown woods like that," Danny admonished her. "You don't know what's out here. There could be wolves."

"Yeah, giant, three-toed ones."

"Um, guys… What did that?"

Alice and Danny turned together to face Elisa. The teen stood on the spot, yet her body had become animated with quivers. She extended a shaky hand up to point behind them.

Nervous but curious, Alice and Danny glanced simultaneously to the right.

Alice immediately pressed her head against her brother with a low groan of horror as she tried to banish the gore before them.

As soon as he looked to it, Danny noticed the stench accompanying it and wondered how in the hell his mind had blocked such a foul odour until now. The metallic scent of fresh blood hung in the air, poisoning the sweet

111

smell of the fall kissed trees surrounding them. The source of the blood appeared to be a bear missing its entire lower end. Shredded fur and deep, jagged wounds in the flesh seemed to suggest something had torn the bear up with its teeth.

Danny swallowed hard and turned Alice away. "Back to the Jeep now," he ordered.

They moved quickly and quietly, all of them aware now of the silence in the air. There came with it a recognition that they had likely stumbled into *something's* territory.

Danny reached for the Jeep's radio the moment he got into the vehicle and called into base. He hesitated as an answer came through and he realised he didn't know what to say.

"I'm on Juniper Lane," he answered at last. "Looks like a large, wild animal has been through here, something big enough and strong enough to kill a bear. Just thought I'd call it in, in case it's a rogue or rabid animal," he added lamely.

Danny let out a deep breath as he released the button on the speaker. He accepted the monotone acknowledgement of the call and ended it.

"Right," he said in a serious tone, "let's get you guys to school. We're all late enough already."

The remaining drive to the school took place in a stark silence. Danny chose not to speculate over what they had found and tried to dislodge it from his mind.

When they arrived at the school gates, the young soldier glanced over his shoulder to the girls and made himself smile.

"Have a good day, and if you're going to that party, don't stay out too late," he cautioned.

"Right." Alice glanced up and nodded at him.

Alice exited the car slowly, almost trancelike as she moved with small steps, and did not bother to adjust her bag when it slipped down her shoulder. She stared ahead at the carved pumpkins lining either side of the path leading up to the school building and swallowed hard. All of a sudden, she had no mood for the holiday; confronting a real horror had her eager for a night in the safety of her home with the lights on and a cheerful movie playing for distraction.

Danny frowned as he watched his sister and Elisa head for the building. He had dealt with a few wild animals in his time, in the jungles and plains of lands at war, and he didn't know of one capable of killing a bear like that.

Alice stared at her reflection with a tired reluctance. The disturbance this morning had poisoned her day with an unease which had drained her. It had only turned six in the evening, and she felt ready for bed rather than partying. The loneliness of her home given her father and brother had both been called to duty for the evening, coupled with the persistent and repetitive barking of the base dogs since she had returned from school, had persuaded her to go to the party with Elisa.

She could see her tension even beneath her costume; her shoulders were rigid, her body taut and her eyes too wide. She supposed, dryly, that her fear actually went with her costume: a plain white bunny. In lieu of a mask she had opted for cheap face paint instead, giving herself a black tipped nose and whiskers that were liable to smear with sweat. White, pink inlaid ears, a pinned-on tail, and a pair of faux silk gloves with pink pads on them, were all that resembled a rabbit when it came to her costume. The short-skirted dress of white was akin to a ballerina's outfit, and the knee-high white socks and flat-soled sneakers didn't add anything to the imagery.

Alice jumped as the doorbell rang. She frowned at her reflection and scorned her unease before she abandoned her cluttered vanity table. She grabbed her gold chained purse from her cushion cluttered bed and headed downstairs.

114

The army dogs were still barking. The sound filled Alice with an unease as she wondered what could have disturbed them to have them agitated for so long.

"Trick or Treat!" Elisa's voice called mockingly as she glimpsed Alice's approaching form through the blurred glass.

Alice slid back the chain and opened the door. "Don't you mean *meow*?"

Elisa had opted for an actual catsuit: skin-tight, black Lycra that had definitely not been parent approved, coupled with a black domino mask with cat ears that seemed more suggestive to feline that outright catlike.

Alice leaned up against her doorway and folded her arms. "And how did you sneak that past mummy and daddy?"

"With the long, winter coat I have in the back seat of my car," Elisa answered happily as she gestured back to her waiting Dodge.

Alice gave her friend an admiring nod.

"Got your invitation?"

Alice raised her handbag and nodded again. "Yeah, not that there's much to it. Hollow Oaks House – where is that?"

"On Gold Orchard Avenue. It's not far from here."

"Right."

"Hurry up and let's go. It's freezing, and this costume isn't as insulating as it looks."

Alice laughed and stepped away from the door frame. She turned to grab a dark, woollen coat off a hook.

"Don't bother with that," Elisa scolded her. "It'll be warm at the house, I'm sure, and you don't want to cover up such a cute costume."

Alice sighed. "Alright." She stepped outside, taking care to close and lock the door behind her.

Alice followed Elisa to her car and was relieved to feel the remnants of heat inside it from Elisa's brief drive over here.

Elisa cranked on the engine, bringing the heaters humming to life along with a corny Halloween-themed song blasting through the speakers.

Alice frowned as the car moved off and she took in the faint fog the headlights bounced off.

"Think that will get worse?"

"Who cares?" Elisa dismissed cheerfully. "We aren't going far."

Elisa started to hum along to the song as she drove, swerving round corners sharply and driving a little quicker than Alice liked considering the elements of darkness and fog.

"Um…you know this place is crawling with soldiers, right?" Alice reminded her in a deadpan tone. "As in well-trained men with sharp eyes who will take in your reg and track you down for this kind of driving."

Elisa shrugged. "I like the challenge."

Alice gripped the edges of the worn seat as Elisa continued to flaunt traffic laws and speed them to their destination.

Alice felt relief as they escaped the barbed fences and the unsettled dogs, as she hoped a party might prove better than an uneasy, lonely army base.

As they drove, she thought briefly of the morning encounter with the strange tracks and the mutilated bear. She had wondered throughout the day if it might be a Halloween prank; either one done exceptionally well or one sinister with hints of sacrificial purposes to it. It was odd, but even the thought of the latter gave her some comfort as it still meant the cause of it all would have a human identity. Trying to consider an animal behind it all had her frightened, as she couldn't imagine the type of creature that could leave those tracks and cause that kind of destruction.

"There it is," Elisa announced happily as they pulled up to the ajar gates of a large property.

The spacious land before the house suggested it had been farmland once. A scarecrow with a ghoulish face loomed down at them from the edge of the path leading

117

up to the house, whilst skeletons danced in a light breeze from the crooked branches of old trees.

The path proved too narrow for the car, forcing Elisa to abandon it against the walls of the property so she didn't obscure the gates.

"Not creepy at all," Alice murmured sarcastically as she stepped out of the car and hugged her exposed figure.

"Well, it wouldn't be much of a Halloween party if it wasn't," Elisa pointed out.

Elisa offered the crook of her arm to her friend. Arm-in-arm they headed up to the poorly lit property.

Their way was lit with lanterns flickering on the edge of the path. Unfortunately, some of the lanterns had toppled over, smashing in the process and leaving them subjected to patches of darkness.

Alice cast her gaze outwards to the wilderness on either side of them as they walked. There was long grass or crops growing wild, she didn't know or care which; all she knew was that it gave her the feeling of wandering through a corn maze, dependent on the path and at the mercy of the flora. Whatever grew out there had barely been kept back from the path, and every so often it narrowed in places where the plants had started to intrude, returning the thin sliver of man's presence back to nature.

Alice shivered and quickened the pace. She could see the consoling glow of lights up ahead and hear the sound of music carrying in the night air. The party seemed so close and yet too far. The house had been built so far back from the gates that, as they neared it, Alice didn't think they were in the same neighbourhood anymore.

A low squeak sounded from the tall grass on the right.

"What was that?" Elisa queried in a low voice.

The noise came again, only this time it sounded more pronounced, as it resembled a squawk. Elisa glanced to Alice and gave a half-hushed, nervous giggle. "Do you think it's a party effect?"

Alice's eyes widened as she saw the grass rustling behind her friend. "I'm not sure. I think we should keep going."

Alice wanted to run but fought the urge. When you ran, things chased you. She dipped her head to the ground to avoid looking at the concealing grass. Her body shook with the cold from head to toe, and she could feel her nose beginning to drip with a watery snot. She raised her free hand to it unthinkingly and cursed as she saw the fresh stain she had made on her glove with the black makeup.

"Nearly there," Elisa reassured her.

The music grew louder as they got closer. Alice frowned as she detected other noises with it. She thought they sounded like screams, but it was hard to tell and she wondered if it might just be more effects.

They reached the front door of the grand house at last. The windows held fading flickers of light suggesting either real candles or faux. The light danced through closed curtains, which kept the party horrors hidden within. Hollow Oaks House had an appearance of a farmhouse wavering on a fine line between vintage and neglect. Two storeys tall, its wooden walls and thatched roof suggested a vulnerability to it, and yet the cracks in its panels and the moss staining its roof proved that it had managed to survive over the years despite its fragile materials.

Elisa knocked on the front door and they waited.

Alice felt a fresh tension in her spine as the squawking sounded again from somewhere nearby.

Elisa glanced to her friend and smiled. "I guess the music's too loud. Let's just try the door."

Elisa reached for the brass knob and turned it. She gave a cry of triumph as the door opened inward with ease.

A cluster of decorations greeted the pair as they stepped through; cobwebs plucked at their hair whilst fake ravens' glassy eyes stared at them from various positions about the lobby. White sheets covered the furniture and bannisters, and candlelit candelabras offered their only light, making the room spookier thanks to the cheap but effective addition of shadows.

"Do you hear screaming?" Alice stared nervously to the left where the sounds seemed to emit from, yells mixed with music in a contrast that would be downright disturbing on any night other than Halloween.

All Alice could see was one of the wooden walls of the house, adorned with Halloween decorations hanging in states that suggested they had become dislodged. The wall quivered slightly with the vibrations of sound but gave no other clues to the source of the chaotic noise.

"All part of the fun I suppose."

Elisa turned the pair to follow the noises, heading up a corridor almost completely in darkness, as the candles had been knocked to the floor and snuffed out.

Alice's right arm was jerked down as Elisa skidded, losing her balance.

Elisa gave a cry of alarm as she turned into Alice and grabbed with her free hand for balance. She gave a gasp as she steadied herself at last and looked down to see what she had slipped on.

Alice dipped her head down too and gave a soft cry. She could see the sheen of a liquid puddle, which glimmered black in the night.

"Well that's a bit excessive," Elisa murmured. "Scary but hazardous."

"Elisa, we should go."

"What? Because someone spilled something? Don't be silly."

Elisa pulled Alice on down the corridor and to a door on the left. With ease, she pushed the door open.

The music and the screaming hit them at once in a loud, violent collision of contrasting noise.

For a moment, all Alice could make out were silhouettes moving in a disturbed animation. Figures were running, falling, tumbling, and hiding. In pursuit of them were things Alice could not identify, leaping through the air and darting in a blur. Yells and screams of terror and pain mixed in the air with bestial chirps and snarls.

The teen just stared as her mind tried to digest what was going on. She could hear squawking again, and low, guttural noises that repeated over and over like a challenge being issued out.

A form lunged out of the shadows through the ajar doorway, revealing a muzzle of snapping teeth belonging to a reptilian head. Alice jerked back from it with a scream, staggering into the wooden panelling of the wall behind her as she evaded the fearsome jaws.

The creature came out of the darkness to pursue her. It stood taller than her without even standing upright and snapped out again as its claws scraped loudly on the floor as it paced forward. Alice had never seen anything like it before: both reptilian and avian, its crimson and sable quilled coat rustled slightly as it was puffed up in warning and it gave her a growl. It swung its head to the right so an eye of golden-green could fix upon her. The only thing the beast resembled to Alice was a creature of prehistoric origin. A dinosaur.

Alice wanted to run, but she somehow knew that the creature would be faster.

The screams were closer, yet they seemed muted now, drowned out by the living horror before Alice. She clenched at the wall behind her with both hands, despairing as she could see no escape.

The creature moved towards her and its head snapped out again. In a reckless move that came from instinct rather than actual thought, Alice let herself drop to the floor. Her body skidded under the creature as it pounced, almost brushing against the claws of its forearms.

It hit the wall with a loud wail of anger and pain, slamming its body into the wood as it attempted to right itself.

Alice pushed herself up quickly, abandoning her rabbit ears to the floor as she stood. She glanced into the room of bloody horrors just once, half-considering aid to the unfortunate within. Seeing the reflective glow of several predatory eyes abandoned Alice's desires for heroism. The guests remaining in there weren't human.

Alice turned for Elisa a second too late. The sound of the snap reached her ears before her eyes took it in. Blood splashed onto the floor as Elisa's throat became dinner for the beast that had attacked Alice.

Alice gave a noise that came out more as groaning than screaming. In a moment of insanity, she grabbed at her hair and shrieked as her friend's sputtered death groan filled the air. Alice turned from the grisly scene and ran.

Alice fled down the shadowy corridor, past cobwebs and false bats that served as obstacles more than cheap scares. She reached the front door and pulled it open to the freedom of the night. In a moment of sensibility, Alice turned quickly to close the door as a snarling beast of dark carmine and black pursued her. As its warm, bloodstained breath brushed against her face she slammed the door. Desperate and almost maddened with horror, Alice turned for the path.

Pushed on by adrenaline, Alice ran. Fatigue and cold were forgotten, secondary points of irritation in comparison to the horror that rattled through her mind and threatened her sanity.

She hugged her chest as it throbbed, laughing and sobbing, causing her ribcage to shake and ache. Could those creatures really be dinosaurs? Had it been some kind of super effective holiday prank? Was that possible? Was the alternative? Her mind buzzed with plausible explanations in an attempt to banish the horror.

She could see the gate ahead; freedom loomed close. Hearing squawks call through the long grass drove her to push her legs faster, forcing herself to gain speed despite the burn of muscle ache.

With a painful gasp of air that dissolved into the darkness in a wisp of mist, Alice raced through the gates. She halted at Elisa's car and a fresh horror dawned on her. She didn't have the car keys.

LIVESTREAM
JAMIE STEWART

1

"The Eiland Dood Event is the equivalent of seeing Neil Armstrong step onto the moon, except while that moment symbolises humanity at its best, uniting the planet in this pioneering moment beyond our world into the stars, the Eiland Dood event symbolises our worst traits as a species. We sat and watched, glued to our devices with mouths agog and watched death…and we did nothing. We watched not some pioneer expanding the realms of what is humanly possible, but some entitled man-child risking his life for attention. In 50 years, we've gone from an event of inspiration to an event of deadly popularity. It makes one lose any hope for tomorrow."

From Steven Johnston, psychologist,
concerning the Eiland Dood event.

2

The crowd of journalists met them on the white steps of the Supreme Court, charging like an army on some

127

long-ago battlefield, banishing their cameras, mikes, and phones like spears that they thrust into his face. David was used to it by now. Still, it didn't stop him from thinking, *so that's what this feels like*, his smile unfaltering and wide with victory.

"Mister Scott, how's it feel to win such a victory against the American legal system?" asked one of the reporters, a man in a crisp suit with a thick weave of brown hair.

"How's it feel to stick it to the man?" proclaimed another in a voice lazy with weed, the pungent smell of which seemed to encapsulate the crowd. Thankfully, there was a wind blowing most of the stink away while ruffling the luscious locks of the journalist who gave the stoner with the iPhone a scowl.

"Mister Scott, how's it feel to win when you clearly broke the law?" This was from a female journalist, older than him, in her thirties. She had a severe look that he found made her features harsher, the frowning forehead distracting from the cute bubble cheeks the colour of honey and the plump pink lips. Even her golden hair was made severe, pulled tight and choked into a bun. David imagined freeing it, plucking the pins that imprisoned it until it flowed in the breeze and wondered how she looked then. How would she look at him?

He felt his father's hand, Edward Scott, clamped down on his left shoulder, knew he would be smiling the same sanctimonious grin he always wore when he won – and why not? They had won big today. David had conquered Goliath. Funny. He wasn't grinning eight months ago when he got the call that his son was arrested for breaking into Area 51.

David knew what that hand meant: *don't talk to this one*. As he had done for the last twenty-eight years of his life, he did the opposite of what his father wished. His Dad, while skilled in the court room, never had any talent for when to seize a promotional opportunity.

"It feels…fantastic," answered David, smiling his perfectly aligned, pristinely white smile that had made him the most watched internet vlogger in the world. "It is fantastic to know that the oppressive tyranny imposed by this nation's privileged elite has been demonstrated for what it is: old, outdated, and out of touch. This is not a victory for myself but a victory for all of us in the community that seeks to find the truth in this world."

The blonde rolled her eyes. David imagined what she'd look like if he reached out and squeezed her throat, not hard, not to the point of choking, just with his fingers gasping the soft flesh at the back of her neck while he pressed his thumb in at the front. He wondered how wide her eyes would get then.

"Mister Scott," said the journalist with the good hair.

"Call me David," David corrected, smiling wider. The male journalist grinned back in appreciation. Why wouldn't he? David was giving him what he wanted.

"After releasing your viral vlog of breaking into Area 51, what's next for you? Are there any secrets out there as big as that? Where are you going next?"

David smiled, his blonde hair golden in the beaming sunlight.

"Where am I going next?" he repeated, enjoying the words on his tongue. "I'm going to Eiland Dood."

The male journalist with the microphone frowned in confusion; most of the faces in the crowd did, except for two. The stoner uttered the word, "badass," while David watched the blonde's frown deepen over her blue eyes. There was no longer contempt in her expression. In its place was concern.

3

Eiland Dood

Discovered in 1685 by Dutch merchants on an expedition to the Caribbean, only to become lost following a storm. It was subsequently this discovery that resulted in the island receiving its name, Eiland Dood, which translates to Island of Death. The Dutch merchants, led by Captain Noah Jenson, found the abundant volcanic island inhospitable on account of an unknown disease. What is known is that when Captain Jenson finally arrived at his destination in Puerto Rico, the majority of his crew were deceased, with the remaining members still dying shortly after – Jenson was one of these individuals. Before his passing, he was able to communicate to documentarians the location and experience on the island that would be later published as a book titled: Eiland Dood – Island of Death.

In total, all 245 members of Jenson's crew died. Uniquely, this mysterious illness did not transfer onto land as there were no documented deaths linked to it around this time in Puerto Rico. Because of this, the island was avoided at all costs by travellers until relatively recently when it was purchased by Charlies Weir, heir to Weir Pharmaceutics, in 1983.

Myth

Despite the limited access to the island, there are many rumours that circulate, mostly through online communities about the disappearances of people that have been said to be visitors to the island. Some of this has become lost in the mythology surrounding the Bermuda Triangle itself, where Eiland Dood is located. A recent suggestion has been made that the island, located in the triangle's centre close to the Milwaukee

Depth – the deepest trench found in the Atlantic, itself may be responsible for these tales. Other rumours state that the island serves as a sanctuary for rare animals. This was supported by the death of Conner Durrant, who, along with his friends, ventured onto the island legally in 1995. Reports at the time indicate that Conner Durrant was 'attacked' by the island wildlife, though those present at the time have since denied their initial statements. Yet, in 2010, an autopsy photograph of Conner Durrant was released online showing that the twenty-four-year-old was mutilated beyond recognition. The legalities of this were settled out of court, with Charlies Weir refusing to provide comment.

Extract from Anna-Marie Thompson's book: A History of the Bermuda Triangle

4

Vlog posted on David Scott's website dated May 5th, 2022.

"And we are on. Hi, everyone, it's your mate David here," said the blonde-headed man into the camera, smiling that forever cheery bright white smile.

In the background is a compact cabin complete with circular porthole and a single bed that's neatly made, its duvet a navy colour. For those watching, they can see that the cabin is moving in a lulling motion that shows at various moments water that's turquoise and clear through the cabin's tiny window. David sits in the middle of this image, at what appears to be a desk. As always in all his videos his age is impossible to guess; physically he appears like a fit young man, yet his body language and expressions are that of someone much younger.

"We are on our way. 'And where are we going?' you might ask," David pauses for dramatic effect. "Why, Eiland Dood, of course. Now I know when I announced this most of you were like, 'what is he talking about?' Well, I'm sure you've all done you're research now, but if you haven't, here's what I know about the island. Eiland Dood is the unicorn, guys and girls. It's the white whale. Eiland Dood is the one place on this planet that is truly left unexplored and I'm the first person, alongside my trusty camera man Jin."

It's at this moment that a young Asian man with a mop of black hair tilts his head into the image from the left. "What's up, everyone," he says, before disappearing off screen.

"Jin's with me right now, making sure, as always, that I don't mess up and making sure that we are the first people to get actual video documentation of this island. Yes, there is some cranky old gas bag living on the place, one of the rich elites, but nobody has heard from that guy in years, and when we reached out to his

133

company requesting an interview, we heard nothing back. But that's not the point. The point is that even though Charles Weir, owner of Weir Pharmaceutics, has been living on the island since the 80s, there has never been any video or photo footage of him or anyone being on the island. And the last time someone did try to visit the place, they ended up being killed. Hashtag RIP Conner Durrant."

"Now you might be saying to yourself, 'David, we have Google. We already know all this.' Ah, but did you know that in 1995 two crew mates from Conner Durrant's yacht also disappeared…of course not, because no one cares about the serving class. Except this guy does. Tina Brewster and Micah Davis worked as part of the yacht's crew during this time, only no one talks about them in relation to this awful tragedy because, unlike Conner, whose friends carried his body back to the boat, they have never been heard from again.

"Their families have never been compensated. They've never even had their faces on the news. There wasn't even an investigation into their disappearance. Why? What's so mysterious about this island? Why is it that when we pulled the construction details for Charles Weir's home on the island, we discovered that he built what sounds more like a military bunker than a McMansion for this tropic haven?

"Well, Jin and I intend to find out. Stay tuned."

David reaches to the side of the screen, switching off the video.

5

The island loomed out of the ocean, beginning as a faint black smudge on the seamless tranquil horizon where a denim blue sky and a vibrant turquoise ocean meet. The crew fell silent as they approached, waves splashing against the bow, though it doesn't appear that way to them; they were not so much approaching the land mass as it was rearing out of the sea like a kraken intend on swallowing them all. They said nothing to David or Jin as they hooted with jubilation.

"Holy shit," cried Jin Bak, springing on the toes of his feet, camera slung around his neck.

David grinned at him – not the grin he reserved for his videos; this one was genuine as he felt the old excitement electrify his nerves. It was that feeling that got him into vlogging in the first place, the feeling of being on the cusp of something new and unexplored.

"This is incredible," he said.

They watched the island grow from a black smudge to a fortress of black mountains that become blanketed with lush emerald jungle. They could see no beachhead, no line of white sand hugging its circumference, yet they could make out a distinct grey colour, unnatural to the land masses colourations. They knew this to be the dock; while the captain of the vessel they've hired had never set foot on the island, she had told them she's been close enough to make out that there is one. This is a lie: she has learned this from other sailors that have journeyed close to the island, fishermen mostly; her seafaring takes the form of Americans wanting to hire a plush boat to show off their bank account to whoever they've bought with. Yet, as they proceeded, they learned that the information was correct.

A concrete jetty extended from the island shore, choked with that same emerald vegetation. It was crowned with a boathouse, also made of concrete that had been weathered and stained, looking more like a bunker than anything else. Its windows made a small, narrow band around the building unlike anything the crew or captain had seen before.

"Are you getting this?" asked David, unable to keep the laughter out of his voice.

"You bet your ass I am," Jin replied in a shout, gazing into his camera.

Neither of them noticed their voices were the only sound to be heard; the captain had cut the engines. They echoed, amplified by the black volcanic rock that loomed above.

David wheeled to face the lens of Jin's camera, his face flushed with energy.

"Let's start exploring."

Captain Jane Kennedy's lips were a thin, white line guiding the boat into the dock, ensuring that the crew had the fenders position right as two of them leapt from the deck onto the jetty to tie the boat securely to it. Though the job wasn't the source of her anxiety; it was the place itself. Like anyone that sailed these waters she knew the old wives' tales the natives told about this place, never believing it herself yet respecting the restrictions placed on its waters until the boys came along. Jane couldn't think of them as men. That had all changed, however, when David Scott had promised triple her normal fee. Now she was here, though she was regretting having ever saying yes.

It was the silence of the place, even the surf which continued to crash seemed to do so with a muted quality. It was…hostile, like the way the eyes of men in those bars on the bad side of town were, the ones that refused to accept a woman as a captain as if she was gate-crashing in a boy's club, which she supposed she was. Jane was good at passing those looks off with a good "fuck you" face back but this was different. The hostility she felt came from the island itself seeming to say, "come on and try," with sadistic relish.

While Jane catered to clients more interested in pleasure cruising, she knew from her personal experiences the type of environment hidden beneath that jungle's canopy. The boys may be whooping now but they wouldn't be for long, trekking through the heat and the humidity. She watched as David, the one in charge, leapt onto the jetty, watched how the other made sure it was perfectly in shot of his camera before he did, and scoffed.

"They're in for a world of hurt," said a voice behind her.

Jane spun, discovering that she was not alone as she previously thought, face flushing as she recognised the third member of David Scott's charter: Amara Chidubem. As far as she was aware, these words were the first the South African woman had spoken during the entire trip. Seeing the rifle slung over the woman's shoulder by its strap, Jane thought, she's the opposite of the two "boys", who, even now, she could hear, David narrating, his voice loud and crass.

"We have arrived, everyone…the notorious, elusive, Eiland Dood, the world's best kept secret."

Jane scoffed, couldn't help it. Amara, who had stepped to the deck side overlooking the jetty, glanced in her direction. To Jane's surprise a wiry grin tugged at the corners of her lips. It was the first warm human emotion she had seen the woman express since stepping

138

on the boat, carrying cases that's heavy weight showed in the corded muscles of the woman's arms. Not that the face behind her sunglasses portrayed any strain. She had viewed the deck, its crew with a stern detachment, surveying everything without comment.

The grin that Jane saw made her look completely different. It suited her, and Jane found the flushed heat remained in her cheeks as the hot sun continued to burn down.

"You think they have any idea what is waiting for them in there?" she asked.

She watched Amara's brown eyes scan the lush green landscape of the island.

"I don't think any of us does," she said.

Jane's eyes swept the jungle canopy, thinking that whatever lurked underneath the vegetation the trees hid it well. Like anyone sailing these waters, Jane knew the island had a reputation, but as her clientele tended to only require sun, sea, and alcohol, she had never paid attention to the half-baked tales and rumours. It had always sat like a dark cloud on the horizon in her mind, foretelling a storm to come, one that she was weary of but knew she could avoid. Now she had sailed right up to that storm, was about to let her passengers plunge headfirst into its dark waters.

She glanced at the black rifle on the woman's shoulder; a woman that was now standing beside her with relative comfortability, which was rare for her.

"Think you'll have to use that thing?" she asked, surprised in hearing the tentativeness in her voice.

Amara observed her gaze, grin growing. It really did suit her, Jane thought.

"Why? Are you concerned for the animals or for them?" she asked, nodding towards the two "boys". There was teasing in her tone, so Jane smiled back in a way that made her feel sixteen again.

"I'm afraid you'll have to use it," she answered.

"Don't be. I know David hired me for the diversity angle on this little adventure, but I'm not some overweight white guy who dreams about taking down a lion while he checks cavities. I only kill what is necessary: the rogues who develop a taste for human flesh. And I am very good at it. That's not what should concern you. What should is how little is known about this island. For all his bravado, David is correct to find this place unusual. Even unpopulated areas around this globe have geographic surveys done on them, have zoologists and like cataloguing every twig and branch. Not here. Here there is nothing."

The waves washed against the ninety-foot boat in a lulling, tranquil motion. Eventually, Jane spoke.

"My father's a dentist."

"That explains how nice your teeth are," said Amara without missing a beat. She looked, unflinching, into Jane's face, whose cheeks soon grew red hot again. She coughed, plucked at her collar, and before she could think to answer was saved by one of the crew.

"Captain, that's us all tied off now."

She spun at the senior deckhand, relaying a series of orders in a chirped, flustered tone that caused the man's eyebrows to rise. When he had fled, she turned back to Amara only to find the hunter gone.

<u>6</u>

"Can you believe this, Jin? We are here. We are actually here," said David Scott, gesturing wildly with both hands at the island.

Jin laughed from behind the camera – an action that's like auto tune now – only this time it was genuine. He felt it too, the excitement of being on the verge of something new. How couldn't they be, just look at the size of this thing. Even if there wasn't some scandal to find, like what really happened to Conner, there must be something.

"And it looks like no one's home."

He said this having aimed the camera's lens at the concrete boathouse. Vines hugged its surface, which was water stained in sections, looking like motionless curtains of dark staining. No one had come out from inside to greet them or tell them they were trespassing. The structure had the air of abandonment.

"Hello...we come in peace," shouted David, stepping close.

His voice resonated out across the water. Several birds shot into the sky from nearby trees, cawing sharply as they did.

Amara, stepping onto the jetty, halted, their sound causing her arms to erupt in goose flesh. The birds were the first signs of life from the island, and neither of the boys noticed.

"Check this out, thing's got a keypad," said David.

Jin trained the camera on the numbered silver square section above the boathouse door handle. He then took several steps backward to take in the entire door. It looked to be made of solid steel that reflected the harsh sunlight like a mirage.

"The thing looks like a vault door," remarked David for the camera.

Just as Jin was thinking why someone would need such a heavy door, David, tracing an imprint on the metal surface with his fingers, said, 'Look at this.' He hadn't seen it because of the light, but stepping closer he watched three ragged scars appear in his camera lens. They weren't deep, yet the gouges in the metal reached across the entire width of the door.

"What the fuck could make something like that?" asked Jin, excitement bubbling in him at the pure gold they were recording.

"I dunno. What do you think Amara?" asked David.

Jin panned the camera toward the third member of their team, only for her to reach out and cover the lens. "Hey."

"Don't put that thing in my face," said Amara, voice deep and deadpan.

Jin took a few steps back, feeling the breeze brush at the nap of his neck. He tried to catch David's eye, tried to communicate again his irritation at having this asshole of a woman accompanying them, but David was still fixated on the scarred door.

This time it was Amara's turn to trace those scars with her fingers.

Z

"What do you think about that?" asked David.

With the boathouse locked up, and no one appearing from within, they had all turned to regard the metal structure at the end of the jetty. It sat to the left of the concrete tongue that extended from the island into the water, bleached the colour of rust. On first glance,

Amara thought it was a dam, but on further inspection she noted the water sieving through slits in the metal.

"It's a grating," she replied.

A staircase rose from the jetty to the island; they could set a gangway over the top of the grating. They climbed them, vision darkening briefly to blindness on leaving the hot beam of the sun. A different heat awaited them in the shadows under the trees, the humidity striking like a gut punch. Beads of moisture immediately clung to their bare skin, puddling in their throats, making them choke. Amara observed the two boys cough and splutter, happy to see that Jin had switched off his camera, the moisture having clouded the lens.

A few steps further into the gloom, and Amara smelt the flora's aroma, a rich, overly ripe smell that was both sweet and sour at once. She had never encountered such vividly overwhelming scent from vegetation before; it was cloying and putrid at once, yet all the greenery she could see looked healthy, though strange. She didn't recognise any of it.

"God, what a reek," said Jin. This was above the roar of the water gushing through the metal grating to their left.

"Smells like sulphur," remarked David.

"This island was formed by volcanic action," said Amara. "Perhaps there's springs nearby, still connected beneath the earth, feeding all this?"

"So, you're saying don't drink the water?" asked Jin, sarcastically.

"Forget the water. Check this out," said David.

From this elevation, Amara could see that the jungle was a fortress of shadows and greenery. To their left was a river, its water high on account of the rust-coloured barrier. Tied to a set of bollards almost hidden by ferns was a boat. Like the boathouse, its grey surface was stained and weatherworn. It was twenty feet in length, a squat, rectangular shape that looked military in design. The pilot house appeared fortified more so than any normal river vehicle she had ever seen. She watched as Jin's stance changed, becoming slightly crouched, filming David as he leapt onto the craft, causing it to bob slightly in the fast-moving stream.

As they explored Amara surveyed the jungle. There was no sign of any visible path having ever existed leading into it, which was odd considering their surroundings. She could visibly see new plants and grass growing in a rectangle area of forty feet before merging with the jungle. Frowning, she looked down and rubbed the ground with the toe of her boot: concrete. Just like the jetty, but the grey stone was stained green there.

"Hey, guys, this thing is unlocked," she heard David say.

Ignoring him, she stepped toward the edge of the jungle, aiming for an area where a slice of sunlight managed to cut its way through, and discovered a fence buried amongst the leaves. Though, on closer inspection, describing it as a fence seemed inappropriate; the word was too small to use in relation to what encompassed the rectangle of land. It was a wall made of metal links, some as thick as her thigh. Amara grasped one of the bars, its surface slimy with moss, and gave it a shake, producing a rattle though there was little give.

"There's even keys in this," she heard David say, his voice now distance.

She was patrolling the length of the metal, discovering that it was perhaps twelve-feet high; that it forked sharply at the top, providing two feet of metal that extended over the rectangle she was in. Eventually, she came to what could only be described as a door, clearly meant for vehicles, yet what caught her attention most of all was the latch. It was close to a foot in size, made of solid titanium that had dulled long ago. She stared through the bars into the jungle, looking for a road and seeing none. If there ever had been, the jungle had reclaimed it long ago. She wasn't standing against a "fence" – she was standing inside a cage.

In realizing that, Amara's head snapped to the left, hearing the motor of the river boat judder, cough, and growl into life with a plume of oily, black smoke. She was running, then, shouting at the smiling, laughing men, a broil of rage at their ignorance filling her with heat as she whipped the rifle from her shoulder to her capable hands.

She observed Jin turn, saw a dull expression sag over his features and knew instantly how much he disdained her. She didn't give a fuck, mind now a red panic of caution.

"Turn it off," Jin shouted into the pilot house.

"What?" David shouted back.

"Turn it off!"

The boat fell silent. David stepped out of the pilot house, brow furrowed with irritation that reduced his age to that of a child about to throw a tantrum. Then he saw Amara, saw the gun in her hands, eyes honed on the jungle above the fencing.

"What's wrong?" asked David after seconds of silence.

Amara didn't respond, eyes shifting slowly from tree to tree, aware that the chorus of bird song that had greeted them under the jungle's shadow had ceased. The only sound was that of the water pouring through the grating. She saw nothing.

147

"We don't know where we are," she replied, speaking just above a whisper, "so, it would be well to be cautious in light of what we have seen so far."

"What are you talking about? We haven't seen anything yet," asked Jin. He was recording Amara, who was too busy scanning the foliage to notice.

"Look to the other side of the river and here," she told them.

"I don't see anything," said David.

"You're standing in a cage," replied Amara, speaking low and slow. "The only reason people build cages is to keep things in or out."

8

"Okay, if you think the jungle is too unsafe to explore on foot why don't we take the boat?" asked David. This was as all three of them stood on the gangway that stretched over the grating, water flowing fast and loud beneath them. They were looking out over the river boat and the river that snaked upstream, its water a dull, metal grey in the dim light beneath the jungle canopy. They saw no sign of any other buildings along its banks.

"Can either of you pilot a boat?" Amara asked. Her rifle was once more slung over her shoulder, though her eyes refused to stop glaring into the jungle.

David and Jin exchanged a glance, shrugging in unison. It was the first thing they had done that made Amara think they weren't just ignorant, spoiled white men. The mirroring gestures spoke of a brotherhood between the two that made her consider just how long they had been doing this together.

"Well, how hard could it be?" said Jin, chuckling. This, she observed, made David smile, expression lit with recollection.

"The last time you said that we nearly died," said David.

"What's this?" asked Amara, genuinely curious.

"Hot stuff here thought it would be fun to trek through the Amazon without a guide one time," said Jin, gesturing towards his friend.

"In my defence, we weren't actually going that far. Just following a trail back the way we had already come," added David.

"Yeah, once…and the second time we were doing it in the dark," said Jin.

"Well, I take it you made it back fine," said Amara. To her surprise, she was amused by the pair's easy back and forth.

"We got lost for ten days before the search parties found us. Ended up catching malaria," said David.

Amara's eyes widened, focusing on the two rather than the trees.

"Being in the jungle was fine. I'd take that over being in a hospital bed beside this one. Dude is such a wimp," said Jin, shaking his head.

"Shut up," said David, laughing.

It was a nice sound, unusually only because of how easy and genuine it sounded. Even his voice was different, Amara thought. It didn't have that gameshow host level of enthusiasm and came across as if he had just snorted cocaine.

"Well, if you don't want either of us trying I take it, Amara, that you don't have any experience with such things?" asked Jin, to which Amara shook her head. "I guess we can ask the captain to take us upstream."

A knot of trepidation formed in Amara's stomach at that thought. It was small – barely noticeable on account of other, more demanding feelings that rose inside at the mention of the captain with the cute grin and golden hair. Had she been overdramatic before when she had told the boys to switch off the river boat's engine? Perhaps. It was true that they had no idea what they were heading into, other than an autopsy photograph of a severely ripped up body, done so with claw marks that she was completely unfamiliar with. She hadn't told the boys that, though, when they had emailed it to her with a request for her services.

The question was, could she guarantee the captain's safety? The answer was no, and that frustrated her – the uncertainty of this entire pursuit frustrated her. They knew nothing of this place, the terrain, the wildlife. Eiland Dood was a complete unknown. That was what had appealed to her in the first place. Not the money, though it was significant, but the thought of exploring a blank corner of the map. It called to Amara as a challenge. She hadn't been aware, until David's email, just how much she had been yearning for such an opportunity.

And she knew the boys felt the same; she could read it in their expressions. She knew voicing her reservations of inviting Jane further along this expedition wouldn't stop the boys seeking her out. They had come too close to not go any further.

"If you're going to ask her, you might as well do it soon, before she leaves," said Amara, moving along the gangway to the jetty.

"She wouldn't do that. She's paid to wait on us," replied Jin, following.

"That may be true, but in the shadow of this place I imagine people can change their minds," said Amara.

9

David stayed, taking it in. The deep, lush world of green that swayed in the breeze, the rich, sweet and sour musk, the constant sound of flowing water. He was here, the next adventure, perhaps his greatest. Unexplored, that's what kept cropping up in his mind. Sure, Area 51 had never been broadcast to 150 million viewers all at once before, but it was old, gimmicky. Only a select few people had ever heard of Eiland Dood and, even then, they didn't understand what it meant.

Unexplored. Uncharted. Unconquered. New.

A crooked grin formed across his face as he turned away.

SNAP!

A tree branch, not some twig that could be halved over a knee, but the snapping of a tree branch resonated from within the undergrowth. David spun, thought of calling the others, then remembered Amara's look of concern and panic as she charged at them. He fell silent, mouth parted, tongue feeling overly wet in his mouth as he gazed into the jungle.

Branches shifted, sections of trees that stood fifteen-to-eighteen feet high shook as something large and unseen, something that had been watching the entire time, moved on.

David's grin grew.

"Ten thousand dollars," said Jane, her voice as firm as her blue eyes, gazing directly at the two boys. Amara smirked at the woman's tenacity.

"That's a bit steep," muttered David, absently.

They were in the pilot house of the yacht, surrounded by plush mahogany that shined under the over lights and modern computer equipment. Outside, the sun continued to beat upon the windows and on an ocean of turquoise, yet in the distance a black smudge brooded on the horizon. Storm, thought Amara, glancing at it.

"Ever since you came aboard this boat, Mister Scott, you have done nothing but brandish that photograph around – the one of the man that's been mauled to death. I value my life very highly, so if you want me to along for the ride you'll pay me appropriately," said Jane, arms folded, legs apart in the bright white captain's uniform.

David glanced at Jin, observed him attempting to hide his amused grin from being seen by Jane. He pretended to look exasperated when he didn't care if the woman wanted double that amount. He remembered the thing that had moved unseen in the trees. It had been huge; the only thing he could think of that would come close to the size and be able to part the canopy like that was an elephant, but David didn't think it was. Not because such animals didn't exist in this part of the world, but how he had felt in that moment. His nerves had strummed with the electricity of danger in a way that was frightening and inspiring.

No, what had been in those trees was a predator. Exactly the type of thing that he could come to expose, and he was giddy to get started. His body was hot with it.

"Fine, ten thousand it is," he said with a fake sigh.

He had never felt more alive in this life.

II

"Think you can handle this?" asked Amara, as Jane flicked switches and checked the dials of the river boat's controls.

"I've been on boats since I was old enough to walk. Trust me, I can manage anything that's on water," she replied, only looking up when she was finished with her inspection. She smiled in a way that lit up her entire face.

"Why? Are you afraid I'll sink us?"

"No…it's not…" Amara's gaze drifted toward the jungle, trying to penetrate the lush green and see any sign of danger. She saw none, yet instinct, which had

154

saved her life more than once when out in the wild, told her there was. Wind continued to breeze through the trees, sieving through the leaves. Birds continued to sing unseen.

Still that feeling of danger remained.

"Don't worry, if we sink or you fall in, I'll make sure you wouldn't drown," said Jane, smiling in a good-natured, easy way that warmed Amara.

With the unknown risk of the terrain, she had not wanted Jane to accompany them, feeling protective in a way that didn't extend towards the others. Feeling the genuine warmth of her presence, a part of Amara felt glad she was coming with. There wasn't any questioning with Jane, no second guessing what her true motivations seemed to be. Amara saw that, like them, she was as curious about this place as the rest of them, her eyes lit with excitement and the prospect of adventure, cheeks flushed red, honeyed skin rich in colour.

To observe her for any length of time was to forget all other things, Amara thought, stepping further into the pilot house of the river boat.

"How kind of you," she replied, and watched Jane's face light up even more.

Outside, the boys were loading their equipment onto the boats, their chests now strapped with cradles for their phone devices. They had informed her that they planned on livestreaming the entire boat ride.

"Don't you need internet for that?" she had asked.

"Yeah, and weirdly this place has the best internet connection I've ever seen," Jin had explained to her, waving his iPhone. "We've got 5G and everything. Also, there appears to be a private link to someone's Wi-Fi."

"What does that mean?" she had asked.

"It means someone is living here," David had replied, his voice giddy and determined.

"Perhaps it's what the reclusive CEO of Weir Pharmaceuticals uses to watch Netflix," Jin had chuckled.

Jane was checking the compartments at the rear of the pilot house. These came to hip height, made of the same stainless steel as the rest of the boat. "Check this out," she said, pulling an A3 size sheet of paper from the top drawer and setting it on top of the cabinet.

It was a map, that much was clear to Amara.

David and Jin had heard her speak and wandered inside to see.

"I thought you said no one had done any geographical surveys of this island?" said Jane, glancing at David.

His face sagged with puzzlement as he stared at the map, only to jump alive once more. The island presented in the map was vaguely heart-shaped; mountains ringed its entire circumference with the interior being dominated with jungle or grassland. Blue veins wormed throughout it indicating rivers, some of which expanded into lakes. The biggest of these was on the island's northernmost point, leading into the sea.

"There are no known surveys of it," he said, emphasising the word "known" as he bowed over Jane's find. "But it looks like someone's been up to something in this place, doesn't it? Check this out," he said, tracing the river they were on further inland.

"This river cuts right through the middle of the entire island and leads right to…well…I say that looks like some sort of complex to me. Perhaps, the home of the person that owns this island, Mister Weir, the one who for the last four decades has been trying to keep this place a secret. Wouldn't you say?"

Neither of the three said anything, partly aware that they were being recorded via the phone on David's chest and partly because they didn't need to. The answer was obvious.

"It looks like we have a destination."

Amara glanced at Jane, any degree of hesitation she had previously felt having evaporated at seeing the blonde woman's bright expression bloom even brighter.

12

The river boat's engine roared to life much smoother the second time, diminishing to a formidable putter noise that sent them on their way. Jane had checked the fuel, finding the drums on deck were full of it. According to the map, it was 95 miles to the northern side of the island where the complex was labelled to be. It may take a few days, but they had enough to get there and back again. She just hoped there was something worth seeing.

The map wasn't clear enough to discern what it was they were journeying towards.

It could be anything, she thought, hands on the helm, eyes on the water. Jane was aware that she had never been on this water before, and anything like a pinnacle of rock just beneath its surface could be lurking to spear through the boats hull. Routinely, Amara would wander across her vision. She had noted that the hunter systematically circled the boat's edge, rifle slung over her shoulder, peering into the jungle, brow furrowed.

Once or twice, she glanced through the pilot house windows and Jane observed that frown smooth out, observed her lips branch out from there and part, observed the sternness in her brown eyes become replaced with a mischievous acknowledgement. When this happened, Jane felt her own expression mirror Amara's, emoting how-did-we-end-up-here while shrugging at the woman, a flushed tingle entering her skin.

You're behaving like a teenager, she thought, giddy. Yes, she was. Didn't seem able to be anything else as if the tall, athletic woman had drilled straight into the goofy side of herself. Amara's outward stern attitude made it even worse, because Jane could see it break, could see the softer side that existed beneath that she doubted many got to see.

They didn't speak as the riverboat ploughed upstream, the only soundtrack that of the boys as David narrated their journey at various stages. They weren't fully livestreaming everything, Jane discovered, merely switching on their cameras at various points whenever they had decided upon a particularly interesting thing to say that sounded tense. All the while, the jungle looked on impassive and unimpressed, a chorus of birdsong fluttering through the trees.

An hour or two later, the river began to widen, the muddy banks drawing further and further away, becoming sloped and less submerged beneath a tangle of ferns.

"Where are we?" asked Amara, referring to the map.

"I think we are about to enter into this lake, the first of three," said Jane, pointing at a rough circle of water on the page.

"All right," cheered David from outside. "Perhaps we'll be able to see something other than just leaves."

It was true that the vegetation was changing, the trees becoming sparser and less like walls, allowing fans of afternoon sunlight to glide through them to the jungle floor. Then, suddenly, the bank on the right-hand side pulled away completely; to Jane it was like seeing the sky again as there were no longer any of the long, drooping branches reaching over them, blocking it out. Even the heavy, sulphuric scent of the jungle disappeared, the air suddenly smelling crisp and clean. Without thinking, she switched off the boat's engine.

"Woah, what just happened?" asked David, a hint of fear in his voice.

"Nothing. I just want to enjoy the quiet of this place," replied Jane.

And it was quiet. Removed from the trees, even the bird noise had reduced as they continued to drift into the centre of the lake. The jungle continued along the banks to their left, but to their right they could see grassland that rose in a series of green waves into the distance before becoming forested once again. Beyond it, for the first time, they could see the jagged ridges of black volcanic rock that ringed the circumference of the island.

"Hey, look, it's an alligator," said David. He was pointing to the riverbanks on the right which fell under the shade of the trees.

Jane observed that he was aiming his chest camera in that direction. To her left, Jin proceeded to take pictures, his camera clicking with each one.

She stared into the shadows, right hand over her eyes, seeing only shadow. Something moved within it, something that she thought was gloom but swished through the air. It was the creature's tail, and it was huge, a muscular lump of thick, scaled flesh as brown as mud. A mouth opened, unveiling the white dirty lining of its gullet and thick, sharp teeth.

"That's not right," said Amara, as if to herself.

Jin snapped pictures of the alligator, though the low light was playing with his focus. As he attempted to adjust it, he noticed frills in the water to his left. They were twenty feet away, and if wasn't for the quiet of the lake he wouldn't have heard them bubbling by. They were aimed at the gator, though when he motioned to say something, they disappeared.

"That's not right," said Amara, louder this time, enough for Jane to hear.

"What do you mean?" she asked.

"It's too big," said Amara. That stern look had fallen over her face with the force of a bear trap. "That's got to be at least ten metres in length."

"And? What's so weird about that?" asked David, turning to ensure she was in sight of his chest camera.

"The biggest alligator ever to be recorded was only six metres in length. Plus, its snout is all wrong. There's no gator or crocodile alive that has that bulbous end."

They could hear it now, a deep, grumbling hiss was emitting from inside its throat, directed at them as they floated by. Jane watched its tail swishing back and forth languidly; it was indeed huge, beyond any animal she had ever seen. Its forelegs clawed the soft soil of the bank, pulling it forward so that its broad snout extended out over the water into the light, it's skin mud brown.

"You think something like that killed Conner Durrant?" asked David.

Jin heard this, meaning to contribute but once more was distracted by bubbles popping on the surface of the lake, closer now to the gator. "Guys," he said.

"No, something that size could swallow a man in two bites. Conner Durrant was slashed to death by something that uses their claws to kill its prey. All that animal needs to kill is its jaws…"

Something giant lunged out of the water to the left of the gator, creating a massive wave that rocked their boat while drenching all four of them in spray. Amara got a glimpse of brownish-red flesh before being hit by the deluge. Blinded, she heard the crunch of bone followed by the abrupt stop of the grumbling hiss that had been produced from the alligators' throat. She wiped at her face, reaching out with the other arm for balance as the boat bobbed beneath them. Vision cleared, she stared at the creature that had leapt from the depths with disbelief; a sense of unreality washed over her, saying that what she saw was impossible.

It stood, its two hind legs in the water up to its thick thighs. She saw that it had a tail that was long and thick, like a fin that stretched behind it into the lake, but this seemed unimportant in comparison to the proportion of its body that was visible. Its body was tremendous in size, immediately giving the expression of a lizard, with a vast sail of red flesh that extended from its back. Amara could see thick spokes of bone, and somehow automatically knew them to be the bones of its spine within that sail of flesh. Its head resembled that of a crocodile's: long and narrow. Within its jaws was the neck of the alligator, still alive, though its massive head moved sluggishly, its open mouth yawning wide in protest before the creature that held it twisted.

There was an audible snap and the gator's body fell limp.

"It's a fucking dinosaur," gasped David.

Suddenly, Amara remembered that she wasn't alone – the sight of the monstrous beast seemed to have snatched all recent memory from her. She whipped the rifle into her hands, knowing she could take down a charging bull elephant with it, yet doubting its capabilities against such a creature. It was just so fucking big. Beyond fifty feet in length, she guessed.

As she fumbled with the drenched rifle, she heard the stomp of footsteps as Jane fled inside the pilot house. It wasn't until she heard the growl of the river boat's motor that she realized what the captain intended to do. "Stop," she yelled, forgetting the scene unfolding before her as the creature threw the gator to the ground, beginning to feed.

She leapt into the pilot house yelling, "Switch it off," knowing she was too late even as she pressed the ignition and the engine cut off mid-growl.

Jane stared at her, eyebrows stretched high, eyes wide with terror. Amara knew that she was doing the same as her, reacting on instinct so powerful it robbed all ability to communicate properly, doing what she knew to do as an experienced captain.

Only what she had done was make noise.

164

Amara heard it, the dinosaur, utter a snort of breath behind them. She observed Jane's eyebrows arch higher, watched as trails of sweat coursed down her face that no longer had anything to do with the island's uniquely humid temperature. She turned slowly, unable to do anything else, twisting at the waist, spine feeling like a rusty bracket.

Through the doorframe of the pilot house, across the water stood the dinosaur, its mighty jaws splashed and dropping blood. It was staring at them. Its eyes were reptilian gold that seemed to glow from the shadows underneath the trees, curious and hostile.

Despite the heat that hugged her, Amara felt her blood turn to ice.

13

It stalked forward, dropping the carcass of the alligator from its three-fingered front limbs, moving with little sound. That's what Amara's mind latched onto, the soundless way it approached. Its crocodile-like snout pointing at them, great, heaving exhalations of breath gusted out of its chest as it sank into the water until its body disappeared completely beneath the surface of the lake. Until it was only apparent by the reddish spinal fin with its yellow, bony spikes. Then even that vanished beneath.

165

"Get the boat started," said Amara, as David and Jin yelled similar shouts of incomprehensible language.

They had all swarmed inside the pilot house as Jane hit the ignition. From the rear of the boat, the engines uttered a series of racketing sounds that ended in a cough of black smoke. "Shit," cried Jane, twisting the ignition again and again.

Only more racketing could be heard. The boat wouldn't start.

All was quiet outside the pilot house as Amara stepped onto the deck, rifle in hand. The river boat continued to glide serenely along, propelled by the previous propulsion. The water surrounding them was as still as glass, showing only the murky depths underneath. At certain angles, sunlight bounced off in blinding amounts. She heard Jane thump the control panel of the boat with a fist, observing through the window that her fringe had fallen over her eyes like a golden hood.

David and Jin joined her on the deck, eyes on the murky water.

"There," cried David from the rear of the boat. "Jesus, it's huge. Must be over five feet tall."

"Where?" said Amara, controlling her breathing now.

He was pointing to portside. Amara rounded the pilot house, rifle stock placed firmly against her right shoulder, only to find the waters deserted of any sign of life. Jane had seen it, though, the animal's fin rising out of the depths, slicing through the water as neatly as any sea creature before submerging once more. Amara looked to her and she said, "It's circling us." The skin around her blue eyes clenched tight with terror.

Again, the water was still. From the shore was the endless serenade of birdsong, broken only by the racketing noise of the engine as Jane attempted to get it started.

"Maybe it's gone?" said Jin.

The sun flashed off the device attached to his chest. Amara felt like rolling her eyes – they were still livestreaming this entire thing.

David took a step towards the starboard side, meaning to peer over the edge. All Amara's instincts, honed from a lifetime of experience of living in the wild, flashed red; she saw the too-big alligator once more on the bank of the lake and said, "No, it's not."

She meant to say more, she meant to say that the dinosaur's behaviour was classic in terms of an animal that is investigating something new to its territory, something that it might have to defend itself against. She didn't get a chance. The creature erupted from the water at the rear starboard side of the boat, the exact same place David was creeping toward. Its snout burst from underneath first, showering them once more in a deluge of water. Once more, Amara's vision reduced under a hail of rain, but she saw enough to understand as the deck catapulted upward that the animal had gripped the riverboat in its mighty forelimbs and heaved it skyward. The rifle was gone from her hands, the deck had disappeared from beneath her feet, and just before she crashed into the lake, she thought of Jane.

14

'Have you seen David Scott's latest vlog? Things are kicking off!'

A comment placed on David Scott's website, one of thousands.

15

The world became replaced with the churn of water. Darkness engulfed her, toyed with her like a puppet on a string. She was directionless, limbs flagging for control, aware of the growing pressure from above pushing down. That pressure came from what had been the floor of the pilot house, which was now somehow directly above rather than below.

Jane knew what it meant: the boat was sinking, and she was still inside.

She floundered blindly in the dark, bubbles escaping with precious oxygen from her lips despite years of experience in the water. Jane found that experience didn't count for shit having seen what she had seen, something that shouldn't exist but did, that was powerful beyond incomprehension and hungry for them. She couldn't think of it as a dinosaur, instead thought of it as the monster she suspected lurked under her bed when she was five, all clawed fingers and spikes. The sight of it had drilled through twenty-seven years of her life's history to that petrified panic she felt clutching onto the duvet as the wind howled outside, seeming to stir the shadows around the walls of her room in a kaleidoscope of reaching, groping talons.

Her heart back then was like a hummingbird's wings, the bed sour and hot from panicked sweat, though she refused to remove the duvet one bit because that's how the monster got you. Well, now she was thirty-two and she didn't have a duvet to hide behind. She was drowning, and somewhere in the murk there existed a creature that had no right to be.

"So you better get moving before it takes a bite out of your ass." The voice was her father's, and for Jane it was familiar to hear in times of stress.

Finding, as she always did, that the hard grit of its tone infused with herself. She reached out into the darkness, hands flailing to connect with something. To her surprise, she felt her wrist bump on metal. Jane gripped at it, found purchase and realised that she was clinging onto the frame of the pilot house doorway, the door having stayed ajar even in the water. Without a thought, lungs burning, she pulled herself through, legs kicking madly.

Jane feels the pressure of the sinking craft leave her, felt that she was now in open water despite the lack of visibility, and felt that spike of terror again. It could be anywhere, the monster that tipped the boat. It could be behind her right now, its long snout just centimetres from her kicking heels. Thinking this made her want to tuck her legs in, an action she knew would lose her power, so she fought it.

It seemed to be the hardest thing, fighting the fear welling within herself. She almost lost, fatigue was setting in, the fire in her lungs having spread into the muscles of her arms and legs. All the while the fear wormed outward from her stomach. It was like lightning striking through her skin, wanting to rip her apart.

Salvation came as she reached out once more with her left hand, meaning to claw through the water, aware that the stroke was feeble, and feeling it slide through air. A second later, she broke the surface of the lake, spluttering and gasping. She heard someone screaming –it was Amara, and she was telling her to, "Swim…SWIM."

From behind came the exhalation of the creature.

<u>16</u>

"The Eiland Dood Event was not a hoax. I've gone through that footage frame by frame. If it was, it utilised some of the best special effects I've ever seen."

From Kelly Torres, Special Effects Artist.

<u>17</u>

The lakeside scene suddenly filled with the roar of gunfire, causing these infuriating birds to launch into flight from the branches above. Six shots rang out, fired from Amara's revolver that had thankfully survived the water on account of her having the foresight to holster it in a waterproof baggie. Not that it mattered.

Amara watched as four of the six shots hit home. Two struck the dinosaur's chest, causing spouts of bright red blood to erupt there. The other two scraped either side of its lower jaw. None stopped it from proceeding forward, leering over the hull of the upturned river boat, and entering the water after its prey.

The prey in this case was David and Jane. She had already clawed her way onto the forested bank of the lake's western side and now stood ankle deep in the water. Jin was floundering out of the shallows to her right, his eyes wide with terror, sharp, gasping yelps hitching from his chest as he waded to the shore. Jane and David were further out, swimming hard, yet it was clear to Amara that David was not the strongest swimmer.

Even as she screamed at them to swim faster, she knew it was hopeless. The creature didn't bother to submerge itself fully this time, its long snout and reddish fin visible on the water's surface as it languidly stalked after David, who was screaming with each weak stroke of his limbs. Its blazing golden eyes peered at him with reptilian curiosity. All Amara could do was watch, diaphragm heaving from the swim, arms limp by her sides, revolver forgotten. She would never be able to reload it in time.

She watched as the creature opened its jaws to accommodate David, its huge teeth visible underneath the murky water. They clamped upon him; David screamed, a high-pitched, thoughtless scream. The creature reared its head from the water, lifting his body, as it opened its jaws once more and chomped them closed, crushing his lower torso. Again, David shrieked, his voice becoming guttural and liquified as blood spurted from his mouth. His arms flailed, grasping at air. His face contorted in incomprehensible agony.

Amara barely recognised him anymore. The happy-go-lucky charm that he exuded every moment she had known him was stripped away.

Jane had reached the shallows now, clambering on all fours up the bank. The creature opened its fanged mouth once more, allowing David's body to slide further inside, before chomping down on him once more, this time crunching over his shoulders. A spray of blood misted the air; Amara could smell that coppery scent mixed with the cloying aroma of the flora and earthy lake water. She blinked as crimson droplets landed on her cheeks.

Amara woke then, the paralysis that came with seeing such a horrible sight vanishing. Suddenly she could feel her body once more, feel the life still in them. She saw Jane wading toward her, could hear Jin panting and crying to the right, watching as his friend was being eaten alive. Amara's legs unlocked; she dove forward, gripping Jane by the underarms, pulling her onto the muddy bank. The creature shook its head, David flopping in its jaws. He had stopped screaming.

Amara observed this with Jane, who turned back to her. Like David, she was unrecognisable, panic having turned her drenched skin to the colour of milk.

"RUN," she yelled.

18

The footage streaming worldwide from David Scott's website continued to play for another ten minutes, though only one of the videos – Jin's – was working. The rectangle section that had previously been relaying the imagery captured by David's chest device showed nothing but blackness. In the centre of this section was the word error.

What played out in those next ten minutes was watched by a million people. Of those million, thousands recorded that footage and reposted it online later. In 24 hours, over three hundred million people had viewed it. A week later the numbers reached into the billions, with speculation raging between whether it was real or hoax consuming the globe.

What was certain was this those that illegally trespassed on Eiland Dood – including the crew of the yacht – were never seen in public again.

AS GODS UPON THE LAND
ETHAN J. POLLARD

The coin glinted dimly as Corven Vancis turned it in his fingers, dull bronze catching and warping the faint light inside his tent. He blinked, eyes gritty with exhaustion. Stared with a kind of detached bitterness at the scatter of tactical maps covering his camp desk, at the lines marking that ever-encroaching wave of enemy incursion.

Nine months of war had brought them here. Nine months of steady retreat, of pitched, desperate battles, the dead left to rot in the fields where they fell. Nine months of defeat.

The invasion had come without warning, an army from across the Grey Mountains, thousands upon thousands strong and arrayed with terrible engines of war. Every battle had seemed like it must be their last, but month upon bloody month they had continued to hold, continued to stand in the hope that help would come at last.

It never did. Their allies gave no answer. God was silent in his heaven. Even the promised reinforcements from the citadel had never materialised. The acres of enemy dead and trail of heroic stands had only delayed the inevitable. They now held at Ebbor's Pass, not two miles from the city walls.

Vancis looked down at the coin in his hand, turning it so that the light illuminated one face. This side was inscribed with a circle of glyphs in a language he did not know, the other with an image of a monstrous skull. Antiquity stained the thing like blood. He could almost feel it on his fingers, grimy and cloying.

Have you truly come to this, commander?

"Commander Vancis?"

Vancis looked up. Straightened his shoulders, sharpened his gaze. A weary-looking officer stooped through his tent flap, hand lifting in a perfunctory salute.

"Lieutenant Forst." Vancis nodded. "Report."

"Column sighted to the east, sir." There was something guarded in the man's expression. Almost fearful. "Svelyet says it's a wagon train."

Vancis' fingers tightened on the coin. A chill plucked at the back of his neck.

"Thank you, lieutenant." He stood, closing the coin in his fist.

Forst nodded and withdrew.

Vancis remained standing for a moment, staring into space. Conscience warred with disbelief behind his breastbone and his belly rolled with something akin to fear. The coin's edges pressed grooves into his palm.

You cannot turn back now, even if you would. Your toes are upon the brink. Your head hangs over the abyss.

He thought of the waiting citadel and its huddled citizens, its weak-willed lords. Of protracted siege, disease, famine, despair. The inevitable collapse, and what would come after. Ruin, rape, and fire.

Would you have this as your legacy? The man who broke when his country's need was greatest. Who balked at the cost of victory.

He thought of his wife's embrace, the grey warmth of her eyes. Of his daughter's small, perfect hands. Always clutching that cheap cloth-and-grass doll she still somehow cherished above all her finer toys.

Mouth firming to a grim line, Vancis slipped the coin into his belt-pouch and strode from the tent.

The half-light of dawn made a cold dreamscape of the world outside, catching eerily in the night's lingering mists. The ring of bridles and scrape of whetstones echoed from the surrounding crags. Men and women moved like ghosts through the murk, busying themselves with those tasks that soldiers on the brink of battle find to fill idle hands.

Uneasy glances followed Vancis through the wavering thicket of salutes, but more than a few burned with a kind of dreadful thrill. All knew for whom they waited today. The desperate gamble they were undertaking. One man met Vancis' eyes and nodded, hard as granite, lifting a fist two fingers short. Vancis returned the nod.

They would stand. They knew the cost.

A narrow stair cut directly into the rock led up to the lookout's post. Vancis ascended, pausing as the view opened out to encompass the valley plain to the northwest. Through the gloom he could make out the vast, bloody constellation of enemy campfires spread through the basin. A number he could hardly credit given the mountains of dead they had left on each battlefield. *And yet there they sit, even so. An insurmountable force.*

His own troops were camped at the top of a steep rise into a sheer gulch of black, jagged rock—the only approach to the citadel from this direction, and a natural defence that had seen them through many a desperate hour down through ages. Heroic stands worthy of story and song.

None will sing of what we do here today. Victory or no.

He turned his gaze southward. The citadel was barely a silhouette on the distant ridge, sprawled across the spreading fields and farmsteads that quilted the surrounding land.

By now the bulk of his army—archers, engineers, most of the infantry—would be back inside those walls under the command of his second. They would lend their strength to the defence of the city in the event that this final gambit failed. Only the cavalry and a corps of elite infantry remained behind.

The lookout on duty was a woman named Svelyet. A half-healed scar scabbed one side of her face, but did nothing to dim the keen burn of her eyes.

She saluted. "Commander Vancis."

"Corporal." He returned the salute. "You've sighted the column?"

The flicker behind her gaze was unreadable. "Aye, sir." She pointed eastward, along the ridge of blade-sharp hills. "Long train, heading this way. It's difficult to make out at this distance, but I can see wagons with them. Large ones."

He could see them now, a long line crawling slowly out of the murky distance, their progress deliberate, unhurried, almost monastic.

The wagons of the Wain-Knights.

A moment of silence based before Svelyet spoke again.

"Sir. Are they truly who we think they are?"

"I imagine we are about to find out."

Another pause.

"How did you find them?"

Vancis grunted. "By more emptied coffers than I care to think of, and no small amount of strange chance. The dredging-up of legend into living flesh is no simple affair, it turns out."

"I had thought they were more legend than flesh, in truth."

The myths spiralled back and back through the ages, stories of brutal feats and unthinkable odds, passed in hushed tones around darkened campfires. Tales to frighten children and men alike. A company of mercenaries, their order cloaked in mystery and arcane rumour, threading through the pages of history like an unholy whisper.

No soldier Vancis knew had ever seen the company with their own eyes, though all claimed to know someone who had, or whose father had, or their father's father. No two accounts were the same, all spun with some uncreditable fancy or other, and yet certain veins of similarity ran through them all. Disquieting details, always recalled with odd specificity— strange, outlandish armour; voices the sound and colour of slate; an indefinable unearthliness to their bearing, an oppressive sense of weight. And, always, the wagons.

None knew their origin—sacred or profane, mortal or divine, flesh or spirit. The Wain-Knights were a spectre in the back of every mind, a curse or an invocation, a legend half-believed or wholly reviled. But all agreed on one thing.

When they took the field, none but their number left it alive.

"Commander Vancis!"

Vancis and Svelyet turned in the direction of the sudden irate bark. A stocky man in grey-cowled robes and tasselled belt was hurrying up the steps toward them, jaw set and brow furrowed.

Svelyet glanced from the man to Vancis, posture stiffening.

Vancis turned back to regard the approaching train. "You were ordered to return to the citadel with the main force, Father Septin."

"And it is providence for you that I did not! What is this I hear of a compact made with devilish forces? Have you taken leave of both sense and piety, Commander?"

"You should not be here, chaplain." Vancis' tone was clipped.

"The voice of God warned me to stay. I will not—"

Vancis' laugh was bitter. "So, he will say that much, at least."

The chaplain's gaze hardened. "Do not add blasphemy to your list of offences, Vancis. You stray close to the edge as it is."

Vancis turned to face the priest, a sudden heat in the back of his throat.

"Do you know how often I have prayed for aid these past months, priest? How I have sweat and bled and begged every day since this war began for some miracle to end it? For the strength to cast these invaders from our homeland?" He flung an arm toward the citadel. "That city is filled with men and women and children who have prayed with no less desperation than I, served with no less devotion. If we fall here today, all of them will be dead or worse by the morrow. And yet, heaven is silent."

A look somewhere between fear and grief drew down over Septin's face.

"And have I not also prayed, Vancis? Have I not wept over every one of our fallen and begged for some manner of deliverance?" He raised his hands in a helpless gesture. "It is not given to us to know all ends. No earthly kingdom is above that of heaven. Every rule must have its end, bitter as it may be for we who witness the passing. God's will may be served in defeat no less than in victory."

He paused, gaze searching. Vancis' eyes were set like stone upon the priest's.

"Commander, would you damn yourself to force that which God has not ordained?"

Vancis looked back toward the city. Weariness settled like a cloak on his shoulders.

"If the price of their salvation is to be my damnation, then so be it. I will not abandon my people to subjugation for the sake of a silent god."

He turned back to the priest, held his stricken gaze for a moment. Then looked eastward toward the approaching train of wagons.

"If God will not answer, then demons must suffice."

The clouds had thickened to iron overhead by the time the Wain-Knights reached their position. Vancis' men had finished checking and re-checking mounts, honing weapons, stowing or mending everything that could be stowed or mended, and now sat mostly in silence, gazing at nothing with hollowed eyes. Some conversed in low tones, casting glances toward the distant enemy, who had begun to assemble downslope with all the urgency of men making ready for sport. The air was hushed, taut as a bowstring.

Vancis and a good portion of his soldiers had been watching the column roll steadily closer for the last hour, and looked on now with a kind of grim wonder as the legends of a thousand campfire tales drew slowly to a halt in their midst.

'Legends' seemed suddenly too small a word.

The Knights walked with slow purpose, every motion an act of domination upon the land beneath their feet, the air through which they moved. They were tall, the shortest among them head and shoulders above Vancis' own height. Some were slender and long-limbed, putting Vancis in mind of stalking birds, their helmets cruel and sharp as beaks. Others were broad as bulls, their armour heavy with flaring spines and thick sawblade ridges. Strange weaponry bristled from every shoulder, and a smell like cold metal and old blood rolled through the air around them. Not one helm was raised; not one face visible.

Mastering an abrupt feeling of light-headedness at the absurd unreality of the situation, Vancis stepped forward, raising an arm to hail them.

"Hold, there. I am commander Corven Vancis of the Free Cities of Yestraiya." He lowered his hand. "You are the mercenary company known as the Wain-Knights?"

No immediate answer greeted him. The Knights continued forward a few more paces before coming to a halt with a creak of great, rolling wheels and the soft thump of hooves on frozen grass. A few of the huge, shaggy oxen pulling their wagons snorted and tossed their heads, hot breath steaming in the cold air. Silence fell. No one moved. For a moment the only sound was the sigh of wind over rock and blade.

Then one of the Knights stepped forward, a massive figure clad in armour the colour of faded oxblood. The eyes in his helm were two boreholes, back as lightless wells.

"Who holds the coin?"

The voice was deep and grating, echoing strangely behind the lowered faceplate. Vancis thought suddenly of stone grinding upon stone, vast cliffs shearing together in the depths of the earth.

"I have the coin." Vancis' mouth was dry, but he maintained a tone of clipped authority. "I am the one with whom you have treated."

The red-armoured figure turned toward him, approached with heavy, silent footfalls. The air seemed to deaden as he grew close. Vancis felt his teeth grate in the back of his mouth.

The figure halted.

"How came you by it?" Each word was a weighty pronouncement, hard as carven stone.

Vancis pulled the coin from his belt-pouch, raising it so that the skull side faced the armoured figure.

"It was given to me in the wake of our correspondence, once the agreed-upon payments were provided and the… sacraments observed. The courier was a woman with golden eyes, and her left hand was of articulated iron, carved with an image like that marking the coin."

Another silence fell. Vancis stared into the empty sockets of the red helm, forbidding himself to look away.

"It is well." Another grinding proclamation. "Hold forth your hand and pluck it unto bleeding. Let the blood run down upon the coin."

Vancis hesitated only a moment. Reaching for his belt-knife, he drew it and cut a small incision in the meat of his palm. Gripped the coin as the blood welled around it.

The red-armoured figure lifted its own hand, unfastening and drawing off its gauntlet with the other. The hand was massive, thick-fingered, the skin dry and strangely colourless. Pulling a curved knife from its own belt, the Knight drew the blade across its palm, dark blood filling the hollow.

A small part of Vancis had begun to wonder whether these creatures were truly men at all, and not rather some arcane construct, dark spirits animating suits of hollow armour. Inhuman things playing at being human. The abrupt corporeality of hot blood steaming in the cold air was almost shocking. He was unsure whether to feel relieved.

The Knight held forth the bleeding hand, palm up. Vancis extended his own and dropped the coin into the pooled blood with a small, wet slap. Smoothly, the Knight drew its gauntlet back on and fastened it in place, swallowing coin and bloody palm alike.

"Thus it is sealed and thus it is done. This day your enemies shall be as ours, and we shall make their flesh a sacrifice upon this hallowed earth. I am Promethyr Zaum, first servant of the Unliving Ones, the Tyrannous Gods, They Who Walk Between Time. I have spoken."

The words rang like a tolling bell over the assembled legion, heavy and terrible, seeming to compress the very air in Vancis' ears. Blood cooled to a crust on his fingers, cracked as he closed his hand on the pommel of his sword.

Thus it is done.

It took less than an hour for the Wain-Knights to assemble their battleline. Incredibly, they elected to abandon the defensible upslope pass where Vancis and his forces had been camped, and instead took to the undefended plain below. Vancis had found himself unaccountably disturbed by the decision. Their company was larger than his own, true, but still dwarfed by the vast horde of the invaders. As the first wagons had broken camp and begun moving slowly downhill, Vancis said as much to Promethyr Zaum.

"We have no need of defence," Zaum intoned. "We take the battle to them."

Vancis looked out at the enemy front. They were assembling catapults, drawing up ballistae, forming lines of horse and footmen, rank upon rank of archers.

So now you will stand aside while another finishes what you could not?

His mouth tightened. The cut in his hand throbbed.

He turned and gestured to Forst, who was standing a little distance away, watching the dark procession with a look of distrust.

"Lieutenant." Forst looked up. "Have the cavalry form up and follow the mercenaries to their position downslope. The infantry will remain here under your command to hold the gap if we fall."

Forst saluted and began to move away.

"It will not be so." Promethyr Zaum's voice, unyielding as granite.

Vancis turned to him, a fist forming on his pommel. "I am grateful to you for your aid in this hour, captain, but I warn you to leave command of my own troops to me."

"What we do is not for your eyes. None may see it." Zaum's tone did not change. "You and your force would do well to return to your citadel. See to your lords and your smallfolk. Be assured that your enemies shall be destroyed to a man before sun-fall. None shall pass your gates."

Vancis felt the words like a spark on the nape of his neck. Something between fury and terror sharpened in his gut. For a moment, the memories of the past nine months swelled somewhere behind the gates at the back of his mind, threatening to breach, spill through, overwhelm him.

He bit down. Stepped toward the towering figure.

"I have given too much to this war not to see it to its end. Every soldier here has bled for their country, their people, their brother- and sister-soldiers. We will not turn aside on the cusp of victory, and we will not accept defeat until the last of us as broken our teeth upon their heels. Honour demands no less. We will ride with you."

The red helm regarded Vancis in silence for a time, unmoving. Vancis returned the stare. His teeth felt on the verge of cracking, jaw clamped as though biting through iron.

Zaum's head turned toward the waiting enemy.

"So be it."

Forst shook himself and hurried away as though snapping out of a spell. Zaum turned and started down the hill toward the rest of his company.

Vancis breathed out, easing the vice-grip he'd had on the hilt of his sword. His hand trembled slightly.

If we are damned already, then let us bring damnation with us.

With a final shove against the doors in the back of his mind, he called for his horse and mounted up, joining his cavalry as they made their way downhill alongside the train of wagons.

As he drew closer to the bottom, Vancis felt a shift in the air. Some phantom energy, a vibration in the earth. He could not lay his finger to it. The hair on his arms lifted, prickling against the lining of his gambeson. He shifted uneasily in the saddle.

Master yourself, soldier.

He straightened, lifted his head to survey the arrangement of troops. The mercenaries had spread their wagons in a widely spaced line at the base of the hill, and a group seemed to have gathered around each of them. He noted the great size of the wagons;

enormous, brooding hulks of resin-dark wood, painted with symbols in faded lines dark red and gold. The shapes struck Vancis as pictographic, but he could not say why, and could make no comprehensible image from the interlocking forms.

He reached the base of the slope and his troop began to gather around him, their expressions caught somewhere between grim determination and wary disquiet. Gazes flicked furtively toward the wagons.

Vancis called out to the nearest of the mercenaries.

"You, soldier. How long before you are ready to advance?"

A helmet of scarred and pitted iron turned to regard him. Horns or crests tapered out from each side of the helm to a width broader even than the pauldrons beneath, giving the figure an unearthly silhouette.

No answer came.

Vancis suppressed a grimace.

"I and my cavalry will lead the charge. We will wait for you to signal your readiness."

A slow nod. The Knight turned away, moving back toward one of the wagons. Vancis turned back to his troops, calling orders in a voice that betrayed none of the unease churning in his own gut.

"Form ranks to the front of the wagon-lines. This charge will be ours to lead. Keska, take yours to the right. Dreym, the left. I'll take the centre." He fixed those nearest him with a hard gaze, each in turn. "Remember for whom you fight this day. Remember whose lives you buy with your own."

Then he wheeled away, breaking into a gallop, heading for the front. Behind, a bristling forest of lances thinned and dispersed, each cohort following their captain with a rising thunder of hooves.

Vancis sensed another shift in the air, a heightening of the sensation he had noticed earlier. He glanced back toward the Wain-Knights. Most of the wagons had been opened, it seemed, and armoured figures were working in groups to unload what looked like large, strangely shaped stones, arranging them in careful piles.

From the far side of the plain came a mounting rumble of distant voices. Doubtless the enemy had taken note of their opponents' new—and far weaker—position and were deciding what to make of it. Vancis prayed it gave them pause, perhaps suspecting some trap was at the core of such a seemingly ludicrous tactic. Far more likely they would see the opportunity for what it was.

And seize it.

With a muted clamour of war-chants and clattering weapons, the enemy began to roll forward in a slow advance.

Vancis looked back again, drawing rein at the head of his newly formed ranks, the great wagons behind them.

Come on, show me you were worth the fortune I paid to get you here. Sweat pricked the back of his neck, his forehead, cooling instantly in the frostbitten air.

The wagons' cargo had at last been fully unloaded, it seemed. Hip-high piles of pale, sculpted stone dotted the grass. The shapes looked strangely familiar, but Vancis could not place them.

Then he spotted a pair of Knights stepping from the back of one of the wagons, bearing between them a monstrous, crested skull.

Bones.

His eyes flicked back to the jumbled piles. With the skull to give them context, the odd shapes became immediately obvious. They were skeletons.

The scale of them dropped something cold through his belly. He saw individual bones larger around than his thigh, talons longer than his forearm. More Knights began to emerge from other wagons, more skulls laid atop other piles. Terrible things—dagger-toothed and sickle-beaked, horned and crested and knobbed, eye sockets gaping, hungry, haunted.

What in heaven and the abyss…?

Murmurs skittered through his troops. He was not the only one who had seen.

A sudden cry drew his attention back to the advancing enemy. They had quickened their march. Perhaps two hundred yards now separated the fronts. They seemed to be raising banners of some kind from their midst.

Another shift. A thrum. Vancis felt it in his gut, his bones, like thumbs pressed against his tendons. He looked back. At each of the piles, a Knight caped in tattered cloth was holding forth a wide bowl, pouring something thick and dark to spatter over the bones below. The others began a glottal, rippling chant, the sound trembling in the air itself.

"Steady!" Vancis had to raise his voice over the swelling chant behind and the tramping boots and battle cries ahead. The enemy had gained yet more ground. A hundred and fifty yards remained. He could see their cavalry picking up speed in the front, forming into a wedge that would split them apart.

Then he saw the banners.

Dead soldiers—his own—their bodies gathered as they had fallen, desecrated, roped to banner-poles and raised in mockery.

Icy rage burned away fear, weariness, uncertainty. Teeth gritted and lances lowered. Horses nickered, tossing their heads as they sensed the storm of emotions in their riders.

"Steady! Hold your positions!"

The drum of hooves rose in the air. The wedge quickened to a canter. A gallop. They would be upon them in a space of heartbeats.

"Lances front! Hold!"

A sudden rush of wind. A clap of silence like an indrawn breath. Then a stone-deep tremor, a rolling wave, a giant shifting in the deep. The air filled with the scent of blood and ice and rot. The Wain-Knights' chanting rose to a grunting, grating crescendo.

Vancis tore his eyes away from the charging enemy.

Red-tinged darkness whipped and swirled around each of the bone piles like pennants caught in a gale. The bones rose on the swirling dark, tumbling, snapping together, lurching slowly upward. Bodies began to form, flesh spun from shadow—grotesque, towering shapes, jaws snapping, limbs flexing. The thrum in the air deepened and moved into the beasts, became their myriad voices, groaning with awakened life, shaking the very earth.

The enemy charge faltered. Cries of horror and confusion rose as their formation broke apart, horses stumbling, men slipping in their saddles. The rigid lines of Vancis' own front began to deform as terrified awe rippled through the ranks, mounts rearing shying.

"Forward! Forward, God damn you! Give them blood and bile!"

Vancis kicked his mount to a gallop, his sword rasping free of its sheath. Behind him, he heard the mounting thunder of hooves, a chorus of rage joining his own bellowing cry, sharp-edged with something between fear and wonder.

One heartbeat. Another. Time seemed to slow.

They slammed into the enemy lines, breaking them apart like a plough through new soil. Blood spattered, lances splintered, men and horses screamed alike. Vancis found himself laughing as something broke free in his chest and he laid about him with sword and hoof, dispensing a retribution long overdue.

A roar split the air.

The sound shook the earth, so loud as to drown even the din of battle. Vancis turned. Felt his jaw go slack.

One great foot lifted and slammed into the earth, sinew flexing beneath pebbled skin. A head swung low, tail lashing behind it. The other leg lifted, drove down. The beast lunged into motion.

"Behind! 'Ware behind, make a path!"

His voice was nearly inaudible in the pandemonium, but others had turned at the sound of the roar and needed little instruction. They hauled on their reins, splitting the ranks to make way for the impossible thing at their backs, lurching into the fray.

The size of it as it passed made Vancis' head swim with momentary vertigo. It was the height of nearly three men, its length at least thrice that. Two enormous, taloned legs carried a body built for destruction, huge head balanced level with a tapered tail, swaying with hideous, deadly grace and moving with uncanny speed. A blunt, wedge-shaped head pivoted on a neck thick with muscle, and two minuscule forelimbs were tucked against its chest. Hunched atop its back was a red-armoured figure, lashed to a saddle and holding a great spear.

Cries of unreasoning terror filled the air. More creatures of equal size and monstrosity were joining the charge, each mounted with their own armoured rider. Some were like the first, narrow-bodied and sprinting on two legs, great mouths lined with teeth like swords; others were broad and low-slung, four-legged, armoured in plates of bone. Here was one beaked and triple-horned, head crested like the rising sun; there another with a tail like a mace, charging forward like a battering ram. A wall of humped, muscled, terrible bodies, scaled and sagging, ridged and tusked and sunken-eyed.

By all the saints and devils.

197

Vancis felt his heart like a hammer at his ribs, throat tight around his breath. Something in the back of his head screamed in atavistic fear, begged him to avert his face, hide, look away; such abomination was not meant for the eyes of men.

He looked toward the enemy line, faltering now into abject terror. They fought each other in their desperation to flee, riders trampling their own foot soldiers, orderly lines collapsing in a panicked crush. He saw a captain urging his troop to stand with furious cries and waving sword taken through the throat by a spear from one of his own men. Vancis watched their grisly, mocking banners topple one by one, the dishonoured dead crashing down on the heads of their defilers.

He grinned with blood on his teeth.

Lifting his sword, he bellowed a command, turning his horse so that he might be heard by his men.

"Form up! Let them pass and follow the charge! Give no quarter; leave none alive!"

Captains passed his orders quickly along, bringing the milling chaos into line, forming the cavalry into tight ranks with wide gaps for the Wain-Knights and their terrible mounts to pass. They thundered through, a ghastly, unholy charge, a myth given flesh and tooth and steel, set loose upon the world of men. They barrelled into the retreating ranks like living siege engines, roaring and bellowing to shake the air, laying about with darting head and swinging tail, crushing bodies beneath foot and talon.

The Knights to left and right spread out, angling their mounts to corral those trying to flee and disperse, driving them back into the killing crush. The air filled with the stink of blood and fear, thick with the cries of doomed men, praying and howling and weeping.

Vancis waited until the line of mounted Wain-Knights had passed, then signalled his own troop forward. They laid waste to any who had evaded the claws and teeth of the great beasts, dispatching the wounded with lance and hoof. Behind them followed the remainder of the Knights, unmounted but formidable in their strange, heavy armour, huge axes and heavy war-hammers gripped in mailed fists as large as skulls.

The charge began to slow as it met the thicker crush of the retreating army. The rout became an inexorable advance, a bloody, foetid threshing floor, thick with blood and shit and soil, the ground mired with crushed bone and pulped flesh. More men began to slip through, terrified and covered in blood but filled with an animal's desperation to live. Some had retained shields or spears, some merely belt-knives or broken swords. A few had nothing but their hands. They attacked like cornered beasts, eyes wild and half-unseeing. Vancis' men dropped lances in favour of sword and mace, and the melee congealed into a battlefield of a more familiar kind, albeit dotted with lone giants in titanic armour, laying about with weapons two men together could not have lifted. Vancis tasted blood and swallowed, mouth fixed in a red grimace.

Time melted to a stream. They drove the enemy back and back, across the plain and at last to the centre of their own camp, the command tents, the supply carts, the picket lines and cold cookfires.

The surge of bodies turned then, a last resistance mounting. Vancis caught sight of a man in a brass-sheathed breastplate as he seized a fleeing horse and swung himself into the saddle with a single expert motion. His eyes were wild, teeth bared like a wolf's, a spiked mace clutched in one hand. Vancis recognized him.

The enemy commander.

A fresh rush of malice burst somewhere behind his chest. He wheeled his horse about and began forcing his way through the churn of bodies.

A group of fleeing soldiers tried to dart past the commander's horse. Unhesitating, he swung down with his mace and dashed the brains from one of them, roaring at the others and gesturing to a line of canvas-shrouded forms. The men stumbled toward them, jerked the coverings free.

Ballistae. Reserves held back from the frontline. The men began loading them, looking about wildly, cringing and flinching. The commander continued bawling commands as more of his men grouped around them, directing them to other war engines, reserve armouries. A semblance of resistance began to mount.

The men loaded one ballista and loosed. The bolt sailed through the air and punched into one of the two-legged monsters, taking it through the ribs. The brute bellowed, rearing.

Another bolt went wide. A third struck one of the mounted Knights, spinning him from his perch in a spray of dark gore.

Vancis roared, at last cutting his way to the open space in front of the ballistae.

Galloping hooves to his right. He spun, raising his sword. Blocked the mace's arc by a miser's margin. The impact rang through his fingers.

The enemy commander's face was a mask of hate, cruel lips twisted in a bestial snarl. He swung again. Vancis blocked, wheeling his mount. He swung back, matching his enemy. Blow for blow, hate for hate.

Another bolt sailed overhead. Another crunch of flesh followed by a roar of fury.

The ground rumbled with a rising thunder. A short, panicked scream cut the air. The men at the ballistae leapt to scatter but made it no more than five paces before two of the four-legged monsters crashed into their midst, splintering wood and flinging bodies like chaff.

The enemy commander flinched, his gaze flicking for an instant to the ruin of his short-lived resistance.

Vancis took his head from his shoulders.

The body began to topple from the saddle just as a shadow swept over Vancis from behind. Vast jaws descended, closing around horse and headless rider alike. The horse screamed, legs thrashing as both were lifted skyward in a triumphant, gloating arc.

The jaws closed. Bone crunched. Blood and viscera pattered down like heavy rain, hot against Vancis' face.

A toss and snap of the great maw, the gullet spasming. Half of the horse tore free and dropped to the earth. The rest disappeared with the headless body of its rider.

Vancis stared slack jawed as the monstrous beast raised its head and loosed a trumpeting roar to the sky, shaking the ground, splitting the very air.

He looked to the rider, a figure in dark red plate. The eyes of the helm were fixed upon him.

Vancis felt his belly churn.

He wheeled his mount away, back to the press, back to the slaughter. The last shreds of frail resistance were unravelling, monsters and men alike advancing upon the doomed invaders, relentless, implacable, inescapable. This was butcher's work, drawn out and dirty. Soiled would be the hands that dealt it, and blackened the heart that bore it.

So be it.

Vancis pressed forward, shoulder to shoulder with demons. Raised his blood-darkened blade. Brought it down like a headsman's axe.

Again, again, again.

Red mist thickened the air. Alien bellows overlaid the screams of the dying. Behemoths stalked the field like nightmares of an elder age, crushing, devouring, making mockery of the strength of men. The sky grew dark overhead and the earth drank deep its offering-blood.

At last it was over. The field was an abattoir, a hellscape of flesh and broken bone, mounded corpses, splintered wood, rent fabric. The cold air steamed with the heat of spilled bodies. Carrion-crows circled overhead, screeching their joy at the lush banquet laid before them.

Vancis sagged in his saddle. He gazed around at the devastation, then slowly back the way they had come.

The pass was visible as a cleft in the distant hills. Somewhere beyond it waited his city, his wife, his child.

He closed his eyes. Slid stiffly from his horse, boots splashing in a thick slurry of gore and earth. Noted idly that drying blood had cemented his hand around the grip of his sword.

He raised his other hand to tangle with the horse's mane. Lowered his head against the blood-sticky fur.

"Home with you," he murmured. "You need not share in this."

He pushed gently against the great, soft neck. The beast nuzzled him once, warm breath chuffing against his skin. Then it turned and started back across the battlefield, head hung low in exhaustion.

Those few of his soldiers who remained had gathered around him, some still with their mounts, some without. All bore the slack expression common to those whose bodies and minds have been pushed beyond their limit—the far side of exhaustion, where weariness dissolves into simple acceptance.

Many of the creatures and their riders still roamed in the distance, devouring the dead, dispatching the wounded, moving like terrible wraiths in the haze. Others were drawing close, making a loose ring around Vancis and his troop.

With slow, crushing footfalls, one of the Two-Legs moved past the rest toward where Vancis stood. The thing's eye seemed to regard him with a strange intelligence; ancient, ponderous, patient as grinding eons.

"You have witnessed that which is not yours to see."

Promethyr Zaum spoke from his perch atop the beast's back. Vancis' eyes swivelled upward, fixed once more on that eyeless gaze. He could summon no emotion.

"You are not permitted to leave this place alive."

Vancis looked around at his companions. A few faces were twisted in some shadow of sorrow, but most were dead-eyed, uncaring. They had known what this would cost them. He shrugged heavily. "Be done with it, then." The words were thick in his mouth.

Zaum seized a saddle-strap and swung himself to the ground, landing with the weight of a boulder, feet planted wide. He strode toward Vancis through the bloody muck. Stopped an armslength away.

"You and yours have fought with valour. Such is not sufficient for salvation, but another gift shall be granted you. If you so choose, you may receive the Revelation."

He raised his hands to his helm, unclasped it, lifted it free.

His face was broad and heavy-featured, bald-crowned, dark-eyed. Rough, grey skin covered most of his head, growing steadily rougher at temples, crown, and jaw, thickening to dark scales that wrapped his neck and what could be seen of his shoulders.

Vancis blinked slowly. A murmur or two of surprise rose from the soldiers surrounding him. A dozen questions flared in his head. One made it to his lips.

"What are you?"

Zaum was silent a moment, black eyes opaque as glittering onyx. Behind him, the creature shifted its weight, the earth groaning beneath it. A low, glottal hum burbled in its throat.

"We are of their kind. Their children. Their priesthood. They lead us in their worship and instruct us in the deep magics, the words from lightless places below the earth. Beyond time.

"We carry their bones that we might feed and strengthen them. Every battle a sacrifice, every battlefield an altar. When at last the skin of this sphere is soaked in consecrated blood, they shall open their mouths and speak the words, and time shall turn back and devour itself, and the green world shall ripen again, and they shall walk once more as gods upon the land."

The words rang as though spoken by the ground itself, thrumming in the soles of Vancis' feet. He saw a few of the soldiers behind him drop to their knees, overcome. A ripple of bone-deep, gurgling hums ran through the ring of towering behemoths. Their eyes gleamed, flickering with the dead stars of incomprehensible epochs. Vancis saw time laid out in a ring vast as the sky. A serpent forever swallowing and birthing itself.

Zaum stepped closer.

"This day's worship is over. Soon their flesh will return to dust. Will you receive the Revelation?"

Eyes fixed on the god-beast above, Vancis sank to his knees. Spread his arms.

The mouth opened. The jaws descended. Darkness engulfed him and vision bloomed behind his eyes, spilling through his blood and belly.

A green land, ripe with life, rich and foetid and warm as blood. Great insects crawled and crept beneath broad leaves, slithered through soupy loam. The sun was golden overhead, broad and diffuse, filtered through shifting mists. Everywhere danced the hiss and cry of half-glimpsed creatures, the buzz of wings, the grunt of hunting beasts. Water flowed in turgid streams.

The smell of rot and earth and leaf and musk thickened and overwhelmed him. Here was life, and life abundantly. Teeming, fecund, overripe. Life in excess untold.

And over all ruled the Great Ones. Tyrant gods, hideous in their looming majesty, their slow strides shaking the earth. They roamed in their herds and hunted in their packs, and bellowed their terrible kingship to the wheeling, golden sun.

The jaws closed. Vision dimmed. Praise bubbled like vomit from his throat.

SAFETY PROTOCOLS
SAMUEL M. HALLAM

"At long last, history comes to life! Do you wish to experience the glitz and glamour of the Roaring Twenties? Maybe you wish to be a brave knight in the Middle Ages, fighting for your monarch? Or perhaps you wish to go back further and walk with the dinosaurs? Well, here at the Woodman Institute, we can bring your dreams to life. Pick any historical era, enter one of our suites, and live out your wildest fantasies! The Other Times Project will break down the barriers between past and present, something humanity has long dreamed of!

"Disclaimer: Any damage to the participants is at your own risk. A full medical must be completed before you may enter.

"The Other Times Project, opening soon!"

It had been years of planning and thinking by Doctor Michael Woodman, to create an immersive experience, delving into the past, to create hyper-realistic situations and scenarios. He always loved history and wanted to share that love with others. But finding someone willing to fund such a bold plan proved trickier than he initially realised, and the Other Times Project seemed doomed to fail, until a silent investor helped Doctor Woodman.

He never asked questions of his investor and never wondered why they funnelled the necessary funds into the project. All Doctor Woodman knew was someone was paying for this project and obviously wanted it to be a success.

When he announced his intention for the Woodman Institute and its hyper-realistic virtual reality suites, he faced a vicious public reaction.

"You're mad! This is science fiction!"

"What you're proposing is absurd!"

"This 'Other Worlds' project is doomed to fail, Woodman!"

Doctor Woodman refused to listen to the naysayers and ploughed ahead with his dream of bringing history to life. Some had called out the potential risks of the project, such as electrical faults and the safety parameters failing, or people overloading the system. The project progressed, and Woodman claimed that all these potential faults and flaws would be addressed by the opening day...

Three days before opening...

"Come on Rose, we're nearly there!" the tall redhead said, pulling her jacket tighter, battling the chilly weather, as she led the way to the Institute. "Dad says it's not open to the public just yet, but you know, being the boss's daughter has its perks."

"Sarah, are you sure this is legal? And safe?" the other girl said, her blonde hair shining in the moonlight, as she tried to keep up. Her teeth chattered, and she could feel the goose bumps sprouting up on her arms as she followed Sarah.

"Sure! I mean, when have I ever got us in trouble?"

"Well, there was that time in school with Mr Herbert. Then there was the Berlin incident, and–"

"Fine, fine, we've had a few close scrapes, but you have to admit, life would be boring without me."

Rose sighed. Her girlfriend had a point. As risky as Sarah was, she brought that excitement and adrenaline rush to their relationship.

In front of them stood a towering, white-bricked building, three floors high, a red door in the centre of the bottom floor, sandwiched between two other nondescript white brick buildings. At first glance, you'd be fooled into thinking there was nothing significant about this building. But appearances can be deceptive, which is just what J.L. Woodman wanted.

"Hang on, I have the key here somewhere," Sarah said, tapping her jeans pockets, trying to remember where she hid it. "Dad probably won't notice. He's been doing sixteen-hour days lately, and when I left him, he was unconscious on the sofa."

"Shouldn't you get back home? I mean, if your dad isn't well, then you should be there."

"He'll be fine! Trust me, all he needs is a good night's sleep, and it's better we're out here. After all, what's today?"

Rose frowned. "It's my birthday, but that doesn't mean you should abandon–"

"Bah-bah-bah. Birthday girl, I know you mean well, but come on. Let me treat you just tonight, please?"

"But what about your dad?"

"He'll be fine! Come on," Sarah said, putting the key in the door and jiggling it. The latch made a dull *click* and swung open. "Welcome to the Other Times Project!"

At first glance, Rose was unimpressed. It looked like an ordinary office, with white walls, lacking any sort of character, with a reception area, only a brown desk and chair to greet people. For such a significant opportunity to experience history up close and personal, it all seemed lacklustre to Rose.

"Is this it? I thought you said–"

"Hang on, babe, this is just the front. The real magic is back here," Sarah said, switching the lights on before grabbing her girlfriend's hand, leading them to the end of the corridor. "Now, what was it, last door on the right?"

Sarah fiddled with the keys, as Rose sighed softly. She'd hoped for a bit of excitement today, rather than being stuck in a pokey office. Part of her wished she stayed home and had a cosy night in, rather than being dragged out like this.

"Can't we just go home?"

"No, I have something special for you, just behind this door. Come along," Sarah said, and revealed the surprise.

Rose stepped inside the room, and it was an empty black space. No lights, no windows, just four walls painted a deep shade of black, with the odd glass dome dotted sporadically.

"An empty room? With glass domes on the wall? This is the 'something special' you got me?"

"Wait a minute. Dad said there was a secret panel in the wall to... Ah, there we go." A small laptop folded out from the wall and Sarah typed on it.

She's up to no good, a voice whispered in the back of Rose's mind. *Stop her*.

"Hey, maybe we should leave and come back when things are all ready and open."

"And queue? No way. Babe, it's your birthday, and I want to do something special for you. Now, shut your eyes, and let the magic begin."

Reluctantly, Rose nearly closed her eyes, keeping them open the tiniest bit, just in case. But a force overwhelmed her, and the two girls fell to the floor, unconscious.

"Sarah? Where are you?"

His eyes felt like they were still glued shut as he flicked on the kitchen light, nearly blinding himself.

"Ugh. Sarah?"

He called out, unable to see any sign of his daughter. He'd been so preoccupied with work at the Institute and the Other Times project that he'd neglected his personal life and Sarah too, something he'd promised his late wife he'd never do.

He found a folded-up piece of paper under a glass on the kitchen counter. He slid the glass away, and read the note, scrawled in the oh-so familiar writing he'd known for so many years.

214

"Gone with Rose to the Institute. Back soon x"

"It's not safe!" he called out to no-one in particular as Doctor Woodman sprinted out the door, not bothering to check if he'd locked it behind him.

When she came to, the black walls and their glass domes had all disappeared, and she realised they'd somehow been transported through time and space.

All around her, she could see thick jungle foliage. Grand trees towered over her, branching out high into the sky, and lower down, little weeds and plants, the likes of which she had never seen before, sprouted all around her. She slowly rose to her feet, trying to figure out where she was. In the air, she could smell something funny, which reminded her of rotten eggs, trying not to gag. All the while, in her ears, she could hear the hoots, grunts, and whoops of animals. But there was something missing from this picture, something important, something personal.

"Sarah? Where are you?"

A clump of bright purple bushes to her left rustled softly, and Rose waited for Sarah to jump out.

"I know you're there, so there's no point being childish. Either you come out, or I'll come in."

The bushes rustled again, and Rose huffed.

"That's it! Come here you! Oh, hello there."

Instead of the smiling face of her partner, the one Rose had seen for the last year now, she came face-to-face with one she had only seen in books. The creature snorted softly and blinked at her in confusion. She wiped her eyes to make sure this wasn't a vivid hallucination.

Rose knew exactly what sort of dinosaur it was as soon as she locked eyes on it; the three pointed horns coming from its skull and the parrot-like beak were big giveaways that this was a triceratops. But, there was something distinctly different about this one compared to the drawings she had seen in so many natural history books growing up: it had dark green feathers, not scales.

She assumed it was a juvenile dinosaur, given how small it was, but she couldn't be sure. Maybe this was how big triceratopses were, and that history had got it wrong.

Instead of running in fear, the triceratops stood there, sniffing the air and looking at Rose. Her hand shook softly as she reached out to pet the dinosaur, stroke its soft looking feathered body, and–

"Boo!"

Rose leapt out of her skin as she felt something clamp her shoulder and let out a deafening shriek. In return, the triceratops stood on its rear legs, honked loudly, and skittered off into the foliage behind it.

She turned to see Sarah's grinning face, satisfied with her work.

"What did you do that for?"

"I thought it'd be funny."

"B-but the triceratops. It came to me. It was going to let me stroke it."

"If you say so."

Rose inhaled sharply and blew the air out of her nose. The triceratops seemed like such a sweet and gentle creature, and she wanted to stroke it. But no, Sarah ruined it, being childish.

"Where are we anyway?"

"The Woodman Institute. Well. We are in one way, but in another, we've travelled through time, back to when the dinosaurs walked on the Earth. Long before humanity came along and ruined everything."

"Time travel? But that's impossible! Right?"

"Not exactly," Sarah said calmly. "We are still in 2022, but the surrounding room has created an augmented reality, recreating what the world was like, millions upon millions of years ago."

"What if we get attacked by a Tyrannosaurus Rex? Or what if there's a stegosaurus which thinks we look tasty? Or-"

"It's all fake. Nothing in here can hurt you."

The two walked along in silence, finding a clearing amongst the thick jungle which surrounded them, pushing through the overgrown vines and bushes of all colours. As they reached the clearing, they saw more of this world.

The sky was a shade of brightest blue, without a cloud in the sky. In the clear skies, they saw pterodactyls flying high above them, their calls echoing into the world as they searched for their prey.

"Woah."

"Woah indeed."

"There is such beauty here."

"I know, right? The world is so, so different now."

Rose and Sarah stood there in silence, just absorbing it all. The world seemed so big, so expansive, never-ending, but deep down they knew it was fake, and it would never last.

All good things come to an end.

As she stood with her girlfriend, Rose felt something bristle against her hand and softly honk.

She looked down to see the triceratops had returned, sniffing her hand. She twitched her fingers softly, not wanting to spook the creature.

"Sarah, look," she whispered, softly nodding at the little dinosaur investigating her.

"Rose. Look up," Sarah replied in a strained voice, and there she could see it.

Stomping slowly through the jungle terrain towards them, a much larger triceratops bellowed out, its horns swaying through the trees. Rose realised what was going on; she had seen it in documentaries of other animals and recognised the signs. The mother was searching for her child.

"Don't. Make. Any. Sudden. Movements." Sarah said, trying not to move her lips as she spoke. Her hand clamped harder around Rose's and her nails dug in.

Rose stood there, biting her lower lip, trying not to scream in agony.

"Hand," she whispered.

"What?"

"Hand. Nails. Hurting. Let go!"

Sarah glanced down at their hands and loosened her grip. The juvenile triceratops continued to hoot back, before returning to softly chew on Rose's right hand.

"Get away! Go on!" she hissed at the dinosaur, but its empty black eyes showed no sign of recognition; it continued to gnaw her fingers. She could feel its teeth nibble at her fingers, and its slimy tongue slither between them.

As the two stood there, unwilling to move as the mother slowly neared them, Sarah's legs trembled softly, and she let out a soft whimper.

"Rose, move," she whispered harshly as the mother triceratops continued to honk softly, unable to see its child, less than a few feet from its face.

"What?"

The mother roared, shattering the peaceful environment, and Rose realised why Sarah wanted them to move – it had seen them. The dinosaur mistakenly believed that they were a threat.

There was nowhere for them to go, nowhere to hide, out in the open.

"Move!" Sarah yelled as she yanked Rose's arm, nearly popping it out of the socket. She made a mad dash away from the two triceratopses and pulled her girlfriend free of the dinosaur.

Rose looked back, and thought she saw tears well in the younger creature's eyes, as it honked sadly. It felt so real, like she really was in the time of the dinosaurs, with how the creature acted around her.

"But Sarah!"

The ground trembled around them as a deafening roar filled the air once more. The mother triceratops, ignoring the soft cries of its child, thumped its feet on the ground, and cried out into the air, before snapping its jaw shut. She locked eyes on the two strange creatures which terrorised her child and prepared to charge.

At first, the dinosaur moved at a slow pace, its legs slowly stamping the ground, gradually picking up the pace, developing into a soft canter, before a full-blown charge. The triceratops, wind blowing through its feathers, crushed everything in its path, in its relentless pursuit of the two creatures.

"This is fake, right? There's no real danger to us?" Rose called out, as she tried to keep pace with her girlfriend.

Shit. Dad said something about the safety protocols. What was it? Think, Sarah, think! her mind yelled at her as they ran.

"Erm, yeah sure," she replied, swatting away a fly, which sprung up in front of her face.

"We're going to die here!" Rose said, tears rolling down her face as she looked behind her. She could sense the prehistoric presence, knowing any moment now it would spear her with its horns.

Sarah wanted to say something calm and reassuring to her partner, as they continued their fight through the foliage away from the triceratops, but it seemed like they were doomed no matter what they tried.

Then she saw it.

"Up there! Jump!" Sarah called out, seeing a ledge, thinking the triceratops would struggle to reach them up here. She leapt through the air, arms and legs swinging as she did so, and gripped onto the ledge with her fingertips.

Rose, all but exhausted, with the last energy she could muster, followed suit. She flung herself at the ledge, but as she did so, a sharp pain ran through her lower left leg. The pain burned, and Rose's mind tried to silence the sensation, hoping this wasn't real.

The words, *"It's all fake. Nothing in here can hurt you,"* swirled around her mind as Rose tried to rationalise the pain inside her.

Sarah lowered her arm and grabbed Rose, pulling her out of the path of the rampaging beast.

"Shit, what's happened to your leg?" Sarah asked, noticing the torn clothing and the wound on Rose's leg. She watched as Rose panted, her breathing erratic, out of sync, as the remorse built. Leaning forward, Sarah inspected Rose's leg wound, gently poking it with one outstretched finger, as though she was a biologist on an alien world, inspecting a strange new lifeform.

"Ah! Don't poke it!" Rose hissed through gritted teeth.

"Sorry, I just-"

"Just what? Thought you'd hurt me a little more?"

"Rose-"

"I thought you said the safety protocols were online?" Rose snapped, making a tourniquet out of her jacket, trying to stop the bleeding. "So how was the triceratops able to do this? Because—" she let out a vicious laugh "—it feels pretty real to me! Or is this fake blood? Am I part of the simulation?"

"No, calm down. You're real. The only thing I can think is… Well, Dad said there were a few teething problems, and well, you know, I didn't know this was going to happen!"

"*Teething problems*?! We could have been killed!"

"If I had known this would happen, then maybe we might have gone bowling instead."

Rose snorted and looked down. The rampaging beast had disappeared now, and there was no sign of it anymore. The evidence it had been here was undeniable; a trail of crushed plants and trampled trees formed a path of destruction, all because the two girls encountered a young triceratops.

"Turn it off. I want to go home," Rose said, a numb feeling running through her body.

"Fine, fine. I thought you would have loved this, but if that's the way you're going to be about it," Sarah said. She couldn't believe how ungrateful her girlfriend was being, especially after all she'd done.

"Don't try to guilt trip me! You're the one who spooked the triceratops, and then put us in the path of its angry mother!"

"It was a harmless joke! You know what one of those is, right? Anyway, how was I supposed to know Mama would come looking for its child? I forget I'm a whatchamacallit."

"Palaeontologist, you mean. Just shut the programme down and let me out of here. I'm not in the mood."

"Wait, which way is North?"

"Sarah!"

"What? Dad told me if you ever end up in the suite and want to get out, head for the northwest corner. I think."

"You *think*?!"

"How am I meant to know?! Dad barely says three words to me on a daily basis and I-I-I-"

Rose watched as a solitary tear ran down her girlfriend's face and softly wiped it away with her finger. Sarah wrapped her arms around her partner as Rose cradled her.

"Sorry," she whispered, and held her partner tight. Rose knew her partner had that clever way of hiding her emotions, and Sarah could easily mask up, hiding her true self away from the world.

"Come on," Rose said, pulling herself away from Sarah for the moment, looking around them for the beast. "I think it's bored with us. What do you say we see what's down here?" She nodded to their left, which seemed to be an opening to an underground tunnel. "It could be a way out of here."

Sarah sniffled and blew her nose on her sleeve, "Okay, sure."

"Programme active – currently playing: Dinosaur expedition. Humans active: Two. Dinosaurs active: Yes. Safety protocols: Off."

"No, no, no. I told her not to go in there!" Doctor Woodman shouted, frantically hammering at the keyboard, trying to end the programme. Every line of the programme's code was corrupted, and someone had tampered with his creation. Alarmingly, whoever the rogue hacker was, switched off the safety protocols, meaning that whatever Sarah was seeing or doing in that room was real.

"Sarah! If you can hear me, find the door! Find your way out!"

He rattled the door handle, but it wouldn't budge.

When a programme is active, the doors are locked unless an emergency is declared. Shit.

He returned to the keyboard, trying to fight the corrupted code and free his daughter from real danger.

"Where do you think this place leads anyway?" Rose asked as they continued down the rocky path into the caverns. It was little more than a foot wide, and the right side clung tightly to the cave wall. To the left of the path was an empty, unwelcoming abyss, covered in smoke. Rose kicked a loose stone from the path down into the blackness and waited to hear the thud as it landed. But she never did.

The faint light of the artificial sun shone a path for them to follow, but ahead, the darkness and the unknown awaited them. As she held her partner's hand, Rose could still hear the faint cries of the various dinosaurs as they gobbled, squawked, and created a cacophony of noises. A part of her wanted to go back out there, explore this world a bit more, but she knew that the terrible triceratops would still be out there, bearing a grudge against them.

"I dunno really," Sarah replied as she led the way down into the cave. Momentarily, she looked back, past Rose, and saw the setting sun, and noticed the dimming light. If they were to get out of here, they'd have to be quick, or face the dinosaurs in the dark.

"I'm sorry, about before I mean," Rose began. "I didn't mean to upset you. I didn't realise things were so bad with your dad. You said he'd been working a lot, but I didn't know that–"

"Let's not, Rose. I'd prefer to get out of here and—"

Honk.

Both girls froze, and once more Sarah's nails sank into Rose's palm, as that oh-so familiar noise echoed around them and paralysed them.

"Sarah!" she hissed.

"Yes?"

"You don't think?"

"No. It can't be. Come on, we'll be fine so long as we keep moving," Sarah said, pressing on through the caves. "What's the worst that could happen?"

"Don't say that!"

Sarah sighed and carried on.

The caves and the pathway ran along for another good ten minutes, with neither of the girls saying a word, listening to the world, and more importantly, the honking triceratops.

As they came to the end of the tunnel, the cave opened into a wide open area, revealing a towering smooth brown wall lit up by a couple of torches. To the right of them, there was a smooth surface sloping down into another section, and to the left, there was a second tunnel.

"Huh. I didn't realise dinosaurs needed torches. Or could make them," Rose muttered as the pair walked into the opening. The world, now silent, still provided them with no escape route from their prehistoric prison.

"Must have been a part of Dad's design," Sarah replied. "It might be part of one of his pathways, and part of a story line for when the programme is up and running."

"But why would anyone come to this cave? What could possibly be down here for anyone?"

"Erm, Rose, you might want to look down there. I think I know."

Rose crouched down into a hidden nest, and saw it: five large green eggs, nestled in a bundle of sticks and twigs, waiting for their mother to return.

"I think Dad might have included a poaching plotline."

"Oh," Rose replied dimly. She didn't get why Doctor Woodman would include such a plotline for the programme. Why would people want to steal from a dinosaur? It was pointless.

"Come on. It might be best to get out of here. We never know whose eggs they are," Sarah said, and grabbed Rose by the arm, pulling her up. "Let's try the second tunnel. There might be a way out of here." Sarah grabbed one of the torches to light the way.

A sense of regret filled both girls' hearts as they headed down the second tunnel, to a destination unknown. Regret for ever coming here, regret for what was said, regret for ruining the chance to explore this world properly, and so much more.

As they walked through the second tunnel, the pair could see the dark brown walls were tall and more than wide enough for any dinosaur to make their way through. On the ceiling, stalactites hung tightly, although part of Rose feared being impaled by one, especially given how the rest of the adventure had gone.

Sarah, agitated by the awkward silence which threatened to drive them apart, began, "Rose, I'm–"

Honk.

"Oh. Shit," Rose replied.

In the distance, faint, but definitely there, the light revealed the three definitive horns of the beast which stalked the twosome.

Honk! the beast cried again, and lowered its head, knowing the two girls were trapped.

No matter however fast they ran, the dinosaur would be a lot faster, and any attempt to hide in the cave was next to impossible.

The pair remained paralysed as the triceratops continued gathering speed, now in a canter.

"Sarah, I-"

"Now's not the time for grand gestures of love. In case you haven't realised, we're about to be gored by a dinosaur!"

The triceratops's heavy breathing filled the air, echoing around the cave walls as it neared the girls. Rose shut her eyes as tight as possible and clung to Sarah in a lover's embrace. If this was the end for them, then this is how she'd want to go out. She waited for the inevitable piercing sensation as–

She felt Sarah being pulled from her arms as she tried to cling onto her girlfriend for dear life.

"No! Sarah, don't leave me!"

"Rose," a deep voice said, but she refused to open her eyes. "It's safe now. You can open your eyes."

Unless the dinosaurs in the programme had the uncanny ability to speak, she was confused. Slowly, she opened her left eye, and gave a quick sweep around the room, ready to be face to face with a prehistoric terror.

But instead of the cave and the triceratops, she found herself in a slightly more reassuring, albeit boring place: the Woodman Institute again. The sight of the black room and the sporadic glass domes were reassuring, and a small comfort considering everything she had just been through, and she knew she was safe.

Rose scanned the room for Sarah, and heard voices coming from outside, slightly muffled by the door.

"What did you think you were doing?!" the bearded man snapped, his voice hoarse with rage. She knew right away who it was. Rose knew Doctor Woodman was a workaholic, and that things with Sarah hadn't been smooth sailing, especially lately.

"It wasn't safe! I told you that! Do you ever listen to me?!" Doctor Woodman raged.

"Sorry, Dad, but I wanted to impress Rose. It was her birthday, and I-I-I-"

"And you thought you'd risk your lives as the ultimate birthday present? What were you thinking?" he said, his voice softening slightly. "I love you and care about you, as you know. You're all I have in this world, and sometimes it feels like you don't realise how much you mean to me. Now come on, home. Both of you."

"Doctor Woodman," Rose squeaked, "It was my fault, really. I told Sarah that I wanted us to come here tonight, and that we should see the dinosaurs. Blame me for this. Your daughter is innocent."

"Hmph."

"Sorry," Rose whispered softly.

"Home. Now," were the only words to come out of Doctor Woodman's mouth, as he rubbed his temples. "I'm not mad. I'm just disappointed."

The two girls slowly walked down the corridor, their heads bowed, looking at their feet as they walked.

"But what about the dinosaurs?" Rose asked, raising her head and turning to face Doctor Woodman.

"I shut the programme down. I'll get to work on it tomorrow. But that's none of your concern. You girls got lucky tonight, and don't you forget that in a hurry."

He locked the door, jiggled the handle, and walked his daughter and her partner out of the building.

Inside the room, the lights flickered on, and the programme started up again...

PLEASE DON'T FEED THE PLESIOSAUR
KAY HANIFEN

It was the idea of the United Kingdom Tourism Board. Every year, thousands flock to Inverness in the hopes of spotting the elusive Loch Ness Monster. Some even dedicate their lives to hunting down the cryptid. So, why not give the people what they want? Why not partner with Resurrection Incorporated and bring back the plesiosaur to live in the famous Loch? "What could possibly go wrong?" asked people who had clearly never seen Jurassic Park.

I tried to warn them in my official capacity as a member of the Environment and Forestry Directorate. We had no idea what would happen if we introduced a fifteen-metre-long apex predator into a delicate ecosystem. If we were lucky, it would quickly die in the cold fresh waters of the loch. If we weren't, the entire environment could collapse. But tourism money during an economic crisis is tourism money that goes to our roads, buildings, schools, and pockets of politicians, so we were overruled, and Resurrection Inc. got to build Scotland's real life designer Nessie.

They stationed me in Drumnadrochit to monitor the introduction of Nessie to the ecosystem. One plesiosaur at a time, of course. We wouldn't want baby Nessies running around making a mess of things. The morning was cold and foggy on the day they were to release her into the dark waters of the loch, but the town was busier than I'd ever seen it. Television cameras and celebrities and even royalty congregated at the ruins of Castle Urquhart to welcome her to her new home.

I stood by the tank, monitoring her behaviour and reactions to the crowds, flashing lights, and chaos. A tracker was clipped to one of her flippers like a pierced ear. This would monitor both her location and her vitals as she acclimated to the loch (and provide tourists a means of finding her). It's a fool's errand to project human emotions onto an animal. They don't think and feel the way we do, and anthropomorphizing them is an easy way to get yourself killed. Nessie's eyes were cold and blank like that of a crocodile or a snake. Scarcely a year old and she could barely fit in a cage used to ferry Great White Sharks between aquariums. If she made it to adulthood, she was going to be absolutely massive.

And, in spite of my misgivings and protests from the perspective of a scientist and someone with common sense, I found myself in awe of the prehistoric creature before me. I am human, after all, and like all humans, I think dinosaurs are cool (even if plesiosaurs are not technically dinosaurs. It's semantics). This creature was a miracle of science, and if I didn't know about the devastating effects she could have on the environment, I could very well have been in the crowd among the other gawkers and looky-loos excited to be a part of history. We've had the technology to resurrect extinct species for a while, but this was the first time one had been introduced to an ecosystem that wasn't controlled by human activities. It was an opportunity for palaeozoologists to see how this species might have reacted if it survived to the modern day.

Though the expressions of her face and body language were foreign to me, I knew better than to assume she was just a stupid animal. Just because they aren't human doesn't mean they aren't intelligent. It's a difficult balance to strike between understanding our differences and not writing them off as unintelligent because of them.

Using a crane, they lifted her tank and carried her to the cliff's edge. People cheered as they slowly lowered her down. Once she was a few feet from the surface, one of the scientists pressed a button, releasing the bottom of the cage and sending her into the depths with a splash.

This is the barmiest thing I've ever seen, I remember thinking to myself as everyone celebrated. I walked slowly to the water's edge where Nessie had swum off.

I didn't blame her. The crowds threatened to crush me with their exuberance, and I wanted nothing more than to join her in the quiet depths of the loch.

She was found dead a week later, her carcass washed up on shore near Lochend with a belly full of plastic garbage. Well, I suppose that answered the question of what would happen if a plesiosaur survived to modern times. It was a bairn that found her while walking his dog. He told me that he thought she was an overturned boat until he got closer and smelled the decay.

When I saw her, my heart squeezed with pity. Lying splayed out as she was, the great mound of her body was taller than me. Her stomach was distended, and I found a plastic bag in her throat. There were almost certainly more than just that. She stared up at me with dead, empty eyes—eyes that I knew on some level were intelligent. But the crows had already feasted on them and much of her face.

She didn't ask to be made into a tourist trap. She didn't ask to be thrown into an unfamiliar environment and forced to fend for herself after spending her whole life being fed by human hands. She didn't deserve this awful, choking death.

I waited until Resurrection Inc. had cleared the body and the beach before I cried for her.

I assumed that this disaster would be the end of it. The mission failed. For a short time, the Loch Ness

236

Monster was real, and now she wasn't. We had killed her. But the UK is nothing if not hubristic. They launched a massive litter clean-up and recycling campaign to "make the Loch safe for Nessie."

And then, a year to the day, Nessie 2 was dropped into the loch at Castle Urquhart. The crowds were smaller and less boisterous this time around, but press and tourists still arrived in droves.

A Resurrection Inc. animal handler sidled up to me while we listened to King George drone on and on about the natural environment and the need to preserve and maintain its beauty not just for us, but for Nessie. "Place your bets on how long she'll last," the handler said.

I blinked. "Excuse me?"

"The last one barely made it a week. We've taught this one to avoid plastic, but who knows if it'll stick." He pulled a carton of cigarettes from his pocket and offered me one.

I shook my head. "Not a smoker."

"Pity," he said, lighting it and shivering in the morning chill.

"I think this is fucking barmy," I said, crossing my arms. "The first plesiosaur died because of us, and now we're going to try again. Either she dies a quick and painful death by plastic or getting hit by a boat, or she'll die a slow one of starvation after ripping up the food chain and flushing it down the loo."

"We already have a backup should something happen to this one," he said, taking a long drag of his cigarette and exhaling. "The definition of insanity, innit? Doing the same thing over and over and expecting a different result."

"We're scientists. That's just how we conduct experiments."

He snorted. "Then I guess we're just the craziest blokes out there. The name's Henry, by the way. Henry Parsons."

"Winnifred McCullough," I replied, offering my hand for him to shake, "but you can call me Fred if you like. Everyone does."

"A pleasure. You know any good pubs nearby? I could go for a pint after all this."

I spotted a ring on his finger and relaxed just a little. It didn't necessarily mean that he wouldn't try something on me, but the odds felt a bit slimmer. I lost count of how many times I went to hang out with a male friend only to discover that it was meant to be a date when he went for my lips, my tits, or my arse. "I might know a couple."

King George announced that now was the time to unleash the beast once more. Henry sighed. "That's my cue, eh girl?" he asked, patting the glass where Nessie 2 swam in tight circles.

The crane lifted her up and dumped her into the water with as much pomp and circumstance as typically afforded to a second try after the abject failure of the first attempt. I watched her disappear below the water as everyone cheered just a little less enthusiastically than last time.

We ended up at the Blarmar Bar in town having a pint with some fish and chips. It was crowded with tourists, but we left the party early enough to score a booth in the back corner. Henry anxiously drummed his fingers on the sticky wooden table.

"What's up?" I asked, wondering what we were even doing here. Admittedly, it was rather lonely in town when you weren't from around there, so it felt nice to chat with another outsider who wasn't just a tourist. I just hoped I wouldn't regret my friendliness.

"I'm just worried about her, I suppose. I've watched over her since she was a pup, and now she's all on her own."

I nodded. "I have no idea what Parliament was thinking by doing this." With a groan, I bit into a fry and said, "Well, not true. I know what they were thinking."

"Gotta bleed the tourists dry if we want to afford more tax cuts for the rich," he replied, taking a gulp of his beer. "I bet Resurrection's got the PM by the balls."

"You don't seem very happy with Resurrection Inc. What are you doing there? Why do you stay? I mean, if you don't mind my asking."

He raised an eyebrow. "Someone's gotta remind them that these are animals, not products. Suppose that someone's me."

I nodded. "I know what you mean. Working for the Environmental and Forestry Directorate feels a bit like crossing the Bolton Strid. No matter what you do or how hard you fight it, you're subject only to the whims of the current politics."

He snorted at the lame pun. "Ain't that the truth." Taking another swallow of his pint, he said, "But that's enough shop talk. What do you do when you're not monitoring the wildlife in the loch or protesting adding in the living monument to man's hubris? You got anyone waiting for you at home?"

Suddenly, my good mood soured. Of course it always comes back to that question, doesn't it? Who are you if you aren't in a relationship? "I—uh—I'm not—" I swallowed, taking note of the half empty glass and his height compared to mine. I'm a fighter, but if he reacted poorly to my rejection, it would be hard to overpower him. "I'm not looking for anyone at the moment, if that's what you're asking."

His eyes widened. "Sorry, I—I didn't mean—I know it sounded like—I mean, I'm married. And gay. So, I was just asking."

And just as suddenly as it appeared, the knot in my chest relaxed. "Right. Right. Good for you." I cringed inwardly at that. "I-I mean I think I'm asexual and aromantic, so, uh, it's nice. You know, to have someone else who is not straight around."

He chuckled. "You know what they say about queers of a feather. We tend to flock together."

We spent the rest of the evening chatting about his life and my experiences at the ministry. On our way out, I offered to walk him to his hotel so he wouldn't get lost. As we passed by the docks, we heard drunken laughter near the water's edge. With an apex predator now in the water. "Here Nessie, Nessie, Nessie," one man slurred in an American accent. Of course.

Doing my best impression of a pissed off copper, I prepared to flash my badge and order them away from the water when one exclaimed, "Look man, there she is!"

"Do you want some fish and chips, Nessie?" the man asked.

"Hey," I shouted, running up to them, "step away from the wildlife."

The guy holding a now empty chippy box turned slowly, his eyes meeting mine in confusion for just a moment before a massive head connected to a long neck sprang out of the water and grabbed him before yanking him under like a crocodile ambushing gazelle at the edge of a river. If I wasn't so horrified, I'd be fascinated. The other two drunks shrieked and ran off, leaving us alone with the rippling water as Nessie dragged the unfortunate soul into the depths of the loch.

"Well," Henry said eloquently, "shit."

"Shit indeed," I replied, staring at the placid surface that only moments before held a monster underneath. "Is there something in your Resurrection Inc. protocols for when a dinosaur eats a tourist?"

Henry shrugged. "Anyone who enters a property owned by Resurrection Inc. must first sign a waiver saying that they're taking on an assumed risk, and unless there's some extreme negligence, it's kind of on you if you get eaten. Plenty have become dino chow, but the company's lawyers are good. I've never heard of anyone getting even a settlement from them."

I blew some stray hairs from my face. "Aye, of course that would be their solution to the whole mess. Anything to cut corners and keep profits up." I groaned, rubbing at the headache forming behind my eyes. "It's like I'm bloody Cassandra, except instead of the curse of prophecy, I have common sense." A distant splash got my attention. She was still lurking nearby, probably hoping for another meal. "I'm reporting this to the police. We'll see about at least putting up signs warning people to stay away."

Henry snorted. "Good luck with that. Dumber than lemmings, tourists are. You have no idea how many people I've had to stop from antagonizing the giant terror lizard before they lost a limb or worse."

"Better than nothing," I replied as I headed in the direction of the police station to make my report. "You coming? They'll probably want your witness statement too."

He grumbled about being tired and drunk but, like a good citizen, followed anyway. The next day, the city erected warning signs for the giant apex predator in the loch, but that didn't stop the whale watching boats from venturing out in the hopes of spotting her. They had her tracker, so they knew her general vicinity, but not how deep she was underwater.

For the next few weeks, things seemed to be going as well as can be expected. A couple of family dogs and some sheep had been snatched by her in the evening or early morning, but no more people had been taken. I wondered if she was perhaps crepuscular and only hunting in those times of day while resting through the daylight hours, but I suspected something else was going on.

During the day, people would boat out to where her GPS tracker said she was only to find still, placid waters. She must have found one of the loch's hidden cave systems, likely one with an air pocket so that she didn't have to resurface until she wanted to. Just about every day, I would pass by a tourist grumbling that they paid thirty quid to see Nessie only for her to be a no-show.

I tell you, I was shocked—absolutely shocked—to hear that a wild animal would want to be left alone and not have a million boats following her around to interrupt her hunting. Who could imagine that?

In their desperation (and against my advice), the boat captains took to chumming the waters in the hopes of summoning her with food. They gave her the tracker so that these boats would know where to look for her, but if my theory was correct, they also completely ruined any chances of her showing up. I'd be annoyed too if someone sat outside my house all day honking their car horn, and this was no different.

Months passed in relative peace. Then one cool, August night, Henry knocked on my door looking panicked. "Fred, these people are idiots. I-I couldn't take it anymore."

I stared at him, taking in the bags under his eyes and lips that looked as though they'd been torn up by his teeth. "Come in, come in," I said, gesturing for him to enter. I sat him down on the couch and put the kettle on. As the water heated, I took the chair opposite him. "What's going on?"

He buried his head in his hands. "The UK Tourism Board has been disappointed by the results of Nessie's introduction to the ecosystem."

I wanted to protest that she hadn't killed anyone aside from the drunk antagonizing her, but that wasn't what he meant. "If they wanted a robot, they should have gotten themselves a robot. Nessie's a wild animal, and shockingly, wild animals tend not to like a whole lot of noise and harassment when they're just trying to live their lives."

"You don't have to tell me."

He groaned. "They're so unhappy with the results, though, that they're introducing another Nessie into the ecosystem in the hope that a second Loch Ness Monster would make it easier to appease the boatfuls of tourists looking for her. That way, they'll get their money's worth."

As if in response to my growing blood pressure, the kettle shrieked, forcing me to get to my feet and prepare the chamomile tea. Two apex predators in a tiny loch when we knew so little about their behaviours and whether or not they hunted in herds or were super territorial. I was mostly just glad that this was a landlocked lake, and they wouldn't be able to escape the confines of the waters. "I don't know how I can help you," I said, handing him his tea and ignoring the queasy feeling in my stomach at the thought of a pair of plesiosaurs being free to travel the world, dining on all the animals vital for the current ecosystem, not one that had been around for a million years. "No one would listen to me anyway. Bloody Cassandra, remember?"

"We still have to do something," he said. "It won't be for a couple months, but we can start campaigning against it. We'll call it what it is, a money sink and a tourist trap that the government is funding instead of paying for things we actually need, like the NIH."

"I admire your optimism," I said, "but I don't think—"

He slammed his mug onto the coffee table, sending brown tea sloshing on the sides. "Dammit, Fred, we can't just sit here and do nothing. Everyone's gonna suffer if we keep putting dinosaurs where they don't belong."

"The only thing I can think of to stop this is if Nessie takes someone else. If she were to grab a bairn, then people might realize just how dangerous she is and turn against this barmy idea." I took a sip of my chamomile, letting the herbal flavour relax me. "But throwing one in to become her dinner isn't an option. I'll do what I can to drum up some local resentment—most of us are sick and tired of the tourists and Nessie grabbing our pets—but we'll need more than that if we want to move Parliament on the issue."

As it turned out, we didn't need to start campaigning against adding more plesiosaurs where they don't belong. Nessie did the job for us.

Henry and his husband, Rami, decided to stay in town for the rest of the week so that we could strategize. He was a charming man of Iranian descent who worked as a genetic engineer for Resurrection Inc. We became such fast friends that I almost forgot the urgency of our mission, because we were having a good time. But two days into their visit, tragedy struck.

According to the incident reports, one of the Nessie Watch boat captains had enough of disappointing his clients and receiving negative reviews online, so he sent down a sonar machine with a camera to better find her. We don't know exactly what happened, but something about the camera and the sonar enraged her. She swam up, ramming herself against the boat at full speed. Her attack knocked it on its side and penetrated the hull, causing it to take on water. Those on the deck were knocked off while those inside the boat drowned.

The ones on the deck were plunged into ice-cold water where she picked them off one by one. The lucky ones managed to swim to nearby boats before the captains could ignite their engines and speed off in the hopes of escaping the enraged dinosaur.

Thirteen people died by either drowning in the boat or being eaten alive by the Loch Ness Monster, including a couple on their honeymoon. And because of this, the capricious public turned on the creature they had loved only hours before. The Prime Minister ordered that she be culled in the hopes of preventing more deaths.

"I say we use that sound device, bring Nessie to the surface, and then shoot her right between the eyes," one of the boat captains said at the town meeting. He had seen the massacre first-hand and even helped a few people on board before escaping her wrath.

"That's too dangerous," I said. "She's already proven herself to be unpredictable with that device, so all we'll be doing is risking more lives by making her mad."

"What do you suggest then, Miss Member of the Environment and Forestry Directorate?" He shot a glare at Henry and Rami standing behind me. "You seem pretty cosy with those blokes from Resurrection Inc. How do we know you don't want to keep her there so the company can keep making money?"

Henry opened his mouth to speak, but I held up a hand. "Henry and Rami only want to help in their

248

capacity as citizens and not workers for Resurrection Inc. And, aye, I do have an idea for how to stop her without putting too many others at risk. She hunts in the early morning and in the evenings, and with her tracker, we'll know where we can find her. I say we feed her a poisoned meal and let nature take its course."

There were murmurs of agreement from the audience, and even the boat captain that lashed out at me moments ago seemed to concur. Sadness curdled in my stomach at the thought of poisoning this beautiful creature. Like the first Nessie, none of this was her fault. She was an animal in an environment where she did not belong, but she was also a dangerous predator, and people were finally seeing it. As awful as it was, this was the only way.

So, it was decided. We would get a whole sheep from the butcher, hollow it out, and fill it with rat poison to be cast out at dawn. The GPS tracker placed her near Castle Urquhart where she was first released. Where it all began. If I believed that dinosaurs had an understanding of poetry and symmetry, I would say that she did it on purpose.

Rami held his husband close, rubbing his back as he cried quiet tears. He had raised Nessie, looked after her, and cared for her even when the company he worked for only saw her as an asset. I heard the couple muttering about quitting, and I understood the need to leave a place like that. Changing it from the inside didn't work, so it was better to just torch it all and build something new from the ashes.

The sky was slowly transitioning from navy to purple to red, reminding me of the old poem: *Red sky at night, sailor's delight. Red sky at morning, sailors take warning*.

I'm not a religious person, but as I watched them chuck the sheep carcass near the spot where Nessie's tracker said she would be, I prayed that the sky wasn't an omen of what was to come.

The ceremony was surprisingly anticlimactic. The sheep bobbed for a moment or two before an alligator-like head popped up, grabbed it, and disappeared once more below the depths. We'd filled it with enough poison to kill two elephants, but, without fully understanding her biology, we couldn't be sure that it would be enough to kill her. Henry and Rami believed it would work, but there was that little bit of doubt in the back of my head telling me that something was going to go horribly wrong.

Henry monitored the vitals from the GPS tracker as the water roiled where she had grabbed the poisoned sheep. I peered over his shoulder, watching her heartbeat rise and rise and rise before stopping. She was dead. We vanquished the Loch Ness Monster on purpose this time, and I could sleep at night knowing that she would no longer pose a danger to the loch's delicate ecosystem.

Three days later, she washed ashore. Her bloated corpse had burst, revealing a foetus inside. I watched Resurrection Inc. take away the mother and the coffin birth feeling both saddened and relieved that we wouldn't have to deal with a population of plesiosaurs in the loch. At first, I assumed that it was parthenogenesis, much like the dinosaurs in Jurassic Park or real-life sharks.

But Nessie wasn't quite done surprising us. Two weeks after her death and the funerals for the poor souls killed by her, I was relieved to be back to my usual duties as a member of the directorate. Now, I could go back to being ignored when warning about the dangers of climate change. I can't believe I missed it. But, while I was working on my study of the loch's fish population after Nessie, I received a phone call that changed everything.

"Fred," Henry said when I picked up the phone, "you're going to need to sit down for this."

"What's up?" I asked, figuring that this would be a good time for a break and taking my seat on the couch.

"Rami finished his post-mortem examination of the foetus inside Nessie."

"Was it parthenogenesis?" I asked, sitting bolt upright. It was the only thing that made sense, but judging by the way Henry sounded, there was a surprise found in the foetus.

"When parthenogenesis occurs, the infant is a perfect genetic copy of the mother because they're basically homegrown clones," he said, clearly revving up for a lecture.

I rolled my eyes affectionately. "I know. What's your point?"

His excitement was palpable even from the other end of the line. I could imagine him jumping up and down like a kid of Christmas. "When he did a DNA test, he found Nessie's DNA, of course, but he also found something else. DNA that didn't belong to any known species of plesiosaur, resurrected or extinct. Fred, do you know what this means?"

I was glad I took his advice and sat, but it didn't stop me from dropping my phone. I was vaguely aware of it clattering to the ground as I said in an awed whisper, "The Loch Ness Monster's been there all along."

AGE OF THE DINOSAURZ
MG MASON

With a groan, the gate closed, enveloping the six occupants – four soldiers and two scientists – in the sealed metal chamber.

A screen dropped from the ceiling, on which the smiling face of a man appeared.

"Can you hear me? Captain Friedkin, please nod because I can't hear you."

She nodded. Everyone else laughed.

"Very good. Welcome to the Chronis device! Sorry that it looks like a shipping container, but we had no budget for interior design." He smiled, pausing for the inevitable laugh.

"Shortly you will hear a bang, which will be followed by a bright light, so I recommend eye protection.

"And that's it! The doors will open, and the research team will greet you with tea and biscuits. I haven't received the handshake from their satellite yet, but it's not the first time. Their Chronis is operational though." The young man leaned back and smirked. "If you have any questions, it's already too late."

The crowd chuckled.

"Ready to go in ten, nine, eight, seven..."

His image disappeared from the screen.

A bang filled the room; then the light appeared, grew, climaxed, and faded into darkness.

Silence fell. The lights came back on along with the air conditioning, and a sigh of relief passed over the crowd.

Captain Friedkin raised her radio. "Attention, this is Captain Friedkin. We have arrived and are ready to vacate the chamber, over."

No response.

"Attention Chronis Operation Team. We have arrived on schedule. Please open the door. Over." She clicked off.

No response.

"Calling Chronis team for a third time. Please open the gates for debriefing, over."

For a third time, there was no response. "Which one of you has the emergency override?" Friedkin asked the two scientists.

The young man smiled nervously and showed her a watch-like device attached to his arm. "We both do."

"Consider permission granted to use it." Captain Friedkin gestured for her men to move aside.

254

"One final time, Chronis Operation Team. This is Captain Friedkin. We are coming through. If there is any reason that door should remain closed, now would be a good time."

When no contact came, Captain Friedkin nodded to the young man. He connected the device to the door, spoke the instructed phrase, then tapped out the password.

"*Lock disengaged. Door will open in ten seconds. Nine, eight...*" said a computerised voice.

"We don't know what's going on, so be ready as we enter the transfer chamber. Formation Alpha," she said to her men.

The door opened.

The four soldiers moved out, keeping low and moving slowly, quietly.

Silence greeted them; the lights were on, but low.

Friedkin led, the two scientists fell in behind her, and the remaining three soldiers took up the rear.

They crept up the metal gangway, steel creaking as they went.

They kept moving until they reached the airlock door; the male scientist opened it and they all stepped through with bated breath.

The decontamination took three anxious minutes in which no Chronis operator attempted to make contact.

Finally, the door opened to reveal a cold, dark, and empty welcome hall.

"Where is everyone?" said Friedkin, looking to each of her soldiers in turn.

"Captain, something moving in there." He gestured at the control room; it was dark, the door firmly closed. "Permission to check it out?"

"Check it out, Second Lieutenant Jones." She nodded at the soldier next to him. "Roberts, cover him."

The door flew open as the two soldiers reached it. A middle-aged man lost his grip on the door handle and fell hard down the steps.

The man scrambled to right himself, wheezing as his eyes darted between the two soldiers standing over him. In the dim light, his skin seemed milky white, veins dark and spiderlike. But his eyes – the whites bloodshot, the iris turned a pale blue.

"Leave!" he wheezed.

"Captain..." Jones pushed aside the collar of the man's boiler suit, revealing a bite on his neck.

"Shit!" said Friedkin. "Roberts, see to the man."

Roberts was already opening the medical kit.

"No!" the man pushed Roberts off. "Leave!"

"I'm just going to see to that wound," said Jones. "If we need to take you back to Earth, we will."

256

Friedkin was only vaguely aware of a whistling sound behind her. But when the man started foaming at the mouth, her attention immediately returned to him. "What's wrong with him?" she asked.

The man started convulsing.

"Hold him down, Jones!" Roberts shouted.

His eyes were now full of fury, teeth aggressively gnashing even as the foam continued to rise from his mouth.

The man took a deep, agonised breath, and went limp.

Roberts checked his pulse, shook his head, and placed the man's arms across his chest.

"Dead?" Friedkin frowned. "From a bite?" She shot a glance at the scientists.

There was a flash of movement and flapping wings from above the main entranceway. By the time this information registered, the thing was already on Lieutenant Allen's back.

Lt Allen swore as he felt the thing impact. He turned quickly, but the thing had already buried its talons in his shoulders. Its immense wingspan was as wide as he was tall. "What the fuck? Get off me!"

The thing sang a triumphal song and bit Allen's neck; he howled and tumbled forwards.

Friedkin drew her pistol and raced to his side.

The creature had the face of a lizard and a long, reptilian body. Its feather-covered wings seemed more suited to gliding than flying.

When she placed the pistol to the creature's head, it stopped biting and turned to face her, revealing long, sharp, pointy teeth.

The thing snarled; blood dripped from its teeth.

"That wasn't very clever, was it?" Friedkin squeezed the trigger. The creature's head exploded, and it fell to the ground dead.

"What the *fuck* just bit me?" Allen placed his hand to the back of his neck, feeling blood. "Shit!"

"Roberts, see to Allen."

"Sinornithosaurus," said the female scientist. All eyes turned to face her.

"A sign-oh-fucking-what?"

"Calm it, lieutenant."

"Sorry," Allen said. "But in case you hadn't noticed captain, an unpronounceable bird just bit me."

"We all saw it. But unless this young scientist bit you herself or told the sign-oh-fucking-whatever-it-was to bite you, don't take it out on her, hmm?"

"Yes, captain. Sorry miss."

"It's all right," the young scientist smiled. "It's called a sinornithosaurus. Largely believed to be the first ever venomous dinosaur."

258

"Wait, dinosaur?"

"Venomous!" said Allen. "Am I going to die?"

She shook her head. "Not from the venom, it's mild. Infection? Normal antibiotics will do it."

"So, what happened to him?" Allen pointed at the dead technician.

The young woman shrugged. "I don't know. To my knowledge, nobody has ever been bitten."

Friedkin sighed. "Until now?"

"We're assuming it's a sino bite. It looks like a sino bite. We have antidotes just in case, but I don't think anyone has ever used it because—"

"...nobody has ever been bitten," Friedkin completed her sentence.

"Can we just backpedal a bit to the dinosaurs thing," said Jones. "Because I don't seem to be the only one surprised to hear that bit."

"I was under instructions to wait for the welcome team to brief you, but," Friedkin sighed. "We haven't crossed the galaxy. We've gone back in time about a hundred and twenty million years."

"Wait, what?" Seeing Jones scowl and glance towards Allen, Friedkin ignored him and turned to the young scientist. "What's your name?"

259

She smiled nervously. "I'm Charlotte. Charley, preferably. Or Doctor Charley if you want to keep it formal."

"Right Doctor Charley – I have an injured soldier and a dead technician. I'm relying on you and – I'm sorry?" she smiled at the male scientist.

"Cyprian."

"Are you a Doctor like Charley, Cyprian?"

"Yes."

"Great. I'm relying on you both to get us to the research centre."

She gestured to Jones and Roberts. "Grab one of those medical trolleys and bring the tech's body with us. Lead the way, Doctor Charley, and Doctor Cyprian."

Dim lights on the floor guided their way across the entrance hall. Two corridors led away – to their left a red sign stated CONCOURSE NORTH CIRCULAR while to the right was CONCOURSE SOUTH CIRCULAR. Ahead, the sign read ALL OTHER ROUTES.

It should have been a bustling transit area, Doctor Charley told them, with civilians and military personnel always passing through, but there was nobody. The only sounds to hear were the occasional flickering of an overhead light, and crackles and creaking of metal.

"How far, Charley?" Friedkin muttered.

"Not far." She pointed to the left. The group followed her direction, down a dark flight of steps. The soldiers lifted the trolley and carried it down. All around them the eerie silence was broken only by the slight hum of air conditioning.

"Just up here," Doctor Charley said.

They passed along a short corridor and turned right.

The double doors before them were wide open.

"Talk to me, Doctor Charley?" said Friedkin, gesturing for her squad to stop.

"That's a high security facility. The doors should never be open like that." She looked to Cyprian, who was already nodding. "And there's usually at least two guards at the security checkpoint. *At least*."

"Right, standard clear and secure."

The soldiers readied their weapons, took their formations, and approached the research facility.

"Huh, did he just move?"

Someone groaned.

"Keep noise to a minimum!" Friedkin whispered.

The tarp fell from the trolley and the tech's eyes now burned with fury, his complexion gone from pale to pure blue, eyes now milky white. With a snarl, he lunged forward, almost falling from the trolley.

"I thought you said he was dead, second lieutenant!"

261

"Well, I thought he was!" Jones snapped, stepping back.

The tech sneered, clawing at the soldiers.

"Fuck, he's strong!"

"Secure him!" barked Friedkin. "Charley!"

Doctor Charley blinked at Friedkin, her mouth agape. "What is wrong with him? What are you researching here?"

"I…I don't kn—"

"What do you think they tell us?" Cyprian shrugged. "We're junior researchers. This is our second deployment here."

A soldier screamed. "Bastard!" Friedkin turned to see Allen swing a punch at the technician's head. Blood and flesh dripped from the trolley-bound man's sneering mouth. Allen released his punch and fell backwards, clutching his left arm which now had a bloodied chunk missing. "Bastard! Bastard! Bastard!"

"Roberts, see to Allen's wound."

A shriek filled the air. All eyes turned to down the long dark corridor.

A shadow appeared.

Friedkin watched the figure take a step forward. It looked like a hunched human, but in the dark she couldn't work out its definition.

And then she saw the shadow was too large to be a human, had a snout, and a tail. At the same moment, the head turned and let out a long and high-pitched shriek. It dipped its shoulders and began charging along the dark corridor.

"Get those doors closed!" Friedkin barked.

Heavy feet thundered against the metal gantry.

While Roberts saw to Allen, Captain Friedkin and Jones rushed to the doors, taking positions up on either side.

"What the fuck is that?" Jones called.

"Angry and hungry!" Friedkin grabbed the side of the door and pushed. It moved a few centimetres. She glanced over at Jones; he too had closed the door only a couple of centimetres.

The dinosaur was just metres away now – not enough time to close the door. Friedkin let go of the jamb, grabbed her assault rifle, and raised it.

With a gurgled scream, the creature launched its body through the door and hurtled towards the back of the room.

"Kill it!" Friedkin wasted no time in letting out a rapid hail of bullets.

Snapping jaws hit Roberts full on in the back. He fell forward into Allen who screamed in pain.

Roberts rolled over onto his back moments before the creature let out a triumphal shriek and tore into his head.

Roberts' scream was cut dead and his body went limp.

The dinosaur rose to full height and turned quickly, the flesh of its victim dripping from its mouth.

Allen took the moment of distraction to move out of the way, crawling quickly behind a table to take up his weapon.

"Why isn't it bleeding?" Friedkin looked on in horror as bullet after bullet tore into its flesh.

"I'll make it fucking bleed!" Jones shouted.

The dinosaur moved its gaze from Friedkin to Jones and snarled.

In two bounds, even while the two soldiers continued firing at the beast, it crossed the floor and brought its heavy bite to bear on Jones.

Realising what was about to happen, he screamed. The creature's strong jaw clamped hard on Jones' throat. His head went limp and he fell silent. The dinosaur tore his throat in two, his head falling limply under the creature's clamped jaw.

Friedkin dropped her assault rifle, pulled the pistol from her side, pointed it at the creature's head and pulled the trigger.

Congealed brain matter sprayed against the side wall and the creature collapsed.

Moments later, the lights and air conditioning came on, and the doors slid closed with a magnetic thump.

At the back of the room, a terrified Doctor Charley whimpered. 'I'm sorry. The system takes ages to boot up. I'm so sorry I couldn't get the doors closed in time.' Tears were already streaming down her face.

Friedkin placed her pistol back in the holster. "Not your fault, Charley. That was really good thinking."

"I'm just…" She rubbed her eyes.

But Friedkin's attention was drawn back to the medical trolley. The tech, still strapped to the trolley, reached hungrily for the two women.

"I thought he was dead," said Charley.

Cyprian went to her and offered her a hug.

Friedkin withdrew her pistol again, cautiously approaching the trolley. The tech's glare was one of both hunger and fury; his teeth gnashed, desperate to gain those precious inches closer to Friedkin. "Charley, what's going on? Has he got rabies?"

"You don't see it, do you?" The question came from Allen. His bloodied hand appeared on the edge of the table. His face was ashen grey, a cold film of sweat on his face.

"See what?"

265

"That flesh is dead, captain."

"What do you mean by 'dead'?" Friedkin asked.

Allen approached the trolley. "Look closely. It's rotting. This is what a body looks like when it's been dead a week or two." He pulled his pistol feebly from his holster and pointed it at the man's head.

"Permission to execute, ma'am."

Friedkin frowned at Allen's choice of word. "What are you doing? Put your weapon away, lieutenant."

"Ma'am, please. I'm going to do it anyway. As long as this man is ali— As long as this man is mobile, we are not safe."

"Explain, second lieutenant."

"Ma'am, I believe the technician is a zombie."

Friedkin laughed. She was the only one who did.

"Ma'am. If I'm wrong, I will own up fully and take all the consequences that command sees fit. But if I'm right, then I won't even be around to face Court Martial and the rest of you are in danger."

"We're talking about a man's life."

"If you don't believe me, ma'am, please check his pulse. We don't need Roberts for that. I'll cover you if he moves."

"I've lost my mind." She grabbed his wrist firmly and held it down against the trolley. He struggled against her grip.

266

Moments later she let go. "Permission to execute."

Allen pulled the trigger and the tech's body went limp.

Charley and Cyprian were already at the dead dinosaur.

"He's right," said Charley. "This deinonychus looks like it's been dead for weeks. But it's been two minutes." She looked at Cyprian.

He shrugged. "This wound on its belly, it could not have been mobile if it was alive. As strange as it seems, 'zombie dinosaurs' is the best answer I have."

"The sino didn't look like this, though," Charley frowned. "It looked perfectly fine."

"What have you been working on here?" Friedkin said.

"Like we said," Charley replied. "This is a genetics lab. We're researching flora and fauna genetics."

"For what purpose?"

"Just research," Cyprian said bluntly. "The usual – medical, bioengineering, crop modification. All mundane stuff we do day in, day out, at any other such facility."

"Military? Bioweapons?"

"Not that we know of," said Charley.

"We're junior researchers. Graduated a few months ago," Cyprian backed her up.

267

"Yes, so you said."

They heard a screech from outside. All four heads turned to face the door. A small bipedal dinosaur stood outside, its snout stopping just short of the reinforced glass, clawed hands pressed against it. Blackened flesh peeled back to reveal the creature's rotting gums.

Any doubts that the creature was already dead disappeared on noticing a significant chunk of flesh missing from its neck, while three gashes from razor sharp claws crossed its chest.

"It's another deinonychus." Charley said, her voice shaking.

"We're safe in here, yes?" asked Allen.

"So long as the power holds up. It shouldn't get through that reinforced glass," said Cyprian.

The thing snarled and hurled its body at the glass. The glass shook. When the thing pulled back, a faint black streak remained.

Cyprian took a cautious step towards the door.

The dinosaur saw him and narrowed its undead gaze.

"What could have made a wound like that?" Friedkin asked.

"Something bigger," said Charley.

"What, like a T-Rex?" Friedkin asked, frustrated.

"We don't have any T-Rexes here, but something like it, yes," Cyprian gave her a stony look.

268

"Or something even bigger than that," said Charley.

"Shit," Allen said.

"Is there any other way out of here?" Friedkin said.

The dinosaur smashed against the door again and let out what sounded like a cackle.

"Fire exits. I think there are three. The nearest is the one in the back lab." Charley gestured through the dark doors towards the back.

"The antidotes," Cyprian said.

"Yes," Charley agreed. "We'll have to go that way to get the antidote too."

"Will it work on me?"

Charley and Cyprian exchanged glances.

"You said it worked on that dino venom," Allen snapped.

"I see no reason why not."

"You don't seem very sure," he snapped.

The dinosaur heard and struck the door again.

"Cool it, Allen," Friedkin said. "They've already said they're junior researchers and don't really know much."

She smiled heavily at Cyprian and Charley. "I've lost two men and there's an undead dinosaur outside that door. If you know anything you haven't already told us, now would be the time. You tell me where we're going, and I'll make sure we get there."

They filtered their way through the back. Friedkin was up front with Charly while Allen accompanied Cyprian.

They entered a room lined with freezer cabinets on both sides and UV lights overhead – all of which were on. Cool air emanated from the freezers.

They swept through the lab and took a right at the back of the room.

A closed door stood before them. It was dimly lit with a sign above the door: HAZARDOUS MATERIALS – AUTHORISED PERSONNEL ONLY.

Footsteps tapped above their heads. There was a brief trilling sound and then silence. Friedkin gestured for them to stop, held her breath, and counted down from ten in her head. When nothing broke the background hum, she gestured for them to move on.

They reached the door. Charley removed a security access card and, with a hopeful sigh, she swiped.

The doors opened into darkness.

"Stay here." Friedkin switched on the torch attached to her assault rifle and moved it slowly across the room. The torch swept over tables, more refrigerator units, freezers, and other cabinets before coming to rest on a bloody streak against the far wall. It snaked around a corner and into a side room.

"Wait here," Friedkin said. "Allen, how are you doing?"

"Not so well, ma'am," he wheezed. "I feel cold and sick."

"Can you cover Charley and Cyprian while they find the antidotes? I'll check this out."

He raised his rifle wearily. It seemed heavy in his hands. "Yes ma'am."

Friedkin nodded uncertainly and followed the blood trail. It turned right and then left, disappearing into a booth.

On seeing a shoed foot, Friedkin stopped dead and brought her rifle to bear. The foot was attached to a leg which was covered in a bloodied and dirty lab coat.

The body was moving, small and barely perceptible jerks around the knee, the lab coat flickering back and forth.

Her eyes followed the torso and landed on a brightly coloured wing.

It was a sinornithosaurus, but smaller – a juvenile. It stopped feasting on the dead man's cheek and, with a menacing song, snarled at Friedkin. It turned and, raising its body to its full height, let out a snarl.

It ducked its head and snarled again, showing small, sharp teeth dripping with human blood.

Friedkin fired a quick burst at the creature. With a shriek, it fell back and erupted in a hail of bullets and a cloud of blood.

She took a step forward to confirm that the man was dead, kneeling carefully.

His eyes shot open and just like the other man, they were milky white and full of fury.

A hand grasped at her ankle. Even through the fabric she felt his fingernails dig in.

Friedkin brought the rifle to his head and squeezed off a single shot.

The man went limp; his grip loosened.

She looked him over, examining the bites and injuries. He seemed freshly dead, possibly no more than a few hours as there was no putrefaction. She became aware of something small and oblong in his other hand – a memory stick.

It was then Friedkin became aware of the shouting from outside. She backed out of the room to see Allen and the two scientists in a struggle with another sinornithosaurus.

The creature was firmly attached to Allen's hand while Charley and Cyprian tried to tear it from his back.

It writhed against their grip, long tail thrashing and clawed wings scratching. But the two junior scientists

272

clung on, desperately pulling against the beast's strength.

With a groan, Allen fell forward.

His head hit the wall and Allen went still.

The sinornithosaurus turned and, with a shriek, lashed out using its wings and snapping jaws at the two scientists still gripping it tightly.

Its long neck darted from Charley to Cyprian in turn. Each time one was able to evade its snapping, it refocused its efforts on the other.

Friedkin rushed to their side, placed the pistol against its head and squeezed the trigger. The sino fell silent.

"Allen?" she asked, but the soldier did not move. She lifted his arm and checked his pulse.

"Nothing," she muttered, shooting him in the head. "I am not letting him come back to attack us. I don't know what you two were here to do, but I will no longer be a part of it. All my men are dead, and I'm declaring this mission over."

"Agreed," they said together.

Friedkin held up the memory stick. "Where is the nearest computer?"

"The booth you just came from should have one. The batteries last days on those things – it's so we can record data in the event of a power outage."

273

Re-entering the booth, Friedkin saw the terminal set into the wall on the left, previously outside her peripheral vision.

It was strange watching the same booth with everything behind her in the video, but brighter and with a male face staring back at her.

He looked tired and scared but did not have the dead look that he had when she encountered him as a zombie in the booth.

"I'm not sure how the security breach started," he sniffed. "It seems the anomalous sinornithosaurus group, that we captured on the island we've called K-6482 because it has no indicators of being anywhere in our time, showed some concerning genetic development."

"What does that mean?" Friedkin paused the video.

"It means there was a group of sinos on an island that had been cut off from the main global population and they had a different genetic structure. Fairly normal – it's how Darwin figured out island population evolutionary drift."

She continued playing the video. "They were kept in a deeper part of the lab here. Their main genetic structure wasn't all that different – the same kind of drift we'd expect in any island group." He rubbed his face. "As mentioned in the previous report, we found all kinds of interesting things about the venom. We even isolated a gene that appeared to have healing properties. Simulations and lab tests showed high clear-up rates for a lot of deadly diseases. The other facility concurred with our findings – as did the tests sent back to our time.

"Most sinornithosaurus are placid, but these were highly aggressive – I suppose they had to be on a small island with limited access to food. We knew they attacked each other, for example, from the research the zoologists did, which wasn't really the case with the main concentrations across the supercontinent. Anyone who worked with them essentially had to wear equipment more suitable to working with sharks."

With a deep sigh, he took a step back. "We administered the antidote and sent the assistant home to sleep it off. 'Zombie' – I hate saying that word because it doesn't seem real, but it seems to be the only word to describe what the people here became. Fully half the population of six hundred people here became infected. That led to mistakes, lack of staff and inevitably the sinornithosaurs getting out and infecting the entire zoological facility. I just hope the spinosaurs were too mean to let them get close."

"Spinosaur? That doesn't sound good."

"Big and mean," Cyprian said. "Probably what attacked the deinonychus."

"At the time of recording, the zombie dinosaurs never made it to the outside – not much can get through all that steel and concrete. If they do, well, I don't want to think about the implications for one hundred million years from now. Someone is going to have to blow the place to smithereens, quite literally. If anyone sees this, go home, and find a way of nuking this place and everything in it. I'm Professor Michael Brightman, signing off."

The screen went blank.

"Blow the place to smithereens. Agreed. We need to get back to the Chronis first."

"Not that one," said Charley.

"Why not?" Friedkin frowned.

"They use so much power and take about twelve hours to cool down and recharge. We've only been here about three hours."

"Is there another?"

Charley nodded. "Across the complex."

Friedkin forced a smile. "Right, lead the way."

They followed a dark flight of steps upwards. Charley explained they were still underground at this point and that the second Chronis was inaccessible using only the subterranean network.

"Dangerous things hide in dark spaces too. Best to be out in the open?"

"Not really. You've seen a deinonychus run," said Cyprian flatly.

Friedkin cringed.

Metal steps in the stairwell made silence impossible. They passed up three flights with no sign of guano. Charley stopped them at a set of double doors and looked quickly up the next flight of steps.

"This is the main level," she said. "If all the dinosaurs are out, this is where most of them will be – especially those that can run like fuck."

"Why would we take this route?"

"Up there," Charley said with a grimace, "are the upper levels. Running things are scary but there should be plenty of places for us to hide and escape – lots of small rooms and units. Up there, flying things plus plenty of open space."

"Benefits of going up?" said Friedkin.

"There were just eight sinos in that island group. Two are already dead."

"So potentially we have just six things to worry about?"

Cyprian grimaced. "That we know of. There may still be land dinosaurs on the upper levels. Or not."

"What level has the best access to the other Chronis?"

"This level. The higher we go, the farther we'll have to come down on the other side."

Friedkin rubbed her chin curiously. "Easier access but lots of running things here, then one up but flying things with cover and maybe some running things, then the top one – dangerous flying things only, but with no cover."

"The layman's explanation," said Charley grimly.

"I've always been a fan of the middle ground."

They moved up a level and stood before the exit door leading to the second level.

"On three?" Friedkin said.

"On three."

Three anxious seconds passed.

Friedkin threw open the door and, with gun raised, stepped out onto the deck.

Above them was a huge glass dome built in a honeycomb shape. Bright blue sky stretched in every direction.

A shriek from behind Friedkin made her turn and look upwards. A broad-winged pterosaur with a long beak, ragged and bony, perched on the upper deck. It bore down on the three of them, undead claws reaching hungrily for live flesh.

"Run!" Friedkin shouted, unleashing a hail of bullets towards the creature's head. They struck, knocking the creature back.

It shrieked again.

In response to the noise, something on the floor below them let out a deep roar. A heavy foot slammed. Whatever it was struck the wall, making the floor shake.

The pterosaur took wing with a pained cry.

"Run!" Friedkin cried again but the two scientists were already at full sprint.

"Shit!" Friedkin said, letting out another burst of bullets before racing after Charley and Cyprian.

Behind her, the pterosaur cried again.

She felt the hairs rise on her neck and threw her body forwards. The thing passed over her seconds later. She could only watch in horror as the pterosaur swooped towards Charley and Cyprian.

Cyprian was just a metre behind Charley and, when Charley changed direction to round a pillar, Cyprian was at its mercy.

With a cry, it struck Cyprian full on in the back. He yelped and fell, but the zombie pterosaur lifted him casually from the floor and carried him over the edge and out towards the centre of the dome, rising all the time.

Friedkin cried out and could only watch as Cyprian struggled against the creature. "Sorry mate, I wouldn't wish that on you." She raised her rifle and squeezed off a single shot.

It hit Cyprian in the head and he went limp.

Charley, realising what had happened, let out a cry.

"Keep going!" Friedkin shouted, giving pursuit.

In the centre of the complex, the pterosaur dropped Cyprian's body. She winced as it tumbled and hit the floor with a crunch.

Creatures raced from between buildings and along streets in the pursuit of fresh flesh.

A small bipedal creature much like the deinonychus, but taller with thinner legs, leapt out in front of Charley, baring its teeth. Like all the others, it too was undead, a horrific life-ending gash along its abdomen leaving entrails hanging.

Charley shrieked.

Friedkin shot it square in the head. The dinosaur screamed and tore its gaze from Charley to Friedkin.

As the thing started to charge, Friedkin squeezed the trigger.

It fell back under a hail of bullets.

"Look out!" Charley cried.

Friedkin turned, her jaw dropping instantly.

A large bipedal dinosaur with a fan on its back and a long snout was just metres away. Strong legs would have made it a fast runner, but tables, chairs, and other debris blocked its way to Friedkin.

She turned and ran, catching up with Charley seconds later.

"Spinosaur?"

Charley nodded blankly.

"How much further?" she asked.

Charley gestured to a door just one hundred metres away.

"I'll go at the back."

They ran, weaving around obstacles while the spinosaur gave hot pursuit, shrieking and snarling as it went.

Several times, Friedkin heard its jaws snap on her tail; each time, she changed direction.

Charley crashed into the door and almost fumbled her swipe card. The door fell open; the two women fell through it together and tumbled into a pile. They scrambled away from the door just as the spinosaur crashed into the wall, mouth snapping, unable to push its way through.

Racing along the dark corridor, Friedkin didn't see the young pterosaur until it hit her in the face, claws digging into her uniform. The rotting smell made her retch, but Friedkin pulled at its small body while the spinosaur's snarls faded.

The young pterosaur clung on tightly, claws grasping at Friedkin.

With her one free hand, Friedkin lifted her leg and pulled her combat knife from its sheath. Unable to twist, and still fighting the creature off, she swung it clumsily. The blade sunk into the pterosaur and it went limp.

Friedkin pulled her uniform collar back up and with a heavy smile asked Charley to lead the way.

Their progress through the facility was slow, stopping every so often on hearing the shuffling of feet and flapping wings.

The only other resistance was a single sinornithosaurus. It was weak and hungry and put up no fight as Friedkin drove her blade into its head.

"I guess they both found their way in by accident?" Charley said.

The facility was the same as their entry point and they were relieved to find the Chronis charged and ready to go.

"There is a time delay built in just in case we needed to evacuate," Charley said, pushing some buttons. "We have three minutes to cover twenty paces."

They walked slowly down the ramp, Friedkin with her gun ready for any sign of movement.

When they reached the Chronis, Friedkin pulled opened the door and gestured for Charley to step inside. "I'm afraid I won't be coming back with you." She smiled sadly and pulled the collar of her military fatigues away from her neck to reveal a bite.

Charley's face dropped.

"I think it was the baby pterodactyl."

"There must be some way?" Charley stepped into the Chronis.

"There isn't though, is there?"

"But...?"

"No. Speak well of me." Friedkin saluted and closed the door leaving Charley in silence.

Hearing the crack, Charley closed her eyes, awaiting the flash. It passed before her eyelids and faded.

Wearily, Charley approached the door and hammered heavily before pressing the communication button. "This is Charley, please open the doors."

There was no response.

"Please, let me out. Cyprian is dead. Friedkin stayed behind because she was bitten. All her men are dead too."

When the door failed to open again, Charley let out an involuntary sob. "Please, I'm all alone in here." She was already operating the remote access.

The door gave a groan and slowly slid open. Bright natural light flooded the interior. Charley stood back and shielded her eyes until they adjusted. With a deep breath, she stepped out.

And found herself on the edge of a concrete structure falling away into the sea.

Thick grey clouds covered the landscape. The water was raging and dark, smashing against the rocky cliffs below her.

"This isn't the London facility..." She looked along the waterside, trying to work out where she was. "Where am I? This isn't even England."

Smoke rose in the distance from the city beyond – several identifiable buildings struck with damage, fallen, broken. Figures walked aimlessly about the landscape.

The thought struck her that they were not human.

That thought was broken just moments later when Charley heard a long and low growl. A shadow passed over her body from behind.

Charley turned slowly and stared into the eyes of an adult spinosaurus.

"How...how did you?"

Its injuries and putrefied flesh made it clear the thing was infected with the zombie venom.

The thing opened its jaws wide.

Charley screamed.

LOST IN TIME
C. D. KESTER

"Shut up you little brat!"

"Brat? Don't call me a brat you big dumb booger eater!"

A thundering voice came ringing out from the front seat.

"Enough!"

Harley and Piper had been arguing throughout the entire day of driving and their father, Scott, was done listening to it. Driving through the desert was tiring enough without the constant screeching and screaming from the back seat. He was also starting to wonder about this shortcut that he had suggested they take, but he didn't want to let Heather or the girls know that or he would never hear the end of it. Scott's outburst did the trick for a moment or two. Before long, though, Piper reached over and pulled Harley's hair. This led to the two of them getting into a slapping match.

Scott turned around and put a hand back to separate the two while yelling, "STOP IT! I can turn this car around right now. We don't have to go to Disneyland."

Heather, who was Scott's wife and the mother of Piper, and stepmother to Harley, grabbed him by the shoulder.

"Honey, the road! The road!"

Scott looked back ahead, and his mouth dropped open. There was a swirling blue mass in the road in front of them. Before Scott could react, the Subaru was pulled into the hole and the car was filled with squeals, screams, and a big deep yell as everyone grabbed hold of whatever they could.

As the car was spit out on the other side, Heather checked on the girls while Scott checked their surroundings in a panic. The road was gone, there were no signs or anything other than the terrain as far as the eye could see. That was besides the little speck out in front of the car that was slowly becoming larger.

The dot grew larger and larger until Scott realized that it looked like an enormous lizard that was taking slow and measured steps. The ground began to shake the closer that it came, and Scott recognized that it wasn't just any lizard. It was an enormous Tyrannosaurus Rex, and it was coming straight for them. The beast let out a thunderous roar and began to pick up speed. The girls and Heather were in hysterics. Piper held her favorite doll close to her chest. It was an Elsa doll that she hoped to show to the Ice Queen herself when they made their way to Disney. He feared now that she may never get that chance.

Scott was doing the best he could to fight through the adrenaline and sweaty palms to keep himself steady. As Scott threw the car into reverse, he turned it around and hit the gas. Looking in the mirror, he could see that the beast was giving chase. They passed a rock formation and a Jeep pulled out from around the other side of it. It was two men who appeared to be in about their forties and were dressed like archaeologists or people on a safari.

The Jeep had no doors on it; the driver was leaning towards the family's car and trying to shout a message. Scott rolled the passenger side window down to see what he had to say while still maintaining his speed and direction.

The driver wore glasses and had brown hair that was blowing in the wind. He shouted, "Follow us! Quickly, there's no time to waste!"

Scott had no idea what was going on and was glad to oblige. Whether or not they could be trusted he wasn't sure, but they seemed to have some idea of what was going on and that was more than enough for him. The T-Rex was gaining speed and reversing away from it wasn't going to cut it for much longer.

The mysterious men waved Scott toward them as they made a sharp turn off to the side. There was just enough time to slam on the brakes and take off forwards before the prehistoric beast came down right on top of them. The girls screamed at the top of their lungs in the back seat as an enormous eye took up the entire back window, before Scott pulled away in a frenzy.

There was what looked like a man-made cave going down into the ground and the jeep disappeared into the front of it. Scott was close behind and was just about to the front of the cave when the car stopped moving.

Heather screamed, "What are you doing? Keep going, we're almost there!"

Scott turned around with a terrified expression. "Honey, I'm flooring it."

The T-Rex had the trunk of the car in its massive mouth. It shook them about a bit as Scott kept a tight grip on the wheel and continued to press the pedal to the floor. As the beast lifted them off the ground Scott had an idea. He slammed his hand on the horn and held it until the dinosaur dropped them and shook its head around in frustration and anger.

As the mangled car hit the ground, Scott was thrilled to find that nothing was wrong with the back wheels. They took off into the cave and beat the T-Rex, which lunged after them once it came back to its senses. When they pulled in past the mouth of the cave, a stainless-steel door came down and slammed to the floor behind them. They could hear the T-Rex slamming into it and trying to get in. He would realize there was no use and wander away soon.

Once they were deep enough into the cave to know they were safe, Scott let his foot off the gas pedal and dropped his head onto the steering wheel. The girls whimpered and cried in the back seat as they held each other, and Heather reached back to make sure they were ok after the encounter.

Suddenly, bright lights filled the cave, and they could see just how immense it truly was. The whole place shined with the same spotless stainless-steel as the door was made in. It was immaculate from top to bottom, as if incredibly maintained or brand new. They were in a lab of sorts with computers, microscopes, Bunsen burners, and the most striking thing was that the walls were lined with displays of wildlife that were much like the enclosures at a zoo.

The wildlife in the enclosures inside were no easier to believe than the T-Rex that just chased them into this laboratory. There was a Dilophosaurus trampling around in its enclosure. It must have been over twenty feet in length. As it noticed them it let out a roar, which was surprisingly loud for it being behind what appeared to be triple-layered polycarbonate or something even stronger.

Harley asked, "I thought that was the one with the big scary frilly things?"

Scott responded while focusing on where he was driving. "You can't believe everything you see in Jurassic Park."

On the other side of the cave there was a long enclosure with little velociraptors that were racing each other up and down the way. Each one of them was not much larger than a chicken in size. Another common misconception thanks to the movies and shows throughout the years. There was a very tall enclosure with flying pterodactyls. When they pulled up behind the Jeep that had beckoned them into the lair, there were two enormous aquariums behind them. One held an Ichthyosaur, which looked like a dolphin with a long thin mouth, much like an alligator gar. The other held a Plesiosaur, which many would see and think of the fabled Loch Ness Monster.

As Scott pulled up to the Jeep, the men beckoned him to get out and approach them. Scott was wary, but he knew the only other option was not very promising. He took off his seatbelt and turned to his wife and the girls.

He said, "We gotta stick together. No matter what happens. None of us leaves anyone, okay?"

The three of them nodded their heads in agreement. Everyone unbuckled and got out of the car, first meeting up near the front of the vehicle, before slowly approaching the men. The man with the glasses and long brown hair that they had seen driving earlier raised his hand in greeting.

"Hello, welcome to our little slice of paradise. My name is Arnold Matthews, and this is my associate and longtime friend Peter Harrington."

The other man had short blonde hair that was combed to the side and elegantly styled. He wore the same outfit as Arnold but stood with a much more imposing stature. Though he seemed intimidating at first, he broke the ice with a smile and a gentle wave.

Scott couldn't hold back his questions any longer. "What is this place? What do you two do? How the hell is any of this even possible?"

Arnold held up his hands in a calming gesture. "Easy, easy. I'll answer your questions. Don't you want to introduce yourselves first, though?"

Scott was beside himself. He couldn't even wrap his mind around pleasantries at a time like this. He did his best to abide by Arnold's wishes.

He pointed to himself. "Scott."

He pointed to his wife. "Heather."

Opening his hand, he held it out towards the girls. "Piper and Harley. They're our daughters."

Harley shot back, "She's my *step*mom! Not my mom."

Scott turned his hand into a stern finger that he held out toward her chest. "Not right now, Harley."

Arnold smiled as if unphased by the family drama. "Great, thank you very much for the introductions. I feel that we know each other now and can continue to learn more. What you are standing in is the life's work of me and my associate.

"To answer your first question. It is not so much where you are, but when. You have found yourself in the Mesozoic Era — the mid Cretaceous Period to be exact. The highway you were on is a very desolate one and not once have we had any issue closing our time warp before anyone stumbled upon it."

Scott fumed, "You left open a time warp into the freaking Jurassic Period! What in the world were you thinking?"

Arnold responded, "I think I said very clearly that we are in the Cretaceous Period, which fell after the Jurassic. I understand your anger, but like I said, my colleague and I have been working on this experiment for decades and have never run into anything like this."

Scott pressed his fingers against his temples as if the whole thing was giving him a massive headache.

Arnold continued, "Right. Well, I think your next two questions can be answered with one explanation. Peter and I are scientists and time travellers. Time travelling has been around for quite some time but is incredibly top secret, as I'm sure you can understand. You need the highest of clearance to learn anything about the program."

Heather raised a finger and questioned Arnold. "How could they keep that so well hidden? It seems like there would be leakers, no matter how high the clearance, at some point."

Arnold smiled as if he expected some type of question like this. "I'm talking about 'a few handfuls of people in the entire world' type of clearance. To your point about leaks, there have been a few in the past. When you're dealing with people on that type of echelon you would be amazed at how quickly they can discredit anybody and chalk it up to conspiracy theories. Anyone who dared to test those waters ultimately met an untimely demise, as I'm sure you can imagine."

Harley and Piper covered their mouths as their jaws dropped in horror.

Scott held their shoulders and looked to the scientists. "Look, the last thing we want is to be tangled up in all that stuff. We were just in the middle of a family road trip. I'll admit this is more spectacular than anything we had up the pipeline, but I don't want to get brought into the kind of trouble you're talking about. We saw nothing, we heard nothing, and I promise that we will say nothing."

Arnold began to pace and stroke his chin. "Oh, what to do, what to do…Sure, you say that you will say nothing. People always do when backed into a corner. That would entail that Peter and I take all that responsibility with the people you speak of on our shoulders." He paused and pointed to Scott & Heather. "Sure, you two comprehend what's at stake." He then pointed to the girls. "But let's say one of these little ones feels a bit gossipy and wants to share what an amazing experience they had on their vacation. One friend tells another, who tells another, who tells their parents. It goes from Facebook to the local news, all the way to the CIA. No, no, that won't do."

Harley responded feistily. "We're not gonna tell anyone! You heard my daddy, now help us get out of here before that monster comes back and tries to hurt us."

She crossed her arms in anger and frustration.

Arnold smiled. "This one has some fight in her. That's good. You're all going to need that type of spirit. Peter…beam them."

Peter looked at Arnold as if he was shocked at the request.

296

Arnold shouted at him. "I said to beam them! We won't have our lives' work ruined by these infiltrators."

Peter reluctantly reached for a device that looked like a remote control. As he held it up and found the button he was looking for, he said, "Sorry," and pressed the button. They had not realized that where they were led to stand had some type of device on the cave ceiling above them. Once Peter pressed the button a beam of light came down from the device and engulfed the family. All they could see was blinding white light, until suddenly they were in the desert next to a large lake.

There were different prehistoric animals gathered around the water, drinking, and resting. Scott knew what this meant. Arnold had sent them to some unknown location in the same period. He had sent them to die, so that they would no longer be a threat to his project...

Some time had passed with plenty of panicked discussion. Scott and Heather were doing the balancing act of trying to keep the girls calm while also planning their next move. Suddenly, Peter appeared in a beam of light. He appeared to be in a rush and worried. He tossed what looked like the fancy remote control he had used to beam them out there over to Scott.

He whispered, "Hide it!"

Scott shoved it into his pants and pulled the girls close. They cowered and held onto him and Heather. Just as Peter was looking over his shoulder, Arnold warped down behind him atop an enormous Allosaurus that he was mounted on like a horse.

The dinosaur opened its giant mouth and reached down to where Peter was standing. Peter screamed in terror as the beast chomped down at about the halfway point on his body, lifting him up off the ground. As it got him into the air, it tossed him as if to bring his legs and waist into its mouth and crunched down as blood spilled onto the ground.

The Allosaurus continued to chomp on the man, snapping his bones and shredding through his muscles and tendons. That's when Scott noticed something. There were two rods sticking up from the top of the animal's head with blinking red lights. He couldn't make out exactly what it was Arnold was fidgeting with, but it looked like he had some type of controls on its back.

Scott knew what he had to do. While its mouth was full might be the only chance that he had. He told Heather and the girls to go and hide behind a nearby tree. They didn't want to leave his side, but they did as he asked.

Scott went up in front of the Allosaurus and started jumping and waving his arms while shouting. The monstrous creature looked down in confusion. It lowered its head toward him to check him out, and as it did Scott jumped up and pulled on one of the rods with all his might. The rod came out from its skull with a wet and gloopy sound as Scott tossed it to the floor.

The dinosaur made a screeching noise, although its mouth was still full of mangled Peter. It chomped back down on its food and lunged its head towards Scott. Scott dodged out of the way and jumped up, grabbing the other rod and removing it from the dinosaur's skull.

This was when Scott took off running towards his family, who had taken shelter behind a large tree. They looked on in awe as the dinosaur thrashed about, tossing Arnold to the floor. The dinosaur romped off towards the water, now focused on finishing its mouthful of food.

Arnold pulled a pistol out of a holster on his side and walked towards the tree the family was hiding behind. He cocked the gun, aiming and ready to fire.

He said, "You come into my world, my experiment, and you have the audacity to ruin my work. Come out and face me like a man and I will give you the kindness of making your death quick and painless."

Scott pulled out the remote and did a quick scan of the buttons. There were so many buttons and knobs and wheels. He had no idea what any of it meant.

"I am giving you to the count of three. One... two..."

Scott saw a button that said '*Warp*'. He wasn't sure if that was the one that he was looking for, but he was running short on options. Scott jumped out from behind the tree and pressed the button with the remote pointed at Arnold. A blue ball of light shot out of the end of the remote and consumed Arnold. As it hit him, he disappeared in a flash.

The girls were quivering, and Heather was holding them close, assuring them that everything would be alright. Scott searched the control for anything that might be of use. After scanning the contraption from the top to the bottom he noticed the word '*Lab*' near the bottom of the remote.

Scott walked back over to Heather and the girls and said, "Ok, I know this is scary, but we have to try to get back to our time. To do that we have to get back to our vehicle first or we will be stranded on a desert highway. I think this button can help us get back to the laboratory, where our car is at. Are y'all ready to give that a shot with me?"

The girls looked up to him with their eyes wet and faces filled with terror. Both shook their heads 'no'.

Scott rubbed the back of his head and, after a moment, shrugged and said, "Well...close your eyes then. Here goes nothin'."

Scott pressed the button with the remote pointed behind them. A portal opened where the blue ball landed that looked much like the portal they had accidentally driven through while still on their way to Disneyland, which felt like a lifetime ago.

Scott grabbed Harley and looked to Heather, who followed suit and grabbed Piper. The girls covered their eyes with their hands while Scott and Heather ran headfirst into the shimmering blue portal. They were all spit out onto the floor on the other side.

As they shook off the rough landing and got to their feet, they realized they were in fact in the same laboratory that they had driven into earlier. Their car was still intact and sitting nearby. There was only one problem: the laboratory was a wreck.

Florescent bulbs were dangling from the ceiling; the whole area was dimly lit as many lights were busted out and had come crashing to the floor. Worst of all, none of the dinosaurs were in their containment chambers. The various screeches and calls filled the air around them as they huddled together. The velociraptors went racing by them and they clenched together tightly.

As the Dilophosaurus stomped into view, Piper shrieked and accidentally threw her Elsa doll onto the

301

floor. Before Scott and Heather realized what she was doing, Piper shook free of their grasp and was lunging forward towards the doll.

"Piper, no!" Scott called as he went after her.

Piper grabbed her doll and clutched it tightly to her chest. Scott was inches away from grabbing her when a Pterodactyl came swooping down and grabbed her with its massive claws. She screamed and pleaded from the air high above.

Scott rushed Heather and Harley to the car and told them to lock the doors and wait for him. The Pterodactyl was circling high in the air. The ceiling was immensely high, and the drop would definitely kill her should the beast decide to release its grip. Scott was trying to think of something, anything, to coax it down to the ground.

As he was contemplating different ways that he could make this happen, the Pterodactyl swooped up into the middle of the ceiling and released Piper from its grip. She held on tightly to her Elsa doll, squeezing it for dear life.

Scott had little time to think. Trying to catch her would surely fail from this height. He reached into his pocket and pulled out the remote. His finger shot instinctively to the 'Lab' button, and he pressed it while aiming at his falling daughter. The blue ball of light consumed her, and a portal opened nearby where they had just arrived moments ago.

She came rolling out of the portal and was tossed like a rag doll across the floor, but the plan had worked. Although she was a little bit banged up, his little girl was alive. He pocketed the remote and ran over to snatch her up. She still clung tightly to the doll and looked up to him with dazed eyes as he lifted her from the ground.

Scott held her close and made a mad dash towards the Subaru. Heather reached from the passenger seat and opened the back door while Harley slid to the other side of the seat to make way. Scott and Piper came crashing into the back seat, and Scott quickly closed the door behind them.

Heather reached back and checked Piper for any signs of broken bones or serious injuries. Just some bumps and bruises. She made it out in good shape considering the scare she had just given them. Scott climbed over into the front seat and adjusted the rear-view mirror. He saw the large metal door shut tightly.

"Crap..."

Scott looked around for any sort of button that might open the door. Then a thought came to him. He pulled the remote out and searched it. There was a button near the top that read '*Open/Close*'. He told the girls to duck and reached back, pointing the remote through the back window and towards the large door.

This time no ball of light came out, but the door did begin to open. Scott turned on the car and turned it around to face the entrance. The car pulled forward through the large door and Scott began to wonder how they would get back to their own time. He handed the remote to Heather.

"Try to find anything that has to do with time travel. Maybe a year or something, I don't know, anything."

Heather tensed as she began to search the remote. That's when they heard the familiar noise. It was the same thunderous and earth-shaking roar that they had heard from the T-Rex when they were searching for safety after being transported to this time. As the beast approached, Scott could see that Arnold was riding on top of his back. He had control rods implanted in the beast and had turned him into another one of his giant remote-control toys.

"Shit. Let me see that thing."

From the back seat a whimpering voice came from Piper.

"Daddy, don't cuss."

"Sorry, baby."

Scott scanned the remote up and down, looking for anything that could either get them out of here or help him with Arnold and his enormous friend. The T-Rex was growing closer by the second. Time was short. Scott decided to run out, away from the car, to distract Arnold and hopefully stop him from growing any closer to his family.

Scott ran out into the desert waving the remote around for Arnold to see. The plan worked, and Arnold abandoned his original path, heading straight for him. Scott's hands grew sweaty; his mind grew frantic.

"Shit, shit, shit. What do I do?"

As the T-Rex grew closer, and the earth began to move with each crashing step, Scott came across a button that sounded interesting. '*Void*,' it read. Scott didn't have time to think. He held the remote up as the T-Rex was nearing his position. Just as it began to reach down to bite him in half, Scott pressed the button.

A black staticky ball of darkness shot out from the end of the remote. The ball connected with the T-Rex's chest and consumed him and Arnold. They swirled into a black abyss that was filled with lightning and pure darkness. The portal disappeared with a pop and Scott fell to the ground, catching his breath.

Looking at the remote, he noticed a knob below a small screen. Below the screen, it said '*Year*'. This was good enough for Scott. He was ready to put this whole thing behind them. Scott turned the knob until the year read '*2022 CE*' and made the trek back to the Subaru.

As he climbed into the driver's seat, Heather, Harley, and Piper all squeezed onto him. He could tell they weren't sure they would ever have another chance to do so. He assured them that everything was alright.

Harley asked, "So where did they go? Where did you send them?"

Scott looked at the remote warily. "I don't know, sweetie. I know where we are about to go, though."

Scott rolled down his window, holding his finger to the button below the knob and pressing it with the front facing the dirt in front of their car. A shining blue portal appeared before them, much like the one that got them into this mess to begin with.

Scott looked back towards the girls and said, "Disneyland."

With that he pulled the Subaru through the portal, and they were back on the same desolate stretch of highway that they had so mistakenly taken thanks to Scott's expert navigation skills. Heather looked toward the remote in Scott's hand as he adjusted the car to face the correct direction on the street.

She asked, "What are you going to do with that?"

Scott smirked, as if he might be thinking of messing with her for a moment, but thought better of it. His window was still open from earlier. As he picked up speed, he reared back and threw it as far into the desert as he could possibly manage. It landed somewhere out in the dirt, away from the road.

Scott rolled up his window and said, "It's someone else's problem now."

They continued down the highway, with the happiest place on earth now within reach. Piper clung tightly to her Elsa doll and, instead of fighting with her, Harley now held onto Piper gently as they drifted off to sleep.

TERROR DAWN
LOKI DEWITT

PROLOGUE

Back when Zach was a kid, he had sat down to watch a movie with his dad. While he had just been looking to spend time with his dad, he would have never guessed that the movie they watched that day would change him forever.

The movie was about a lone warrior who travelled the harsh roads of a post-apocalyptic wasteland, striving to fight off all manners of marauders and bandits, while they were just trying to get what they needed to survive.

This opened up Zach's mind to a whole new world of possibilities.

Growing up in a small corner of the suburbs, Zach had never even considered racing across the desert on some wild adventure. The idea of this whole new world, which was so unlike his own, stuck in Zach's imagination and never really left. As he got older, he got a mundane job, and even a nice apartment, and was doing pretty well for himself all things considered.

Despite all of that, though, the idea of getting to be that wasteland warrior, even if just for a little while, was always in the back of his mind. He wasn't sure how or when, but he knew that one day he was going to leave his normal life behind and finally take his first steps into the wasteland.

<u>I</u>

Thirty. It still felt a little crazy to Zach to think that he had reached such a milestone in his life. It seemed like only a few years ago he was back in college doing keg-stands and trying to pick up girls. He couldn't believe how much had changed since those days. He had gone from frat boy to management in what felt like the blink of an eye.

Every day he put on that suit, tightened up his tie, went in there, and dazzled clients with his smile and that college-educated vocabulary. His bosses loved him and the job he did. In their eyes, he was the dream candidate to lead their advertising company into a bright future. While he was happy to be factored so prominently into their future plans, he knew that none of them had the slightest clue as to the kind of future he really wanted.

He couldn't help but feel a rush of excitement as he shut the water off in the hotel shower. He knew what the actual future held for him, but that wasn't what this week was about. This week was not just about celebrating his life and all that he had accomplished in it. This was the moment where he got to step away from working for everyone else's dreams for him and start working on his own.

He looked down at the water as it swirled the drain. It had a slight crimson tinge to it that made him smile even broader than he already was. There was a part of him that still couldn't believe he'd done it, but he also knew that it was something he had to do. His hand reached out and grabbed the towel that he had placed just outside the shower. As he dried off, he made his way over to the mirror. He chuckled as he saw his reflection.

Normally his hair was well groomed and very nice looking. That wasn't the case anymore. In the place of his normal do was a mohawk, coloured with a shock of red. He grinned seeing it. It was everything that he hoped it would be. He grabbed his phone and snapped a quick selfie to post on social media later, before finishing getting ready.

2

It was still dark outside as he rolled up to the site where they had all agreed to meet. They had found a spot in the New Mexico desert that had little light pollution and decided that it would be amazing to watch the sun come up together. It blew Zach's mind just how peaceful and serene the desert looked around him. It was all so still and calm, and somehow just as beautiful as it was in the daylight.

Knowing that this was a once-in-a-lifetime kind of trip, he had made sure to arrive a little bit before the others so he would have the chance to truly appreciate it before things got going. He shut off the truck that he had rented for the week and sat there for a moment, taking it all in. For all the noise that they had planned, there was something magical about the quiet.

He hit the little button that sent all the windows rolling down and the soft desert breeze came rolling through the truck. His eyes closed and he took a deep breath, letting the sensation wash over him. As he let it carry him away, he could swear that he could hear the desert come alive around him. Little rodents scurrying, sand shifting slightly, and even the sound of flags flapping in the distance.

Then came a more specific sound, one much more aggressive. His eyes opened and a smile spread across his face. It was the sound of engines.

Moments later came the headlights, and then the trucks and SUVs that the rest of his friends were riding in. He reached into his pocket, pulled out the small little box, and flipped it open.

He hadn't just invited all his friends out here to help him make his childhood dream come true – he had also invited his long-time girlfriend, Kimberly. It took a special kind of girl to come out here to the desert and play wasteland warrior with him, and he knew that was exactly the kind of girl he wanted to keep around.

He grinned as he snapped the box closed and stuffed it back in his pocket. While he hadn't told anyone else, he planned on making two of his dreams come true while they were out there. He jumped out of the truck and held his arms wide to greet the others. The time for quiet was just about over, and then it was going to get really loud.

3

All of the four-wheelers and dune buggies had been unloaded and were in the process of getting one last check over. Zach looked over everyone. They had all done their part and put together some pretty impressive post-apocalyptic gear. Everything was already perfect, but all the spikes, leather, and goggles somehow made everything even better.

Of all the creative outfits, though, his favourite that wasn't his own was Kimberly's. He had never really considered pink or purple to be very fallout flavoured, but she had managed to make it work well. He had made sure to tell her so, and she complimented his mohawk while running her fingers through it.

While she played with his hair, he looked deep into her eyes. "I'm glad you came." His words made her smile, which made butterflies flutter in his stomach.

"Me too. Can't let you boys have all the fun, right?"

He chuckled and nodded. The two shared a tender kiss before they heard one of the others whistle.

"Everything is good!"

The announcement was met with a chorus of cheers. Everyone moved to their respective vehicles and got in place. Zach took Kimberly's hand and walked her to the four-wheeler that had been placed at the front of the herd.

As he neared the vehicle, he pulled two flares from the pack that had been secured to the back. With the flares in hand, he turned to face the crowd. Everyone was in the vehicles and ready to go, they were just waiting on him to give the word.

He lifted the flares high in the air and smirked. "Wasteland Warriors!" He took a deep breath, savouring the moment. "Hit the lights!"

He struck the flares, which erupted to life with a red glow. The others began to hoot and holler as they started their engines. Zach handed the flares to Kimberly and climbed on their four-wheeler. Once he could feel her behind him, he started his engine. With a whoop of excitement, he and the others set out across the predawn desert, ready to make some noise.

4

The wind rushed through Zach's hair, and he smiled as he listened to Kimberly hoot and holler behind him. Out of the corner of his eye, he spotted something sailing past him. As soon as it hit the sand, he recognized it as a glowstick and motored off toward it. As he picked up speed, he leaned back toward Kimberly a little bit.

"Start the tunes!"

She nodded and quickly went to work. A few moments later the sounds of old Bay Area thrash filled the air.

Zach's eyes lit up with mischief as he pushed the throttle forward. The four-wheeler lurched forward as it picked up speed. He could feel Kimberly waving the flares in the air behind him, and he could hear the others zooming about as well. They didn't come out to just ride around the desert, though. They came to conquer it.

He turned the vehicle suddenly, causing the four-wheeler to turn sideways. He knew the risk of what he was doing, but risks were part of the game if you wanted to make it in the wasteland. The four-wheeler came to a stop and he jumped off, with Kimberly right behind. The others in the group came to a stop shortly in front of them. He looked them over. They all looked at him with their war paint-streaked faces and waited for a command. He didn't have a command to give them – he had a challenge.

"All of you have followed me out here, far from the safety of society. Out there is no air conditioning. There is no internet. There are no deadlines. There is only freedom! That freedom won't just be given to you though. No. In the wasteland, freedom must be taken! To get that freedom, you will face danger. You will look death in the face. When you see the Reaper coming, though, remember one thing: he has to catch you first!" The group laughed and cheered, but fell silent again when Zach raised his arm. "He won't catch you, though, because we ride together, and the wasteland is ruled by Siberia and Big Daddy Cinder!"

The group cheered loudly at his proclamation. As he jumped back on his four-wheeler, Kimberly slid in behind him.

"Siberia, huh?" He nodded. "I like it." She leaned forward and cooed in his ear, "Alright, Big Daddy Cinder, let's ride."

His eyes lit up with mischief, and a little more, as he revved the four-wheeler engine. He took off at full speed, leaving the others scrambling to catch up. He wasn't about to slow down, though. The wasteland was wide open and they had a reaper to outrun.

5

They had been riding around for hours with only brief stops to refuel the vehicles. The sun would be coming up soon, and Zach knew that they were going to have to stop for a different kind of fuel soon.

He had Kimberly wave the others back to camp with flares. The pack fell in line behind him, and it didn't take long before they were all gathered back where they had started. As soon as everyone was back at base camp, they wasted no time in getting everything together to make a hearty breakfast.

As the meal was cooked, Zach made sure to check in with each person, make sure they were having a good time, and thank them for coming. He made sure to give extra thanks to Kimberly's friend Kelly. Kelly was a New Mexico native and had helped secure the area they needed to put everything in motion. After he had made his rounds, he settled in beside Kimberly, who was helping some of the others with the food. He put an arm around her and kissed her on the side of the head. "Thank you for all of this."

She stopped what she was doing and snuggled into him a little. "I'm glad you like it…" She looked up at him with those eyes that always drew him in. "Big Daddy Cinder."

The two shared a laugh and she waved him off so she could get back to helping with the meal. Once away from the others, Zach took a short walk away from the base camp and just looked out at the expanse of desert.

He inhaled deeply and closed his eyes. While the impending sunrise meant that it wasn't quite as quiet as it was when they had shown up, he was still able to pick out some sounds beyond the general commotion of the group. The sound of the soft breeze was still there, and so were some of the scurrying animals.

The sound of flags waving was still there, too. In fact, it seemed to be louder than it was earlier.

He opened his eyes and turned to look back at the group. Something caught his eye as he turned, something that didn't seem to quite belong against the horizon. He ran past the group to see if he could get a closer look at it, and as he did, the sound of waving flags seemed to get louder. As he got closer, his eyes widened. He wasn't just getting closer to it, it was getting closer to him.

He stopped dead in his tracks and just stared. As the thing came more and more into view, his mind was less and less able to process what he was seeing. Its massive wings beat against the dawn, causing it to pick up speed as it got closer. Its eyes were locked in on the camp, and behind it, the thing's skull came to a sort of stalk. The thing led the way with its pointed beak.

Zach stood there, petrified, his mind desperately trying to figure out how the thing rushing toward him could even exist. His lip quivered as he tried to form the word. Even if he had found the word, it would have been drowned out in the deafening screech that the creature let loose. The sound drew everyone's eyes to the same spot that Zach was looking. Immediately, they all began to scramble and try and react to the impossible thing they were seeing.

The creature zoomed past Zach and into the crowd, taking several of them off their feet as it crashed into them. As the mass of humanity tumbled and fell, several of them landed on the firepits that they had been using to cook. Screams filled the air as flesh seared, and panic spread. Some moved to pull their friends out of the firepit while the others were moving in self-preservation and doing their best to get away from the winged monstrosity.

As all of this was unfolding, Zach regained his composure and rushed back to see if he could find Kimberly. It took him a few moments to locate her in the chaos, hiding behind one of the dune buggies. "Kim, we gotta go. I don't know how, but there's a damn pterodactyl in our camp."

Hearing his voice brought Kimberly out of her shocked state and she realized what Zach had just said. "Pterodactyl!?"

Zach nodded and grabbed her hand. He knew that if he could get her in the dune buggy then they could go get help, and at the bare minimum get to some kind of safety. He didn't have time to explain and dragged her to the passenger side of the dune buggy.

As he made his way around the other side, he caught sight of the winged beast grabbing up one of his friends by the neck and shaking them violently. They tried their best to try and get free, but the creature jerked them hard to one side. This caused their neck to crack sharply and their fighting to stop as their body went limp.

Zach jumped into the dune buggy and turned the key. The engine roared to life and the winged monster responded by shrieking loudly. Without thinking, Zach stepped on the gas and sped away from the scene, trying to put as much space between himself and the prehistoric invader as he possibly could.

6

The others at the camp scattered in different directions, completely oblivious to the fact that the one who had drawn them all out there had fled the scene. Even if they had known, it wouldn't have mattered much at the moment. They were more focused on getting away from the beast that had decided to literally crash the festivities.

Though the sun was still slowly emerging, the beast cut an intimidating silhouette as it chased after the fleeing partygoers. The creature was able to move through the air quicker than the cosplay wastelanders could move through the sand. Just moments earlier, Kelly had been so happy that she was there to see her friend's childhood dream become a reality. She might have regretted it if anything other than fear filled her mind as she fled from the predator.

Her heart pounded in her ears, but she could still hear the death and chaos behind her. It was difficult to run through the sand, but adrenaline kept her moving. The further she ran, the more distant the sounds became.

A new sound filled her ears, though – the sound of flags flapping in the wind. She turned to see what was making the noise. The looming form of the creature's beak opening would be the last thing she ever saw.

Her head was caught in the open beak and the beast had gathered so much speed chasing her that her head was severed from her body in an instant. The headless corpse that was Kelly collapsed to the sand as the creature turned to head back to catch more of the others.

The scramble of humanity was no match for the sleek predator. One by one, they faced the brutal force of the beast that seemed to have come out of nowhere but made itself undeniable.

Some were lifted high into the air and dropped back to the ground with bone-shattering force. Others were impaled by the sharp beak of the thing. A few were shaken violently until their bodies couldn't take anymore. One or two even joined Kelly on the ground, headless, staining the sand with their blood.

Soon enough, any of them who weren't dead would be before too long. The monster circled the carnage it had created, making sure that no one had remained. It seemed content with its work. Then the sound of an engine powering a vehicle across the desert hit its ears. Its eyes looked in that direction.

It had come to hunt, and nothing was going to escape it.

Zach glanced over at Kimberly. She was still in shock from what had just happened, but at least she wasn't there with them. As he kept driving aimlessly across the dunes, his mind began to race in an attempt to figure things out.

Where was he going to go? Who was he going to get for help? How could they help? Could they stop that thing? What even was that thing? Where had it come from? Why was it there? Was it really a pterodactyl?

Kimberly spoke the last word of the question as he thought it. It was the last word he had heard her say before they fled the camp, and it was the first one he had heard her say since. He looked over at her again. The look on her face told him that her mind was trying to process everything too.

As unreal as everything had been, there was something about hearing the name of the creature said out loud that somehow made it even more bizarre.

"How though? All of them died out millions of years ago." Even as he spoke the sentence, his mind raced to formulate some kind of an answer.

While none of it made any sense, he knew that whatever had attacked them back there was certainly real, regardless of where it had come from or why it struck. He glanced back to Kimberly and the gravity of the attack seemed to hit her as she began to sob uncontrollably.

Zach wanted nothing more than to pull over and comfort her, holding her close and letting her know it was all going to be okay. At that moment though, he knew that he couldn't do that, and even if he did, he would just be lying to her. The best he could do for both of them would be to keep doing what he was already doing: putting as much distance between them and that creature as possible.

He turned his eyes forward again and looked out at the seemingly never-ending sand. Out on the edge of the horizon, the sun was coming into view. Purple, red, yellow, and orange streaked across the sky, blazing the signal of a new day. As terrified as he was, Zach couldn't help but feel a twinge of sadness. Seeing the sun come up with so many of the people closest to him was supposed to be something truly special.

That creature had taken it all away.

He pushed his sadness aside. As beautiful and special as that sunrise was supposed to be, he did not doubt that if he and Kimberly could survive to see another one, it would be more beautiful than any other.

He glanced behind him to see if the winged monster was still pursuing them, but much to his surprise, he saw nothing. There was no creature, there was no campground littered with carnage, and there was only sand as far as the eye could see. Zach laughed in relief as he faced forward again. He could feel himself start to relax as he took a hand off the wheel and put it on Kimberly's shoulder.

"It's going to be okay. We got away." He squeezed her shoulder and took a deep breath.

The sunrise was looking especially beautiful, and the breeze blowing across the dunes felt better than he could describe. He felt happier to be alive at that moment than he had in a very long time. Everything felt so crisp and amplified to his senses, the sound of the dune buggy engine, the tires digging into the sand, the sound of flags flapping.

The last sound made his blood run cold, and he couldn't help but look up. He didn't see the creature, though. Instead, he saw the headless corpse of Kelly falling out of the sky. There was no time to avoid the dead body as it crashed into Zach and Kimberly. Despite this, Zach tried anyway, jerking the steering wheel hard to the side. Between the impact and the speed, this sent the vehicle veering out of control, eventually tumbling end over end across the sand.

8

Pain screamed through Zach's body as he slowly regained consciousness. His vision was blurred and his head throbbed as he tried his best to assess the situation he was in.

As his hands groped about in the sand, they eventually settled on something warm and thick that coated his fingers. Slowly, he brought his fingers closer to his face so he could see what he had put his hand in. It took him just a second to realize it was blood.

He turned his head gingerly to try and see if he could find where the blood was coming from. First, he spotted small splatters, and then a larger pool. The pool was still forming, and he followed the pouring blood up to find the source. The blood was pouring from Kimberly's head, which was not only turned at an unnatural angle but also had shards of glass from what used to be the headlights sticking out of it. What made it even worse, though, was her mangled body was twisted up with the corpse of his dead friend.

He felt a scream of anguish rise up in his throat, but the vomit made it out first. The contents of his stomach spilled out on the sand followed by several gasps for air. The smell of the vomit and blood mixed to make a putrid odour that had his stomach turning again, but the chemical smell of gasoline quickly overpowered it.

He wasn't sure where the gas was coming from, or if there was something in the wreckage that could ignite it, but he knew he wasn't going to stick around to find out. Though the injuries he had sustained were begging him to stop, Zach crawled through the puke, the blood, and out of the twisted metal.

It took him several minutes, but eventually he freed himself from the remains of the dune buggy. Looking back at it, he briefly wondered how he had survived.

The frame of the vehicle was badly mangled, as were the two less fortunate souls who hadn't been as lucky as he was. Free from the wreckage, he sat in the sand and began to cry as the pain from his injuries and the gravity of his situation refused to be pushed aside any longer.

Tears streaked down his cheeks, washing away the sand that had covered them, and his body shuddered. He screamed into the emptiness of the desert around him, the sound lost in the vanishing moments of the dawn. His fists clenched and he drove them into the sand as he screamed out again.

This time though, something screamed back. The high-pitched shriek of the beast that had caused all this cut through the air, announcing its impending arrival. Zach's heart rate picked up again and adrenaline began to course through his body, allowing him to somehow scramble to his feet.

As soon as he was standing, Zach realized that his ankle was broken, and nearly collapsed back to the sand. A look back over his shoulder at the terror barrelling towards him kept him upright, though. He moved across the dune as quickly as his wounded body would carry him.

Unfortunately, the adrenaline in his system wouldn't last long, as the pain of his injuries forced him back down. As he fell to the sand, he could feel his consciousness starting to slip away again. He wanted to fight it, but he couldn't, and the last thing he heard before everything went black was the sound of flags flapping in the wind and the triumphant screech of the prehistoric predator.

2

Zach's eyes opened once more and were immediately greeted with the brightness of the sun. Instinctively, he squinted his eyes and began to look around. He wasn't sure where he was or why he was still alive, but he knew that he was somewhere other than the dune he had collapsed in.

He barely had time to look around before he heard that all-too-familiar shriek cut through the air.

This time it was close, and that meant it was loud. Loud enough to be near deafening.

His head snapped toward the sound, and he saw it. The creature stood there in all its terrifying glory, wings spread wide, its head turned to the sky. Somehow, seeing it stationary filled Zach with even more terror than it chasing him. If it wasn't moving, then that meant it felt comfortable that he wasn't going to get away.

His mind tried to process the creature in front of him, and it kept coming back to the same conclusion: it was indeed a pterodactyl.

Before Zach could give it another thought, the creature lowered its gaze onto him. Frozen in fear, Zach closed his eyes and waited for the death that he knew was coming. He didn't hear another screech though. Instead, he heard several small peeps. He opened his eyes to see what was making the noise, and instead of the large beast that had brought him there, he saw several smaller pterodactyls moving in toward him, hunger in their eyes.

DANIELLE AND THE DIPLODOCUS
MEGAN KIEKEL ANDERSON

Danielle was going to have to go to Science City smelling like sour milk and Monday's rotting lunch. They'd thrown her into the dumpster. Again. It's one of those bullying tactics that's always played for laughs in movies. But in real life, it has some real freaking consequences. You think no one wants to sit beside you when you're unpopular? Try finding a friend when you smell like mouldy lasagne and you have a clump of fermenting mystery meat tangled in the back of your hair. A clump of fermenting mystery meat that no one has the decency to warn you about.

Those ignorant jocks probably don't even think it's a big deal. In fact, Danielle doubts they spare her a thought after they've tossed her away like a hunk of uneaten meatloaf. It's just a game to them: catch the nerd, toss her away. That task checked off the list, time to go after the next victim: stuff tiny Aaron Williams in his locker, burn sure-to-be-valedictorian Kristy Millsap's homework in the bathroom trash can. Push further than cheerleader Leslie Parker is willing to go on a Friday night.

They weren't people to them, not really. They were just a joke. A light-hearted way to spend a morning. And they were, each and every one of them, untouchable. Feted, even.

Danielle groaned and tried to get to her feet, a difficult task with the refuse shifting and sliding underneath her. Her back had hit something hard, sending a sharp pain through her body. She now saw it was the arm of an old, broken projector. That was going to leave a huge bruise. Hopefully the dull pain radiating through her back now was the worst of it. If she'd broken something, there's no way her parents would be able to afford to do anything about it. She'd have to suffer through the pain, whatever deformities may come from any bones improperly knitting themselves back together.

And that was the crux of it, wasn't it? She just had to accept it. She had to accept that she was here to suffer. That she was the only one who could heal herself, however mangled the results.

The bus ride to the museum was predictable. Danielle sat in the front of the bus, near the chaperones, so no one could do anything to her without getting caught. The seats behind and next to her remained empty. The smell was much more noticeable in close quarters, but there wasn't much she could do about that. She'd tried to wash off as much as possible in the school bathrooms, had even started keeping an extra pair of clothes in her backpack, since she'd been thrown in the dumpster so often lately, but the scent of garbage still clung to her hair.

Danielle could tell the teachers were trying to be polite, trying not to show how much the smell bothered them, but they had a clipped way of talking to each other. They were smiling too wide, clearly trying to breathe only through their mouths. It was sort of sweet, Danielle supposed, that they didn't want to show that she was having an effect.

One of her teachers had even slipped her some deodorant last week, somehow mistakenly thinking the problem was *her*, that this was *her* smell, that this was an issue of *poverty* and *hygiene*. Again, she appreciated the concern—sort of—but she didn't understand how the truth wasn't glaringly obvious. Everyone knew. How could they not? She didn't really believe it. The only explanation she could think of was that they were fooling themselves, because believing the problem was her was easier for them than trying to untangle the mess of the truth. Because then, they'd have to actually do something. And it would be a lot harder than picking up a stick of deodorant at the dollar store.

The bus dropped them off at Union Station. Danielle was the first kid out, basking in the few moments of fresh air before they had to go into the grand building, where the hum of her own smell returned. Danielle wished she had one of those Black Plague doctor's masks that look like some kind of evil bird, that she could stuff flowers in the proboscis-like nose, that she could escape her own smell, breathing in gentle florals, while still inflicting it upon others, a reminder of their fault. Their complacency.

She understood those doctors. It made sense to her, the trade-off. It made sense to look like a monster to escape the smell of death.

There was none of that old-timey, spooky sort of science or pseudo-science to be found at Science City. Designed for kids—they were all way too old for it really; Danielle had no idea who the hell thought it would be an appropriate field trip for a bunch of juniors—Science City was a sparkling expanse of hands-on STEM learning opportunities, sectioned off into distinct areas, made to look like its own little contained city square.

Danielle rushed past the little black light neon maze, the various doodads that taught the science behind sound, the fake motel full of optical illusions. Let the jocks go torture the rabbits in the animal section, find someone to make out with in the sewer-themed tunnels

334

and slides that taught about water cleaning processes, show off on the high-wire bicycle that was supposed to convey something important about Newtonian physics.

Danielle wanted to hide away in the dinosaur corner on the ground floor. There was a pit filled with those tiny pieces of rubber they put on playgrounds sometimes. The kind that clings to your socks and never lets go, that somehow turns up in the dirty laundry months later. Kids could don goggles and grab brushes from bins and sweep away the rubber granules, uncovering faux fossils.

Mosasaurs, pterosaurs, Mesozoic fish, ancient ocean creatures. Danielle repeated the fossils that could be found in the Dig Site like a mantra.

The huge dinosaur depictions on the wall annoyed her; the theropods, at the very least, should have been depicted with feathers. The first feathers on dinosaurs were discovered in the 90s, with more and more research piling up over the 2000s and 2010s. There was consensus; why did the inaccuracies persist? When she'd asked a worker about why a *science museum* would perpetuate incorrect imagery last time, they'd said they hadn't updated it because they were planning on replacing the dinosaur section soon, so it wouldn't be worth it. *Wouldn't be worth it*. To actually teach kids accurate science. Unbelievable.

Danielle wondered where the lab would go if they were getting rid of the dinosaurs. The lab was the best part. Plus, what would a kids' science museum be without dinosaurs? It didn't make any sense to her. She must have misunderstood. They must be planning on shuffling things around a bit, moving the dinosaur section, not getting rid of it altogether. They did seem to like to keep things fresh, offer new exhibits often, but you can't just get rid of *dinosaurs*.

Behind a wall of viewing glass, there was a real palaeontology lab, in partnership with the university. No one was working in there right now, but there were camarasaurus fossils in various stages of repair scattered throughout the workspace. Casts were being made, fragments pieced together. To Danielle, it was magical. Almost holy.

She'd loved dinosaurs since she was a little kid. In first grade, she'd run out of books at the school library. Every single book on dinosaurs: Danielle read them all.

No one around her got it.

"Why can't you just read them again?" her mother had asked.

"I can. I do. But I know them already. I want to know more."

Her mom had sighed at that, but she gave in. She started taking her to the public library, requiring that she check out one non-dinosaur book a week. She soon ran out of books there too, but luckily a kindly librarian taught her how to use the inter-library loan system.

Danielle felt a pang for the kid she was then, rubbing her fingers along the plastic ridges of the feathers on her *beipiaosaurus inexpectus* toy, which she kept in her pocket. Feeling its familiar grooves soothed her anxiety. It was wild how much she loved them then, how she could rattle off the complicated names at will. They must have sounded so strange in her small, seven-year-old voice. But she quickly learned that her obsession made her a target, and she'd let it fade away. Now she needed pronunciation guides to even be able to say the names of dinosaurs outside of the popular (inaccurate) *Jurassic Park* cluster. Where had all that knowledge gone?

She'd lost that special interest, and in return she'd gained nothing. Letting go of dinosaurs hadn't stopped her from getting thrown into the dumpster several times a week. She should have just embraced the weird.

At least being here, now, around them, just the idea of them, still brought her comfort. Comfort was so hard for her to come by. She let herself fleetingly imagine that dinosaurs were real, that she could cuddle up with a squishy one, something like a mini iguanodon, in bed at night. Like a stuffed animal. The iguanodon shifted into a velociraptor in her mind—a real one, knee-height, feathered, not the giant things—more closely

337

resembling deinonychus raptors—that had invaded the popular imagination. The raptor curled at the bottom of her bed in her mind, a ready attack dog, in wait to protect her from her enemies. If only.

She peered into the palaeontology lab, trying to see if she could read the papers on the desks, see if any of it meant anything to her. And if it didn't, well, it wasn't too late to change trajectory. She could get back into dinosaurs. No rule saying she couldn't. She could dive back into the deep end of dinosaur facts, get accepted into some state college with a good program, maybe even be out on a dig this time in five or so years. Assuming she could hang on that long.

She scanned the notes, looked at the depictions of the various Missouri and Kansas sourced fossils they'd worked on.

I could really do some damage with some of these things, she thought.

She heard rustling behind her and turned towards the sound. She thought she'd find some kids brushing enthusiastically in the Dig Area, but it was still empty. There was no one else in this section. Her fellow teenagers seemed to be the only other field trippers in the museum, and they were all far too cool to be seen here. Must have been the air conditioning kicking on or something.

She returned to scanning the lab, but she'd no sooner turned her back than the sound started up again. Had she been imagining things? No, that time she definitely heard something.

"Hello?" Danielle called out tentatively.

There was no response. She walked out of the little alcove that cut into the lab—to give a more immersive experience, she assumed—over to the Dig Site.

Do you want to play? a voice whispered.

The voice seemed directionless, or at least like it was coming from the wrong direction, like a ventriloquist throwing their voice. There was nothing over there. Just a giant tibia on a stand, from some sort of sauropod. Danielle looked all around her. Maybe someone's voice bounced off the walls, making it seem like the question had come from the fossil's direction. Little kids often sounded creepy when they were playing, especially if it was somewhere echoey.

"Who's there?"

She peered into the barrels that housed the goggles and brushes for the dig, thinking that there could be a kid hiding away in there. But there were only goggles and brushes.

That was when the rattling started. The sound reminded her of the beginnings of earthquakes in movies, but this was Kansas City, and unless

Yellowstone was blowing the big one, tremors were unlikely here.

Danielle looked around, a quizzical expression on her face. It was the tibia. It shook, battering into the stand that held it erect. Curious, Danielle started to move towards it. She had no idea what could be causing it to move, why it would be rigged to do such a thing. This was a science museum for kids, not a haunted house.

The tibia broke free of its stand and clattered to the ground. Danielle gasped, expecting it to break. Were fossils of dinosaur bones hollow like the bones themselves were? Fragile, like birds'? If it cracked or shattered, Danielle expected to be blamed, but the impact seemed to not alter it in any way. Instead, the tibia fossil rolled along on the floor, end over end, seemingly of its own volition. It travelled in that way over to the lab. There it tapped on the glass, like a giant finger trying to get attention.

Plink. Plink. Plink.

Danielle could no longer believe that there was some sort of hidden effect causing the tibia to move. Either she couldn't trust what she was seeing and hearing—couldn't trust her mind—or something very, *very* weird was going on here.

The tibia tapped against the glass separating the dig zone from the palaeontology lab. Something about the sound had an effect on the fossils in the lab. Many of them started to shake, just like the tibia had, and a resounding crash came from somewhere deep within the lab, somewhere out of public vision.

Danielle began to back away. She didn't know what the fuck was going on, but she knew she sure as hell wasn't going to get blamed for it.

Other fossilised bones, bones Danielle couldn't name, began tumbling toward the tibia, banging against the glass along with it. The *plink*ing sounds turned thunderous. Danielle felt like she was stuck under a metal roof, waiting out a hailstorm. The bones hammered relentlessly. A hairline crack began to creep across the glass, jagged like lightning, then crept outward in fractured ripples. The glass wall fell all at once in a rain of small pebbles, quiet destruction compared to what it took to get it to break, a sound akin to pouring a shovelful of snow.

Why wasn't anyone coming? Wouldn't the noise have tipped someone off? Was Danielle the only one who cared there was something seriously wrong here?

Transfixed, Danielle slowly backed into a wall—the back of the elevator—she'd forgotten she'd even been moving. She needed to move to the side. She probably should have turned to run, but there was something holding her gaze with magnetic strength.

Don't you want to play?

341

There was no mistaking that the whispering voice came from the fossils this time, the fossils that were now joining together, sprouting sockets, stitching ligaments from thin air, collecting impossibly. Forming a skeleton. But it was more than that, because the bones that had found their partners were wrapped in muscle, sinewy and stretching, wrapping and wrapping around the limbs of the beast like an invisible hand was mummifying it, only this was the opposite of that, not a death rite, but life made from death.

Danielle realized too late that it wasn't going to fit. The creature was forming itself from the bottom up, the pelvis or hip bones or whatever they were had found their place, and the legs were in a crouching position, but even so, it was poised to break through the ceiling of the lab. The vertebrae crept up the parts that were already being formed, some already brushing against the tall ceiling. It was going to cave in on them.

The ceiling began to feel as if it were pressing in on her. Her chest mimicked the feeling, putting her in a vice. Danielle finally found the will to move away from the elevator wall, to peel her back off. Pressing up against the wall had grounded her as she witnessed the impossible, but she needed to get away from the impending crashing debris. She backed away, still unable to turn from the sight of the creature forming itself.

Outside of sections tucked under a perimeter of wide walkways, the museum was open every level, all the way to the glass ceiling four or five stories up. The Newtonian bike-on-a-rope was overhead, as well as the safety net stretched under it. Danielle was standing on a painting of a maze, but it was the museum itself that now felt maze-like, a labyrinth no one would be able to escape in time.

Danielle imagined the life-sized plane bursting from the thick cables that secured it to the ceiling beams, plunging into her tormentors. Her lips flicked briefly into a smile, though her round, child-like eyes were still wide with fear.

I thought we could be friends. Don't go away.

Could it be the dinosaur that had been talking to her? Talking, somehow, without vocal cords, without a tongue, without a mouth, without any part an animal requires to make sound? That, somehow, seemed even more impossible than dinosaur necromancy.

The creature bent its neck around the elevator shaft, bones already fused, snaking impossibly fast towards Danielle as muscle and flesh knit its way up the skeleton's long neck. It was a sauropod. A dinosaur. A real dinosaur, forming in front of her eyes.

She couldn't have outrun it, even if she could have moved her cemented feet. She squeezed her eyes shut,

343

waiting for impact, expecting to be obliterated, expecting to be hit with the force of a speeding train.

She tensed at the sound of screaming all around her, could tell that people were rushing for the exits. Again, she wondered what had taken them so long. Metal creaked and groaned, crashed and clanged. The dinosaur had busted completely through the lab, then. And Danielle was still alive. Why was she still alive?

There was a terrible smell. Humid, like rotting plant matter. Compost with too much green and not enough brown material. She ventured a peek out of one eye. Nothing could have prepared her for what she saw.

She was face to face with a living, breathing, dinosaur, mere inches from her face, filling her entire field of vision.

Danielle could not wrap her head around the scale of it. Its neck alone was three times the length of a giraffe's. Its tail was as long as its neck and body combined. What the fuck was it? She flipped through her memories of the sauropods. Was it a brontosaurus? No, it had narrow spines along its back, which made it look kind of like a giant iguana—if iguanas had elephant legs that were themselves as tall as a whole elephant. The scales on its legs reminded her of a crocodile's, but the shape of the scales changed, were different on different parts of the body. She tried to remember which sauropod had spines. Dip-something? Dipla? Diplo? Diplosaurus?

Diplodocus.

That was it. Diplodocus.

There was a diplodocus standing in front of her. It had moved away slightly, laying its head on the ground, like an animal bowing to the dominance of another. She had to look down at it. The head seemed so small for how massive its body was. It met her eye, then moved along, head low to the ground, the long neck snaking past like an anaconda. She looked down the length of its body and could see the tail was still forming. It was moving so it would have room to grow.

The diplodocus picked up a humongous foot, seemingly light on its feet for an animal of such a size, and Danielle saw smears of guts and viscera attached along with something that looked like a clump of hair. It had been alive again for mere minutes and it had already crushed someone into an unrecognizable pulp. The power of it! She was in awe.

Danielle wondered if the diplodocus would raise its neck now. She didn't see any other way it could fit in the building, even if it knocked everything out of its way. It didn't seem to be able to lift its head very high, despite the long neck. Or maybe it just didn't want to try to fit.

The diplodocus started ramming its head against the glass wall that led to the outdoor play area. It didn't take much for the wall to come crumbling down, no effort at all compared to what it took for the bones to break the palaeontology lab glass.

The diplodocus began to move its head and neck outside, but stopped when its body was aligned with the steps to the indoor treehouse, which held animal pelts and posters with facts about local birds.

What are you waiting for? asked the voice in her head. *Hop on.*

The voice was no longer a whisper, but a normal speaking voice. Now that it was speaking clearly, she realized that it sounded British, the kind of accent she associated with aristocrats, with broad as and missing *r*s at the end of words. Things just kept getting weirder.

I won't bite.

Danielle hesitated for a moment, but climbed the steps to the treehouse. It was a ready-made way to the dinosaur's back, like those little portable staircases for people who can't otherwise hoist themselves up onto a horse. Danielle balanced herself on the railing at the treehouse landing and launched herself onto the diplodocus. She grabbed hold of the last spine between its neck and body and used it to clamber up. She straddled its body, wedging herself between two spines, wrapping her arms around the spine in front of her.

I am riding a dinosaur, she thought. A hysterical laugh burst from her.

I suppose you are, said the voice in Danielle's head.

"How can you understand me?" Danielle asked aloud.

You pick up a few things, spending all your time in a museum. There's no need to speak. I can hear you.

A telepathic diplodocus? This was some weird fever dream. She'd wake up in a hospital, connected to tubes and wires. She couldn't accept it.

You were conscious, Danielle thought-asked, *as a fossil?*

Yes.

So you've been basically trapped. For millions of years.

Hundreds of millions, they tell me.

Almost like a djinn, trapped in a lamp.

I'm not familiar with—

Never mind. Were you at a British museum before?

I've been here since the dig. Why do you ask?

Accent.

The way you hear my voice? Is that what you mean?

Danielle projected a feeling of assent.

That would be the voice of the woman who put me together, Dr. Holbrook.

That made a strange sort of sense. But it still didn't explain why the diplodocus was focusing on her. Why it didn't just crush her like the poor soul now smeared under its foot.

Your pain called to me. I can help.

Danielle couldn't form a coherent thought. The wheels of her mind were spinning, but they couldn't find any traction.

We can play.

The thought came with a burning feeling of rage, of glorious vengeance. The word play suddenly took on a new meaning.

She didn't mean to answer. She meant to think to herself.

What kind of damage can a sauropod do? It's an herbivore. Not exactly among the frightening class of terrible lizards. Sure, it crushed a kid, but I bet it didn't even mean to. I wish I'd accidentally summoned a giganotosaurus, an allosaurus or something. Something with teeth.

The diplodocus swung its head to the side, crashing through a seating area for playing board games, and looked back at her. It bared its peg-like teeth menacingly. Its teeth pointed forward and only seemed to be present in the front of its mouth. Danielle wondered how it chewed, if it chewed at all, or if it just used its teeth for tearing.

There are benefits to being one of the longest dinosaurs to have ever existed.

I'm so sorry if I offended you, Danielle thought to it, *I didn't mean—*

I can hear everything. But do not worry, I will prove myself to you. When playtime starts.

It clicked its long claws, which Danielle understood to be an impatient gesture, onto the tile floor. There was only one claw on each front limb. It was weird enough that it had any claws at all, but only one per front foot? Whatever could those have been for?

Why prove yourself to me?

It didn't answer. Danielle had a million more questions, but the diplodocus began to move forward and she had to focus on swaying with its movements, learning to ride. She worried she'd be knocked off at the wall, that the hole the diplodocus had created wouldn't be big enough for her, but the spines seemed to work almost like a cat's whiskers. The diplodocus crouched as it walked to allow its body to pass without scraping her off.

The outdoor play area was fenced in. People were everywhere, running and screaming. Something ignited inside Danielle, lit by the pure thrill of their terror.

Terrible lizards, she thought.

Indeed.

The diplodocus knocked down one of the fences that closed off the outdoor play area from the non-paying public. A crowd of teenagers, chaperones, and workers clambered over each other to try to escape. The first of them to break free ran for the parking garage.

Like concrete could protect them from this massive monster.

Danielle huffed in amusement. One of the jocks—part of the dumpster crew—cowered within the crowd. Danielle drank in his fear. A look of recognition came over his face and he began to throw smaller kids behind him, clearing a path for only himself.

A torrent of rage flashed through Danielle.

The diplodocus felt it too.

Revenge? they asked.

Danielle radiated joy.

The diplodocus moved away from the terrified group, crushing the climbing structure that looked like giant red and white Pringles trapped in a net. They moved together towards the train tracks. Danielle looked over her shoulder. The relief on the jock's face was so palpable.

Had the diplodocus misunderstood? Did it need her to give a verbal confirmation?

Don't worry, it told her.

The diplodocus waited for the jock to break free of the crowd, letting him run through the parking lot. Then it lifted its whip tail and brought it down on him. The crunch of his bones was incredibly satisfying.

How many are left? it asked.

Danielle thought of the jocks that dumped her in the garbage over and over again. She pictured each and every one of their faces. But her mind then trailed to the people who watched and did nothing. The people who stood by. The teachers who looked the other way.

So many.

But they had run away. They were hiding. How many of them could they reasonably hunt down? And how many others would they squash in the process?

They reoriented, toppling a train parked on the tracks behind Union Station. The play area was empty now, except for someone crouched inside a globe structure with climbing gear on the outside. The one that was supposed to teach about a wheel and axle—the play area was simple machine themed. The diplodocus stomped towards the parking garage, squishing the globe flat, and the person inside with it.

I understand you're large, but could you try to…not squish innocent people?

How many of these humans are innocent?

Danielle didn't know how to answer.

They moved through the play area and towards the parking garage in a whirl of destruction. Its tail whipped into the giant letters on the side of the building, sending them crashing to the ground. There was really no way for it to move without destroying things. Godzilla came to mind.

I'm not familiar with this predator, said the diplodocus.

Oh. It could read images from her mind too, not just words.

It's not real, Danielle responded, trying to decide how to describe movies—fiction even—to a millions-of-years-old creature.

The diplodocus spanned its neck in an arc, taking in the view of the city.

Where is the food?

Plants, you mean?

Yes. Plants.

They're all over. There are lots of parks and stuff. But I can see why it'd seem sparse from your perspective. This is where we live and work, how we get from place to place. We kind of have to cover over the plants for that.

The diplodocus's voice in her head turned low, trembling with anger, almost a growl.

I should crush them all for what they've done.

There's a big lawn across the street, in front of the memorial. There are trees. Do you eat trees?

The diplodocus cantered towards the park in answer.

It didn't slow when it reached the streets. Cars swerved out of the way. One crashed into the entrance sign, another smashed into the back of the first car. Danielle hadn't thought fast enough to explain traffic lights. The diplodocus briefly got its neck tangled in telephone wires before bringing the poles down. It was not made for this world.

Squirrels in the park across from Union Station barked in warning. The diplodocus began to strip leaves from branches, inhaling a nest of chirping baby birds along with it. Danielle could feel its pleasure as if it were her own.

Police sirens began to blare in the distance. Was that the sound of a helicopter?

We should go, Danielle thought to the diplodocus.

She realized what was coming. Tanks. Nets. The National Guard. She did her best to project understanding of what they would face.

The diplodocus sighed. *At least I got a meal. You don't realise how much you miss eating until you get to taste something green again after hundreds of millions of years.*

The diplodocus moved with dragging, reluctant steps back to the museum. Crossing the road was no problem this time; there must be a blockade set up somewhere. It was like moving through a ghost town.

Danielle dreaded what was coming. She wanted them to stay together, maybe even take over the world. But the government would nuke the whole of the Midwest rather than let that happen. There are jocks at all levels.

The diplodocus had already begun to unknit its flesh when it stopped back at the faux treehouse so she could climb off.

It lumbered off without a word. Danielle watched it fade from sight, back to the palaeontology lab. Back to bones. She suddenly felt so, so alone. Her hair fell into her face, and she brushed it aside. It didn't smell like garbage. It smelled like blood. Danielle smiled.

The memories would sustain her for a long time.

CONTENT WARNINGS

The following list of content warnings does not and cannot cover all topics.

Read at your own risk.

Terror on Central Park West
Child (under 18) endangerment; child (under 18) death.

Burning Dawn
Animal injury; animal death; guns.

The Hidden Grotto
Gore; caving.

The Beast from Before
Animal death; alcohol; gore; guns.

A Primitive Party
Animal death; gore; child (under 18) death.

Livestream
Gore; guns; animal injury.

As Gods Upon the Land
Battle; gore.

Safety Protocols
Caving.

Please Don't Feed the Plesiosaur
Animal death; smoking; alcohol.

Age of the DinosaurZ

Gore; animal death; animal injury; guns.

Lost in Time

Child (under 18) endangerment; animal injury.

Terror Dawn

Gore.

Danielle and the Diplodocus

Bullying; child (under 18 endangerment); child (under 18) death.

ABOUT THE AUTHORS

A. W. Mason

A.W. Mason lives in Florida with his cat Wallace, a retired extreme parkour artist (who looks so dapper in his little helmet and knee pads). He enjoys all the nachos, getting lost in the woods, and naps.

He is a graduate of the University of South Florida with a degree in communications with a focus on health.

His first book, *A Haunt of Travels*, is a short story collection with tales of horror, terror, suspense, crime, and science fiction. His second book, *The Cleanup Crew*, is available now. Mason has also co-authored the extreme horror story, *The Scampering*, with Alana K. Drex.

WESLEY WINTERS

Wesley Winters is one of several pseudonyms used by a private writer who has been publishing fiction and nonfiction for nearly two decades. He started in music journalism by regularly appearing in such national and international magazines as *Hails & Horns*, *AMP*, *Outburn*, *New Noise*, and *Alternative Press*. He then stepped away from journalism to begin focusing on his fiction in 2017. Since then, he's published more than 100 stories spanning horror, crime, fantasy, mystery, science fiction, and whatever hybrids have tickled his fancy. In May 2024, Slashic Horror Press will release his grim collection *Nobody's Saviour*. He can be found on Instagram, Threads, and Wintry Monsters Press, where he posts reviews, writing opportunities, press releases, previews, and more.

SOCIALS:

Instagram and Threads: @wesleywintershorror

OFFICIAL WEBSITE:

www.wintrymonsterspress.com

CONTACT:

contact@wintrymonsterspress.com

DEREK HUTCHINS

Derek Hutchins is a writer for the Bad Vibes Podcast and author of the novella *The Darkness* and of a collection of short horror stories, *The Undertaker and Other Macabre Tales*. Raised in Connecticut, (the most haunted state), he developed a love for horror and the fantastic at an early age.

Derek has an MFA in Writing for Film and Television from Emerson College and lives with his wife and daughter in Utah.

Follow him on Instagram @themanwhoknewjustenough or Twitter @derekmhutchins for updates.

ANDREW JACKSON

Andrew Jackson is a UK-based student and writer with a love of dark fiction. He experiments across various genres, but most of his work embraces science fiction, ranging from space opera to the claustrophobic terror of sci-fi horror.

Drawing on influential films such as *Alien* and *Event Horizon*, and video games like *Dead Space* and *Mass Effect*, he's happiest in space with something unspeakable hunting him. Most of his stories are bleak, gory, and a little bit weird.

His science fiction and horror stories have appeared with *Black Hare Press*, *Night Terror Novels*, and *Dark Matter Magazine*. Additionally, he has recently published *Project Jotunheim*, an aquatic horror novelette, co-authored with Samuel M. Hallam. Look out for his debut sci-fi horror novella, *No Life Signs*, coming in 2024!

Find him on Instagram @authorandrewjackson where he posts all the books he hopes one day to get through, and occasionally some writing too.

NICOLE NEILL

N. S. Neill lives in Britain with her husband, dog and cat. She is an avid fan of crime and horror novels and anything featuring dinosaurs. She is the author of *There's Something in the Woods* and a *Deadly Dinner Party* and is currently working on the sequels to both.

JAMIE STEWART

Jamie Stewart is a horror author and editor. His books include *Montague's Carnival of Delights and Terror*, *Price Manor: The House That Bleeds*, *I Hear the Clattering of the Keys and Other Fever Dreams,* and *Mr. Jones*. He has co-edited such anthologies as *Welcome to the Funhouse* and *The Sacrament*. His short stories can be found in various anthologies, podcasts and YouTube channels.

This latest book *Something Wicked, Something Dark* was released in 2023.

Jamie lives in Northern Ireland with his wife, Claire, and dog, Poppy. He can be found on Instagram @jamie.stewart.33 where he reviews and promotes books.

ETHAN J. POLLARD

Ethan J. Pollard is a writer and graphic designer living in Oregon with his wife/editor and an assortment of rabbits. He is the author of the dark fantasy novella *Sanctum*, as well as a number of short stories in different publications. He enjoys reading, woodworking, dark coffee, old scotch, the sense of cosmic enormity experienced when staring into the depthless void of the night sky, and the music of Peter Gabriel.

He can be found on Instagram @theinksmithe, and online at ethanjpollard.com.

SAMUEL M. HALLAM

Samuel M. Hallam (He/Him) is a British author who dabbles in horror, sci fi, and on occasion fantasy. His previous works include *Haunted Souls*, *On The Trail To Vulture's Gulp*, and *Project Jotunheim*, which he co-authored. He has also had his works featured by various publishers including *Night Terror Novels*, *Strange Elf Press*, and more.

You can find him on Instagram, @Still_Reading_Sam or @TheIndieHorrorBookClub which he runs supporting indie horror authors.

KAY HANIFEN

Kay Hanifen was born on a Friday the 13th and once lived for three months in a haunted castle. So, obviously, she had to become a horror writer.

Her work has appeared in over forty anthologies and magazines. When she's not consuming pop culture with the voraciousness of a vampire at a 24-hour blood bank, you can usually find her with her two black cats or at kayhanifenauthor.wordpress.com.

MG MASON

MG Mason is a mixed genre writer from southwest England, born in Wiltshire and now living in sunny coastal Cornwall with his partner of ten years.

While his most popular work is humorous cosy crime fantasy series *Salmonweird*, deep down he is a horror writer at heart. His proudest work is *Phobetor's Children* – a science fiction horror set during the Roman Empire, a book he describes as the world's first sword, sandals, sci-fi and scares epic.

The current he's working on is a steampunk zombie horror called *The Forever City*. *Studio Salmonweird* (the third book in the series) will be out later in 2023 while his last release was a short story horror and dark fantasy collection called *Spooky Salmonweird*.

He's one of the lucky few who write for a living – though fiction doesn't even come close to paying the bills. He's a content writer, mostly in the education sphere but also dabbles in website content for fellow creatives, product listings, and any other written stuff small businesses and creatives need. Other creative outlets include photography and video.

C. D. KESTER

C. D. Kester is an author of fiction who does most of his work in the horror genre. He lives in Kingwood, Texas with his wife and two children.

He is an active member of the HWA and is attending SNHU for his BA in Creative Writing. Kester has published a novel, *Chasing Demons*, and a novella, *The Bunker*. He has also had many stories published in anthologies, ezines, and read in podcasts and YouTube videos.

You can see his work and find him on social media via his link tree at https://linktr.ee/cdkester

LOKI DEWITT

Loki DeWitt has lived in a number of different places but currently lives in Arkansas. He has loved horror since a very young age when he was introduced to the genre by watching a number of 80s horror movies with his dad (despite his mom's protests). Years later he began writing in the dreaded land of fan fiction. While his stories were not original, they let him sharpen his skills for the days ahead when he would tell his own stories. Now an adult, Loki retains his overactive imagination and takes great pleasure in unleashing it on readers.

In addition to horror, Loki carried his childhood love of dinosaurs into adulthood and is thrilled that he can bring his loves of horror and dinosaurs together to help birds (which he also loves).

MEGAN KIEKEL ANDERSON

Megan Kiekel Anderson (she/her) is a nerdy queer neurodivergent dark fiction writer. Her work can be found in such places as *Flame Tree Press*, *The Arcanist*, *Dark Recesses Press*, and *Monstrous Books*. A dinosaur lover since childhood, Megan enjoys visiting their fossils at museums and even has a dinosaur themed bathroom, complete with a photo of her in front of the "Wall of Bones" at Dinosaur National Monument. She'd love to be able to ride one, though she'd be sure not to let her dinosaur steed squish anyone. She lives in Kansas City with her chaotic family including too many cats, chickens (modern dinosaurs!), and foster kittens.

You can find her on Twitter and Instagram under the handle @megan_nerdnest.

Visit her website at www.megankiekelanderson.com, where you can sign-up for a weekly Reader's Newsletter of reviews and story recommendations or her Writer's Newsletter, which includes weekly submission opportunities and tips.

Thank you for picking up and reading this charity anthology.

Please help support these talented authors, and the Royal Society for the Protection of Birds (RSPB), by leaving a review for this anthology online. Reviews are the lifeblood of indie authors.

Word-of-mouth recommendations hold immense power, too.

We can't do this without you.